THORNS IN SHADOW

BOOK 2 OF THE CHOSEN OF THE SPEARS

SANAN KOLVA

*To Chloe and Jerome, Shelby and Jacob, Kit and Kim, and all the rest of
my awesome cousins.*

1

By mist we walk
By shadows run
From shrine to wood
From rest to none

Cold, pale mist wrapped around Lyan, stealing him into its depths. The trees and stone arches of the Shrine of Equinox vanished behind him, swallowed in white. The songs of birds cut off. He saw only muted light with no source as his friends and companions disappeared. The mist thickened until he couldn't even see his stallion Shadowstar, though he could feel the horse's confident steps.

Where am I? Where are Kithr and the others? Fear gripped his chest and knotted his throat as he looked over his shoulder into gray haze. The doorway was gone.

"Peace, Lyan." The reassurance was more a sensation than actual words, like a soothing drink of clear water on a summer day.

The touch on his mind made him jump. Lyan was far

from accustomed to not being alone in his thoughts. He felt down the stallion's shoulder, to the weapon strapped to the saddle, assuring himself that it, at least, remained close.

Another reassurance, tinged with amusement, brushed his mind, then withdrew. Lyan found a thin smile. "Thank you—" The mist muted his words and clung in his throat.

He raised his eyes, as if the mist might somehow reveal the sky while it hid the land. Assuming there was anything to see at all. His understanding of magical portals was limited at best. No stars glowed overhead, but Lyan did see shadows forming through the fog. They resolved into branches high overhead. Mist faded, and Lyan found himself gripping Shadowstar's mane with one hand, the other resting on Equinox.

The Spear stood nearly as tall as him, etched with arcane runes. The serrated head shone, flawless, as if it had not seen centuries of battle. Even lacking expertise with weapons, Lyan could admire its craftsmanship and deadly beauty.

From the Spear, a sensation brushed Lyan's mind, like a bird preening its feathers. He smiled faintly. Until a few days ago, he'd never thought Equinox, one of the two Spears of the Stars, most powerful magical weapons in the world, could be vain. Not until Lyan had taken the Trials and become bearer of the Spear had he even considered that the Spears might be aware and have thoughts of their own.

Shadowstar turned to look at Lyan and tossed his head, snorting as if to assure his rider that their method of travel was perfectly normal. Lyan let out a breath that became a soft laugh. Releasing the stallion's mane, he reached forward and stroked Shadowstar's neck. "Even my horse is more familiar with magic than I am."

Shadowstar snorted again, then lowered his head to investigate a patch of ferns. Lyan drew a deep breath, filling his nose with the scents of fir and pine. Cones littered the ground, and when he turned his gaze to the sky, he saw tangled and twined branches casting the forest floor in shadows. Despite the heavy shade, summer's heat pierced the air, stifling after the chill of the mist. Insects buzzed and whined in the still, heavy air, but no birds sang, and he heard none of the expected rustling of animals aside from Shadowstar's movements.

Much as Lyan wanted to rejoice to be under a forest's sheltering boughs, these trees loomed with malice rather than welcome. He instinctively tried to sense the spirit of the place, as he would have at home in the elven forest of Eilidh Wood. To his surprise, the wood reacted to his touch, pushing back with sharp warning. Branches shifted, dropping dry needles down on him. Lyan raised an arm to shield his head, but no larger missiles fell from above.

Raking fingers through red hair, Lyan shook out most of the needles and tucked straggling locks behind his long, pointed ears, careful not to tangle them on his ear cuff. He eyed the trees, wary of further reaction. "I'm not here to bother you. Just… passing through."

Branches rattled like dry bones, then settled. Lyan felt the forest watching him—just watching.

"Do you know where we are, Equinox?" Lyan asked in a low voice. "Are we still near your shrine? What about my friends?" At the Shrine of Equinox, the Guardian who opened the portal had told Lyan it would take him "where he needed to go," but offered no clues as to where that would be. Lyan had intended to accompany his human companions and help them retake their homeland. What part did this malevolent forest play in that goal?

Equinox responded with reassurance. Lyan's questions would be answered soon.

A jingle of tack and the heavy step of a horse made Lyan turn, gripping Equinox. His shoulders relaxed as a cloud of mist resolved into a grim elf in brown leathers astride a chestnut horse. Kithr had been Lyan's friend for nearly a hundred fifty years, since they were both children. When Lyan had left Heartshrine Village a few short months ago, Kithr had tried to convince him to abandon the idea, not trusting the humans Lyan chose to accompany. When he could not convince Lyan, Kithr had followed, revealing himself to the [illegible] and no longer avoid doing so.

Kithr was a study in brown—hair the color of acorns, well-traveled leather clothes, tanned skin. Like Lyan, he surveyed their surroundings. His brow furrowed in a frown that held more surprise than irritation, and he turned to Lyan.

"I don't suppose we've lost your Tathrens?" Kithr asked in a low voice.

"I hope not," Lyan said. "And I doubt it." He nodded at another mist cloud forming to Kithr's right.

"A pity." Kithr watched the mist, bow in hand.

When Lyan left home, Kithr would have followed no matter who he accompanied. However, Lyan hadn't left with simply *any* humans. He had left in the company of men from the country of Tather. The country that, sixty years before, the elves of Eilidh Wood had invaded. As apprentice to the village astrologer, Lyan had been too essential to be sent to fight. Kithr, however, had answered the muster of Heartshrine Village. He'd fought and killed Tathrens. He'd lost his father and many friends to them. To humans, the war was history. To the elves who had fought, it was recent memory.

The mists revealed the first of the humans: their leader, the Tathren lord Cailean Dev'gilla. His golden brown hair was trimmed short and his face clean-shaven. To Lyan's eye, Cailean looked close in age to him and Kithr, and he sometimes forgot the human had seen only twenty-six years, not one hundred and fifty. Cailean glanced around, then nodded to Lyan and Kithr. Lyan counted him as a friend. Kithr tolerated him, a vast improvement over Kithr's initial hostility, and nearly miraculous considering Cailean wielded

Solstice, the second Spear of the Stars, and the impetus for the elven attack on Tather.

According to tradition, Solstice had been granted to Tather for safekeeping, and Equinox to the elves of Eilidh Wood. Solstice had passed from generation to generation through a noble family of Tather. Equinox, however, had been hidden in its shrine, far from Eilidh Wood, protected by Guardians and demigods. To find the shrine, seekers had to solve a riddle written in the stars. Many had tried. Few had succeeded. And none who had sought the Spear had returned in over a hundred years. Resentful of the Tathrens and determined to right a perceived insult and inequality, elven warriors had fought, killed, and died in an effort to find and claim Solstice. They had ultimately failed, but at the cost of blood, hate, and chaos that could benefit no one but the Mad God himself.

Trees shifted and swayed, spitting prickly pine cones at Cailean. He eyed the forest and shivered. His horse edged closer to Shadowstar without urging. "Hardly an auspicious greeting."

Lyan was less glad to see the next person who appeared. Cailean's steward, Aikan, was a stern man in his sixties who had never hidden his dislike of elves in general or Lyan in particular. The lines of his face told of a man more apt to frown than smile, and he fixed the familiar scowl on Lyan. "What gods-forsaken abomination have you whisked us into, elf?"

"I did not control the portal we entered, Aikan," Lyan answered tightly. "At a glance, though, I would say a forest."

Kithr snorted a laugh, earning a glare from Aikan. "Shade, shelter, and cover in one place. Why should we be anywhere else?" He and Aikan held each other in mutual disdain, though Kithr usually managed to restrain himself from needling Aikan too often.

"Bah. Just like an elf." Aikan's jaw tightened.

Cailean scanned the forest. "Aikan, the rest of my men followed you?"

"They should have, my lord," Aikan answered. He gave Lyan another suspicious look, not convinced he wasn't somehow responsible for the delay of the other four members of their group.

A mist swirled into existence beside Aikan, and the gray-haired man's horse drew back from it. Torqual and his mare appeared. The blond warrior rubbed at the perpetual stubble on his chin as he studied their new surroundings. When on foot, he stood equal height with Lyan, though on horseback he seemed shorter. Of all the Tathrens, he was the only one Kithr nominally respected, as one warrior to another. He was sparing with words, respectfully cautious of Kithr, and usually polite to Lyan.

After him came the brothers Dalrian and Shiolto, hunter and stable hand from Cailean's keep, respectively. Both greeted Lyan with nervous smiles. Shiolto was the youngest of the group, still in his teens, while Dalrian had several more years, just cresting twenty. Of all the Tathrens, they had been the most welcoming to Lyan when he joined Cailean's search for Equinox. At the same time, neither felt at ease amid quests for ancient magical weapons, meetings with demigods, magic portals, or actively hostile forests. Shiolto claimed such adventures were meant for men better than common peasants, but Lyan knew few he'd rather have at his back.

The final member of their group appeared moments after the brothers. Unlike the rest of the humans, Yion was not Tathren, but a mercenary who had attached himself to Cailean for reasons he'd never completely explained. He was shorter than the others, and his features flatter. His eyes seemed to slant slightly. When caught in the right light, the center of Yion's forehead had an odd oval divot he sometimes rubbed when thinking. At a glance, he drew little attention, carrying himself with calm ease, but Lyan knew that hidden under and in his plain, unrestrictive clothes, he bore an impressive arsenal of blades and throwing weapons to complement the short sword at his waist.

"We're all here," Lyan said. He paused. The forest had, if anything, grown darker and more threatening as his companions arrived. "Wherever here is."

Dalrian shivered, gripping his sword. "Can we leave? This place feels creepy."

"And if we leave this forest, perhaps we can find landmarks, or a village… something to help us determine where we are." Cailean walked his nervous horse in a tight circle. "And how far we have to go to reach my home."

Unexpectedly, Kithr laughed. "You mean to tell me you can't tell where we are? Tathrens, and you don't even recognize it?"

"Then enlighten us, if you are so much better informed," Aikan snapped.

Kithr smirked. "I know quite well where we are. I once lived here, plotting and raiding your people. This is Malgor Forest." He shook his head with another, softer laugh. "This, *this* is Tather."

2

From blood to blood
Rage and hate
By blood and blood
Shall you know your fate?

"Malgor Forest?" Dalrian repeated. "Lord Cailean, we're in your lands!"

Shiolto gaped. "That's at least four month's travel from where we were."

"Not just in my lands." Cailean said, grim. "Malgor Forest lies in Ewart's holdings."

Lyan's spirits had begun to rise at the news that they had reached Cailean's homeland, but Cailean's reply sent his hopes crashing to the ground. Ewart Col'renn was cousin to Cailean's deceased father. Not content with his place in the hierarchy, and wanting Solstice's powers for himself, Ewart had gathered an army and risen against Cailean. He besieged and eventually took Cailean's keep. Cailean and a few men had barely escaped after the walls fell. Worse, in the midst of the battle, a powerful mage in Ewart's service cursed Cailean, amplifying the strength it cost him to call on Solstice. Even a small use of the Spear's power left Cailean drained, while greater effort left him unconscious and weakened him for days after.

"Ewart," Kithr said. "He's the one who chased you from Tather?"

Cailean answered with a curt nod.

"What are the chances he's still busy looting your keep?" Kithr continued.

"I can't be certain, but high, I suspect." Cailean's voice was tight and his eyes smoldered with anger at the thought. "If you are suggesting we attempt to take his fortress in his absence, chances of *that* succeeding are not worth mentioning. I may be their liege lord, but his men are unlikely to open the gates and welcome me in. No doubt Ewart left someone behind to handle affairs."

"But if we could get inside, perhaps we can discover something that will help us defeat him," Lyan offered, guessing Kithr's intent. "There must be a reason we're here and not closer to your stronghold, Cailean. The Guardians of the Shrine of Equinox said the portal would take us to a place we need to go."

"Then why in Ahebban's Hammer are we in this accursed forest?" Aikan snapped.

Cold wind swept over them, rattling branches like dry bones. Shadows drew closer as the forest closed around them and blocked the patchy sunlight. Lyan gripped Equinox.

"Don't invoke your gods here," Kithr ordered. "They are as unwelcome under these boughs as Tathrens are."

Cailean reached for Solstice as he eyed the forest. "Let's not linger. We'll discuss Ewart's keep once we're free of Malgor Forest. Kithr, do you know your way through?"

Kithr nodded. "I know it. Stay close." He scowled at the trees and spoke in Elven. "Back off. I have business here."

To Lyan's surprise, the forest grudgingly complied. Brambles untangled, opening paths between the pines. Kithr kicked his horse, pointing her head toward one of the paths. The animal balked, and Kithr gave her another firm jab of his heels. She reluctantly obeyed.

The other horses felt the same foreboding, hostile air. Only a combination of coaxing and cursing convinced [illegible] all the horses but Shadowstar. Lyan's stallion viewed their surroundings with the same self-assured calm that Yion did. Shadowstar's confidence didn't carry to Lyan, though. He'd thought the Forests of Cossette, far to the west, uncomfortable for their absence of spirit, but this place was different. The spirit of Malgor Forest was awake and aware of them. It did not offer welcome. Lyan was as much an intruder as his Tathren companions.

"This is even worse than Eilidh Wood," Shiolto whispered.

"Eilidh Wood simply distrusts you," Kithr said with a touch of scorn. "Malgor Forest actively hates you."

"Then you *elves* should feel right at home," Aikan snapped.

"It doesn't like me any more than it does you," Lyan said quietly. "Try not to aggravate it further."

Kithr led, followed by Torqual and Cailean. Lyan followed them, and behind him, Aikan, Dalrian, and Shiolto, with Yion bringing up the rear. Brambles grabbed at their clothes as they passed, and branches dipped low even as riders ducked under them.

Lyan winced as a branch scraped his arm. *Elves did this. Someone with talent fed their anger into this forest. How long did they live here, to drive their hatred so deep into its core?*

The silence hung heavy enough that the first whistle of birdsong made Lyan jerk. He started to relax, feeling foolish, until he saw how abruptly Kithr stiffened.

"Kithr?" he whispered.

"Trouble." Kithr said nothing more, but drew and nocked an arrow as he kicked his horse forward again.

Lyan rested a hand on Equinox and glanced at the trees. The oppression grew stronger, joined by an itch between his shoulder blades as if someone intended to put an arrow in his back. *What kind of trouble? What might sound like a bird, if not a bird? The forest hates us, but the elves who used it returned home when the war ended.*

Unless they didn't.

A chilling understanding filled him. *That wasn't a bird.*

Lyan gripped Equinox more tightly and focused his thoughts toward the Spear. *"Can you protect us from missiles? Please?"*

A pulse of warmth and a momentary sense of agreement answered him. Nothing else seemed to change.

No second call gave warning of the arrows. Like a flock of deadly birds, shafts flew down from the tree branches. Kithr rolled from his horse and searched for targets. His bow rose to release lethal arrows in return, but he didn't loose, seeing the arrows deflect off an unseen barrier just overhead. The Tathrens grabbed for weapons.

Startled Elven curses rose from the trees as not a single arrow found its target. Another arrow hit the barrier harmlessly.

"Enough!" Lyan shouted in Elven.

Silence. Absolute silence. Then, finally, a cold, hard voice answered in the same tongue. "Who are you?"

"Lyan, astrologer of Heartshrine Village."

To his left, someone dropped from a tree and stepped forward. "Get off that horse."

Shadowstar snorted disapproval at the sharp tone, but Lyan complied with the demand, swinging down from the saddle. Equinox in hand, he faced the thin, grim elf dressed in mottled brown and green.

"What in the names of all our fallen are *you* doing *here* with *Tathrens*, you witless idiot stargazer?" His fist rose to swing at Lyan.

Kithr caught the other elf by the wrist. "Try to hit Lyan and you'll lose that hand," he warned in a tone as cold as ice.

Lyan stepped back. "I am here… we are here because we were sent here." The other seemed to know Lyan, but Lyan didn't recognize him.

"Sent? With Tathrens? Bah!" The elf jerked away from Kithr. "The only Tathrens sent here are those sent to die. Who would send you?"

"Don't bother arguing, Lyan," Kithr said before Lyan could do more than feel anger rise at the dismissal. "He won't listen. Let's go. Whatever the Guardians thought, there's nothing for us here. Especially not with this lot."

"You won't leave this forest alive," the other elf snapped.

Without batting an eye, Kithr drew his bow, arrow aimed at the other's heart. "Watch us."

"Archers, aim for the stargazer," the other retorted, eye locked with Kithr's. From the trees, bows creaked.

Lyan slammed the butt of Equinox against the ground. "That is enough!"

Branches trembled, and elves voiced alarmed surprise as they dropped to the ground. With a sharp twang, every strung bowstring snapped. Kithr cursed his stinging fingers. Lyan steadied himself on the Spear, weariness washing over him as if he'd just run a race. He drew a deep breath, let it out, and forced himself not to shout.

"Do I have your attention now?"

All eyes focused on Lyan, and few were friendly. The elf before him answered. "It seems you do, stargazer."

"We were sent here—all of us, even the Tathrens—by the Guardians of the Spear, the demigods who guard and protect Equinox and its shrine. They said we would arrive where we needed to be. Their magic sent us here, and we did not come to fight you."

Angry murmurs rippled through the forest. "You allowed *Tathrens* on sacred ground, stargazer? We fight them for Solstice while *you* invite them to the other Spear?"

"Lyan didn't let them enter," Kithr cut in. "The

Guardians did. So if you have a problem with that, Milosh, take it up with the demigods who've spent centuries at their duties."

Milosh. I recognize that name. He's from our village—one who never returned. But I don't recognize him at all.

Milosh sneered at Kithr. "And what are *you* doing in the company of this filth, Kithr? You never hesitated to slaughter them before. You were as eager as any to claim their heads as your prizes. Have you become a coward?"

Kithr's fingers curled as if he would wring Milosh's neck. Lyan spoke first, before Kithr's rage could burst free. "The war is over, Milosh."

Milosh spun on Lyan. "Over? Tell that to the Tathrens who hold half our men in their dungeons. Tell that to the Captain and the rest of our warriors as Tathrens torture them. Tell *them* the war is over! Pull your head from the clouds and see how the world is."

"I do see the world, and I do know of torture and pain, Milosh," Lyan responded in a low voice. He drew a deep breath. "The war is over, and we are not part of your vendetta. We have no part in your battle."

"You're here. That makes you part of it," Milosh said. He gestured, and elves appeared from the shadows—gaunt, scarred elves. Only a few had restrung their bows, but all carried other weapons. "You will come with us."

Lyan glanced at Kithr, who answered with a short nod. Lyan swung back on Shadowstar. "As you wish. But we're not giving up our weapons."

Milosh's eyes narrow. "You claim no part in the war."

"That doesn't mean I'm stupid enough to enter a hostile camp with no means of defending myself," Lyan retorted. "Lead the way."

Shadowstar eyed the warriors surrounding them, but Lyan patted the stallion's neck and urged him to follow. Some elves vanished back into the forest, but most remained on the edge of sight, making their presence and their displeasure known.

Cailean moved beside Lyan and spoke quietly. "Lyan, where are we going?"

"To their camp, I think," Lyan answered as softly. "Don't tell them who you are—not even family name. Have your men avoid using titles, for your safety."

"I understand." Cailean nodded.

No, you don't. These elves aren't like Kithr. They're worse. They will kill you without a moment's hesitation, and if they know you carry Solstice… They must never suspect that.

Though sounds returned to the forest, its hostility only deepened. Kithr spoke to Milosh as they rode. "Who's in charge? Not *you*, I hope."

"Captain Nylas leads us," Milosh snapped. "Just as he did before you abandoned the war."

"Nylas?" Lyan repeated, sitting straighter in the saddle. "My cousin is here?"

"No. The Captain was captured. By *Tathrens*." Milosh glared at Lyan.

Lyan looked at the trees again. *Nylas is skilled with plants. Is this his doing? Is this how he's used his magic?*

How long has it been since anyone spoke of him? He's my cousin, and even I hardly thought about him.

Milosh led them to a towering, thorny bramble wall. The twisting, wicked branches reluctantly peeled back, forming an entrance and granting them access to the elven camp. Trees formed living shelters, and openings had been carved into the rock wall that formed one edge of the camp. A few elves stood guard on the bramble wall, and they watched the newcomers with open hostility. Others hung tanned hides to dry. Lyan's gaze swept the camp, and he sat straighter in surprise. A group of youths sat on the ground, sorting feathers for arrows. At the sound of hooves, all five looked over sharply, expressions wary and as guarded as the warriors. Three boys and two girls, Lyan guessed their ages ranged from seven to fourteen. Their ears were less pointed than elven children, but more so than human ones. All were as thin as the warriors around them. The oldest girl met Lyan's eyes as if challenging him to say something about the blotchy purple birthmark running down the right side of her face. Then, oddly, she smiled at him.

Kithr turned to Milosh. "Kids?"

Milosh shrugged. "Some whores don't care what shape your ears are if you have coin. The mothers of half-breeds dump the infants at the forest's edge. If they're strong enough to survive until we find them, we take them in. Most haven't seen a live stranger before."

"I have," said the girl with the birthmark, standing and walking to them. "The Captain took me hunting."

Milosh grunted. "True. Those you saw weren't alive for long even so." He nodded to the girl. "That's Patch. She's got the forest skills. Some guess she's Captain Nylas's."

Patch studied them. She was tall and thin, her golden brown hair cut short. "Why are humans here?"

"Tathrens," Milosh spat.

"No. Not that one, at least." Patch pointed at Yion. "Why are they here?"

"Because Lyan the Stargazer claims neither he nor they have part in our war. The Captain should judge that himself," Milosh responded.

"But the Captain is gone." Patch continued to study Yion like an exotic creature. No one else spoke. The other elves and the children all watched, awaiting the conversation's outcome. "And we can't keep them here."

"We could just kill them," Milosh said. Lyan listened. He heard the words, but more than that, he heard how Milosh spoke to this girl as if her decision mattered. As if, in the absence of Nylas, a half-Tathren child who might be Nylas's daughter held authority.

Patch shook her head in answer. "We don't kill our own people. If they claim to not be part of the fight, and not to be our enemies, then they should prove it." She tilted her head and looked at Lyan, then smiled. "If they free the Captain, they cannot be our enemies."

A murmur ran through the elves, some agreeing, some disagreeing. Lyan glanced at Kithr, but his friend's face was an expressionless mask. Lyan's eyes moved to Cailean and his men, relieved that none of them understood Elven. If Aikan had followed the conversation, Lyan knew the older man's temper would have flared, and here, surrounded by the very elves who fought the war, the response would be deadly.

Milosh spoke in Tathren. "Get off your horses and follow."

Lyan dismounted, taking Equinox. "Shadowstar, watch over the other horses." Gaunt, hungry elven eyes warned him of the fate of any unprotected animal. He couldn't say why he trusted Shadowstar's ability to protect the rest of the animals, but Lyan was confident the stallion could.

Shadowstar snorted in answer, nosing Lyan's red hair. The stallion waited until all the riders dismounted, then herded the mounts together. Lyan saw Shadowstar take a warning snap at an elf reaching for a saddlebag on the packhorses. The elf glowered, but backed away.

Milosh led them through one of the openings in the rock wall and down a maze of passages dug underground. Massive roots formed supports and braces. Lyan shivered as glowing elven lamps replaced the daylight. Earth surrounded him, too close and confining. Looking around, Lyan saw evidence that the elves lived in these tunnels. The air smelled of infrequent bathing and years of accumulated odors of living and dying. Clothes hung from pegs on the walls. Blankets lay spread on the floors; some rooms even held beds. In other rooms, Lyan saw stores of dried plants, followed by a collection of traps. He peered at the traps, and glimpsed movement.

"Rats?" he whispered to Kithr.

Kithr glanced toward a trap, then answered simply, "Food."

Milosh ushered them into one of the few rooms with a door. Scowling, he spoke in Tathren. "You will stay here until we decide what to do with you."

Milosh slammed the door shut as he left, and a bar thumped in place after him.

Wooden crates littered the room. Cailean looked at them and sighed. "So *this* is what became of my missing wine shipment." He tested the stability of a crate, then sat. "What's the situation? I expect it could be worse, given that we're still alive, armed, and not restrained."

"Lyan made the argument that neither you nor he is part of the war. He made it effectively enough that they're considering it. Which is worthy of note, since they live by killing your people," Kithr said.

"Tathrens captured their captain and some of their men," Lyan added. "The girl, Patch, suggested we prove our good faith by rescuing the prisoners." He braced for reactions.

"What?" demanded Aikan, shaking with anger. "Prove our 'good faith' by attacking *our* people? Why would we want to free any bloodthirsty murderers? So they can continue attacking us?"

"Do you know what Tathrens do to captive elves, Aikan?" Lyan asked quietly. "I do. Vynzent taught me. Where do you think he learned?"

A long moment of silence answered him. Aikan looked away, silently acknowledging the reminder of Lyan's capture by Ewart's bastard son. In the days he'd held Lyan, Vynzent had tortured Lyan in an effort to discover the location of the Shrine of Equinox. Lyan shivered at the memory of searing metal against his skin.

"The 'why' is simple enough." Kithr leaned against the wall. "You should want to free them because it's how you will leave here alive and without a fight. Not only that, let the elves loose, and Ewart's men will have to deal with them. Can't focus so much on chasing us down if they're liable to be ambushed by elven warriors."

"You think they'll follow a child's suggestion?" Torgual scoffed.

Kithr scowled. "Watch what you say about her. She has power, and she's earned her place. Bear in mind, this might be your only chance to show her Tathrens as something other than enemies before she and the other children become the next generation of this war."

More blood, more death, more trophies no elf of Eilidh Wood should prize. Lyan sank down to the floor, back against the wall as weariness caught him. "Kithr, how long do you think they'll keep us here?"

"Hard to say. Long enough to try to search our gear for anything they can use, at least."

Lyan smiled. "That'll take a while. Shadowstar's watching over the other horses." He rested Equinox on his shoulder and let his head rest against the Spear as his eyes drifted shut. "Wake me when they come back."

"We're surrounded, in this camp of *elves*, and you're going to *sleep*?" Aikan demanded.

"Let him be," Cailean said.

Lyan neither heard nor cared about further conversation. He slept.

~

Someone shook Lyan's shoulder. He started awake and opened his eyes. Kithr stood over him, and for a moment, in the shadows, Lyan lingered in a dream where Kithr proudly presented grisly war prizes as if Lyan would accept them.

"Lyan. Nylas's men are ready to talk."

Lyan rubbed his eyes. Kithr's hands were empty, no heads

hanging in his grasp, no blood staining his clothes. Cailean and his men stood unharmed, watching Milosh and the three other elves who had taken posts just inside the open door.

Stiff muscles protested as Lyan stood, clutching Equinox and trying to ignore the gnawing hunger that woke when he moved. "Have you decided?"

"Normally, there would be nothing to decide: we would kill the Tathrens," Milosh answered in Tathren. "But as you insist on complicating matters, stargazer, we have to offer some alternative. If you free Captain Nylas and our comrades from the keep of a Tathren called Ewart Col'renn, we will allow you passage through this forest." He paused, eyes narrowing. "To ensure you do this, one of you will remain with us until the Captain returns."

Lyan's breath caught a moment. He saw the glitters in the eyes of the elves as they looked at the humans, and knew whoever stayed faced a far more certain danger than those who left on this rescue. Cailean and his men exchanged uneasy glances.

I could stay. Cailean and his men will be safer away from here. I'd be down here, but I can manage, if I must.

Lyan opened his mouth. "I—"

Kithr cut him off. "*You*, Lyan, will go with them. Milosh and his lot insult us by claiming our word has no value and we have no honor? Fine. Then I'll stay."

Milosh and the other elves gaped at Kithr in open disbelief. Kithr crossed his arms and glared at them. Milosh found his voice. "*You* will stay, Kithr? In place of these?"

"I will stay," Kithr said coldly. "And if you're too stupid to understand why, there's no point in explaining."

"You're a fool if you think they have any reason to return for you."

Kithr's eyes narrowed, but Cailean spoke. "I no more intend to abandon one of my companions than you do to leave your captain imprisoned."

Milosh barked a sharp laugh. "Do you know anything, Tathren? Anything at all about your 'companion' and what he's done in the war?"

"I know enough," Cailean answered, voice flat. "And I know both sides inflicted tortures aplenty. Kithr is one of us, and we will [illegible] for him."

Milosh spat on the dirt floor. "Fine. Let's see if a stargazer and a handful of *Tathrens* can succeed without their only warrior."

"Do you think I'll leave Lyan here with you?" Kithr said. "He's endured your insults long enough. I will not subject him to more. Now get out. We'll come up when we're ready to go."

Lyan saw an angry tic in Milosh's forehead. The elf spun on his heels and stormed out with his companions, slamming the door.

"Kithr, are you sure?" Lyan began.

"I'm sure it's better than *you* staying here," Kithr answered, voice flat. "And you stand a better chance of keeping the prisoners from killing your Tathrens once they're free than I do. Remember, Lyan: the elves you rescue will not hesitate to attack, regardless of whether or not those Tathrens help free them. If you have to choose between saving them and saving your Tathrens, pick your Tathrens."

Lyan started, staring at Kithr. "What?"

Kithr switched to Elven. "Look around, Lyan. You see what these winterborn have become. You know it. They are Lost."

Lyan drew a sharp breath, chills running icy fingers down his spine. He cast an uneasy glance at the door, as if Milosh would burst in demanding retribution for the insult. Only elves who turned so far from the ways of Eilidh Wood that the forest itself refused them were called Lost. Unless they found their way back, Lost elves went insane, eventually becoming little more than savage, murderous animals. "Kithr—"

"They are," Kithr said harshly. "These should hardly be

called elves. They are Lost to Eilidh Wood. Keep your Tathrens. At least they have honor." He paused, gaze hard and serious. "One more thing, Lyan. Don't trust Nylas. He was a cold-hearted bastard the last time I saw him, even before the war ended. I don't care that he's your blood kin. Do not trust him. Do you understand?"

Lyan lowered his eyes. "I don't like it, Kithr. But I understand."

"Good. Don't like it. You shouldn't like it. When you start to like it, you're on your way to becoming one of them. Don't like it. Just do it."

3

Ahebban, Watcher on the Walls
Lay your hand upon our work
May your eyes be ever on these halls
That never may magic one stone move

"Lord Cailean, this is madness! We cannot seriously be planning to free elves!" Aikan burst.

"From Ewart's keep," Cailean said. "From my enemy's stronghold. If that is not the last place he would expect to find me, it's close. The Guardians sent us here for some reason; there must be opportunity here."

Shiolto, Dalrian, and Torqual listened to the argument. They looked between the two men as if expecting someone to throw a punch and start a brawl.

"And how will we enter?" Aikan countered. "Will they open the gate at your asking?"

"They *should*," Cailean growled. "Ewart's rebellion or not, I'm still their lord. They *won't*, but they should."

Kithr leaned back against the wall. "Your mercenary found his way into your keep, didn't he?"

"By the guidance of my god," Yion answered. "I will pray

for his further leading, but I cannot say whether or not he will grant it."

Kithr grunted. "Enemies got into your keep as well, as I understand it."

Cailean looked at Kithr. "The ones who came swarming over the walls and took the gates did, certainly."

Kithr watched Cailean through narrow eyes. "And those are the only enemies who found a way in?"

"All the entrances were guarded," Aikan snapped. "If anyone got inside, they did so by magic."

Kithr laughed. "Magic to enter a Tathren stronghold? If that worked, we would have razed your peoples' strongholds to the ground."

Aikan fumed, but Cailean frowned. "What do you mean, Kithr? Why do you exclude magic as a possibility?"

Kithr eyed Cailean, then gave another short, sharp laugh. "Don't tell me that I know more about your gods than you do. When your strongholds are built, you ask the protection of the Watcher on the Walls. It's part of the dedication of the keep. That ritual ensures magic can't be used against a besieged keep. No hostile magic, whether fireballs, or roots to undermine the foundation, or spells to allow an intruder to appear inside the keep, work when the caster is outside the walls. Once they get inside, no restrictions exist, but first, they have to get in."

The Tathrens all stared at Kithr. Finally Cailean asked, "How do you know this?"

"When we found something blocked our magic, we questioned some priests. They proved very informative."

"But," Shiolto cut in, "mist covered Lord Ca... the keep when it was attacked. That wasn't natural."

"Then someone grew creative. The mist's origin must have been outside the walls, and they let the wind move it," Kithr said.

Lyan knew Kithr told him all this for a reason, and he

knew he should understand why, but his mind wasn't on the attack on Cailean's keep. "Well, we aren't trying to get into Cailean's keep, we're trying to get into this one, and our access to magic is limited."

"Then we must go and see for ourselves what means we can find to achieve our goal," Yion said.

"That means we can leave, right?" Shiolto asked hopefully.

Cailean looked to Kithr. "Will you be all right here?"

Kithr snorted. "Worry more about yourself, Tathren, and about what I'll do if you let anything happen to Lyan."

"I haven't forgotten since the last time you warned me," Cailean answered dryly.

Kithr pushed away from the wall and walked to the door. "Then hurry up, before these fools manage to get around Shadowstar long enough to eat one of your horses." He paused to look at Lyan and spoke softly in Elven. "One last thing to remember, Lyan: show them no weakness. Act as you would with any wild, dangerous, starving animal—don't give them reason to think you're vulnerable."

One of the elves who'd been with Milosh stood guard in the passage outside the door. He scowled at them, but Lyan had yet to see any other expression on the other's face. "Are you ready?" snapped the elf.

Lyan met the glower without flinching. "Yes."

Without another word, the elf turned and marched up the tunnel. Lyan followed, and heard the others behind him. The return to the surface felt faster than the descent had been, and Lyan breathed a sigh of relief once he stood under open sky. He blinked rapidly, one hand raised to shield his eyes. Afternoon sun shone through the trees, painful after the dark tunnels, leaving Lyan to wonder how long he'd slept.

All around the camp, elves watched them. The children had cleared away their work and joined the adults in hostile study of the Tathrens. Lyan clutched Equinox. No matter how he tried, he couldn't ignore that they were his people, some even friends he'd grown up with. He couldn't ignore the accusations in their eyes when they looked at him in the company of Tathrens.

How can I make them see that the Tathrens don't have to be our enemies? How can I make them see I haven't betrayed them?

I can't change their minds in a day. If we help them, maybe they'll listen. Lyan considered what Kithr had told him. *But if they really are Lost, there's nothing I can do.*

He looked around the camp. "Our horses?"

Lyan heard Shadowstar snort before any elves answered, and the stallion herded the rest of the horses to their group. Reaching Lyan, Shadowstar roughly butted his nose against Lyan's chest, and Lyan rubbed his head.

Patch spoke, breaking the stillness. "Is that a horse, or a guardian spirit?"

Lyan turned to her, surprised by the question. "Shadowstar is a horse. But the herders of the Appret Plains say he's roamed the grasslands for as long as their history tells."

"Has he?" She walked to Lyan and brushed her hand over Shadowstar's shoulder. The girl reached into her pocket and pulled out an iron key. "Take this. Perhaps it will open something for you. The man who carried it before doesn't need it any longer."

Lyan held out his hand. She set the key in it and folded his fingers over it. "Thank you," he said.

"Do not lose it," Patch told him, surprisingly serious.

Lyan nodded, though he couldn't begin to guess what it would unlock. "I won't."

"Lyan. You're wasting time," Kithr cut in.

Lyan jerked his head in understanding. "How far to this keep?"

Milosh watched him warily, on edge the longer Patch stood beside Lyan. He pointed. "A day's march east."

Lyan looked to Kithr. His friend met his eyes and gave a short, curt nod. Then Kithr turned and walked back to the tunnel. Patch stepped back to rejoin her people.

Shadowstar snorted and nudged Lyan impatiently. Lyan complied with the unspoken order and climbed into the saddle, then nodded to Callean and his men. He didn't have to ask if they were prepared. Even if they weren't, the Tathrens were eager to leave.

The wall around the camp peeled open to let them out. Thorny branches grabbed at clothes and slapped at faces. Lyan glowered at the brambles. "Enough. We know you don't like us. The longer you delay us, the longer you have to suffer our presence."

The branches rustled angrily, and once they passed the barrier, it sealed behind them with a hiss of leaves. Lyan suppressed a shiver. Shadowstar chose the path, and the other horses followed. Lyan glanced over his shoulder, and realized all the horses had followed, including the two pack animals and Kithr's horse. He recalled the gaunt elves and knew if they'd left any animals behind, they wouldn't have gotten them back.

Lyan patted Shadowstar's neck. "Thanks for watching over them."

Shadowstar snorted and tossed his head in reply, stepping up to a swift walk. No one broke the stillness for a while.

"I don't like leaving someone behind," Shiolto said in genuine concern. "Will Kithr be all right?"

Aikan laughed sharply. "You're worried about an elf who invaded our country and murdered our people? He's back in the company of fellow killers. You should be asking whether he'll greet our return with anything but arrows. Just like the rest of those filthy scum."

Lyan gripped Equinox's shaft tight.

"How can you say that, Aikan?" Shiolto demanded.

Aikan sneered. "Are you blind? What do you really think he'd rather do: travel with Tathrens, or kill them?"

"He'll come with us," Shiolto snapped. "He said he would. And he isn't going to abandon Lyan."

"Having returned to the brotherhood of the invaders and killers who have continued their attacks on our people, despite the war being 'over', as Lyan is so fond of telling us, I have doubts that elf will be interested in keeping our company." Aikan's voice was cold.

Shiolto made a sound of exasperation. "Lyan, tell Aikan he's wrong."

Lyan said nothing. *I'm a fool to think I can convince these elves to see Tathrens as anything but enemies. I can't even convince Kithr. What makes me think I can change anyone else's mind? He's right. Kithr would be happier staying here than continuing with me. I've been forcing him to follow me on a mission he'd rather end by killing Cailean and all his men.*

"Well?" Aikan scoffed.

Lyan gritted his teeth. He wanted to lash out, to strike someone, to wipe the smug sneer he could hear in Aikan's voice off the man's face.

"Aikan, shut up," Torqual said. "Your every word announces your ignorance of what it means to be a soldier. Kithr will do his duty."

Lyan glanced over his shoulder at the men. Aikan glared daggers at Torqual now, and the weight of his gaze no longer pressed on Lyan. Shiolto walked his horse by Lyan, concerned.

"Are you okay, Lyan?" Shiolto asked softly.

"I don't like being here," Lyan answered as quietly. "This whole forest is steeped with hate. It oozes from every fiber of every plant." He shuddered.

"It does," the Tathren agreed. "So why in the gods' names do you think Kithr might want to *stay* here?"

Lyan didn't answer.

"Come on, Lyan. You don't actually believe what Aikan said, do you?" Shiolto pressed.

"No," Lyan lied. From Shiolto's expression, his tone failed to convince.

Shiolto just sighed and shook his head. "Kithr's not going to stay here, Lyan. If nothing else, he's as stubborn as you are, and isn't going to back down on his vow to protect you from *us*. All right? Trust him."

Lyan nodded and said nothing. Shiolto shook his head and fell quiet again.

When Shiolto spoke again, it was on a different subject. "Lyan? Why do you think Kithr said all that about magic and our keeps? Was he just warning you, so you wouldn't try to get inside using…"

"Using the power I've been given?" Lyan finished as Shiolto searched for a way to not announce that Lyan carried Equinox. The Tathren nodded, and Lyan thought. "That might have been his reason, or one of his reasons."

"I don't understand his interest in anyone sneaking in during Ewart's attack on us. That didn't have anything to do with elves at all." Shiolto shrugged. "I guess that's good to know, though, even if it doesn't mean much now."

Lyan nodded distractedly. *Why did Kithr tell us that? What am I supposed to understand from knowing Cailean's enemy couldn't have used magic to get inside?*

His breath caught. *When was Cailean cursed? During the attack on the walls, or before? Did the mage get in before the breaching of the gates?*

Did someone let the mage inside?

His gaze drifted over his companions again as he recalled another whisper of treason. For much of their journey, Cailean and his men had been pursued by a pooka. The shapeshifting monster took an interest in Lyan, taunting him, even daring him to attempt to bind it while it played tricks and games for its amusement. The pooka had even hinted to Lyan that someone among Cailean's men served Ewart. *Did the pooka tell the truth about a traitor in our group?*

The forest reluctantly gave way as the sky darkened to night. Lyan looked to the sky as clouds shrouded the moon and hid the stars, as they had without fail for too many nights. He rested a hand on Equinox. The Shrine had given him the stars, but not for long, and not the true sky. Cailean's enemy still hid the stars, still denied Lyan his astrology. Did the signs reveal Equinox had been found? That his search would lead to nothing? Or did he search as much for the Shrine as for the Spear itself? Venycia, leader of the Guardians of the Spear, had said minions of Murdo, the Mad God, sought the Shrine in the hopes of taking Equinox when the Spearbearer died. Lyan shivered again, then looked over his shoulder at the forest. Thorns and brambles choked even the path they'd followed.

How can my people keep fighting when these clouds tell of a far more dangerous enemy? Don't they look up? Don't they see? Or have they lost their way so completely that they hold nothing sacred any longer? Do any wonder why the astrologer of Heartshrine Village is in Tather and not performing his duty to his village?

"Lyan." Cailean leaned over and rested a hand on his arm.

Lyan started and tried to collect himself, realizing he didn't know how long he'd been staring blankly at the sky. "Sorry. What did you say?"

"Are you going to be all right?"

"I'm just being the fool stargazer again," Lyan said. "I'm fine."

"You're no fool, Lyan, and don't believe anyone who says otherwise, whether they're your people or mine."

Lyan shook his head. Cailean's men had moved ahead, using the muted moonlight to guide their way. Shadowstar waited patiently for Lyan to signal him to continue on. "Cailean, I need to ask you something."

"What is it?"

"When Ewart attacked your home, the one who cursed you—did he reach you before the assault on your walls, or after?"

Cailean stiffened. "Lyan, why ask about that now?"

"Because of what Kithr said about magic and Tathren keeps. When did it happen, Cailean?"

Cailean's voice dropped to a whisper, though none of his men should have been close enough to hear. "Before. Before the assault on the walls. I could hear it starting outside." He shuddered, hands closing in fists. "He laughed. Said no one would hear me or help me."

"Why did he leave you alive?" Lyan asked, a question that had lurked in his thoughts. "If he wanted the Spear, then why…?"

Cailean gave a thin smile. "I couldn't call for help, and no one knew I needed aid. But before he could take advantage of my weakness, my men found me. He vanished when my soldiers burst in to alert me to the attack." He let out a deep breath. "If they hadn't come when they did, though, I think they would have found a corpse. Why are you asking, Lyan? What does it have to do with this?"

"Only that he had to get inside by some means other than magic. Either he found some path, like Yion did, that no one knew, or…"

"Or someone let him in." Even in the moonlight, Lyan saw the Tathren lord pale. "Are you implying one of my men, maybe even one with us now, betrayed me, Lyan?"

"Only that it's possible, Cailean. I don't know anything for sure, and I have no proof."

"You think one of my men is a traitor?"

Lyan said nothing.

"I trust my men, Lyan."

"Then perhaps you should not try so hard to convince me

I'm not a fool." Lyan nudged Shadowstar, and the stallion joined the rest of the horses.

They found a road, and the horses followed it at a quick walk. They could have pushed faster, but the darkness hid holes and stones in the road, and the thump of hooves on packed dirt in the middle of the night would draw attention. They passed a few villages, and left the road to give them wide berth. Even so, a dog started barking at one village, the sound following even after they left the hamlet behind.

The first faint pale light of dawn touched the sky when Cailean ordered them off the road. Lyan wondered why, but Shadowstar followed after Cailean's horse. Lyan's looked again to the sky and sent a silent prayer to the elven gods. He hoped they could hear him so far from Eilidh Wood. To properly pray, he should be kneeling at a shrine, but he doubted he would find any such sites dedicated to his gods in Tather.

Soldarr, Feyra, Tesseia, please watch over and guide us. Help us free these prisoners. And please, keep Kithr safe.

They topped a rise, and Lyan stared ahead. He'd heard of keeps and fortresses, great structures of stone walls. Kithr had described some he'd seen, and Shiolto had talked about Cailean's keep, but Lyan's mind had conjured foggy images of rude rock walls such as he'd seen around villages. His first sight of the massive wall, with towers and parapets, sent his feeble mental images crashing to the ground. Lyan stared up at the forbidding structure commanding the hill—a barrier as immoveable and unyielding as a mountain.

We have to get into this? How?

His gaze moved over the wall until he found the gates. He drew a sharp breath.

"Lyan? What is it?" Cailean asked.

Lyan swallowed hard, looking at three shapes dangling over the gates. "Bodies."

Cailean grimaced, then turned his horse back down the rise. "Let's go before someone notices us."

Lyan followed him, and the hill blocked the structure from sight once again. They stopped under some trees and tied the horses. Lyan sat against a smooth trunk, feeling small and insignificant. *How can anyone imagine attacking something like that?*

Cailean paced, shaking his head and looking deep in thought.

"Have you been in the keep, Lord Cailean?" Dalrian asked.

"Not for many years," Cailean asked. "I learned a few less obvious ways to get around when exploring with Ewart's bastard, but I doubt I could find them now."

"All right. We might find a servants' entrance along the wall, or, possibly, the sewer." Dalrian grimaced at the thought.

Cailean raised an eyebrow. "Oh?"

"I used the ones in your keep all the time," Dalrian said. "Even managed to hunt twice during the siege."

Cailean's eyes narrowed. "You left passages open into my keep while we were under siege?"

Dalrian hesitated. "No sir. They were always guarded, even when someone went out. I thought you knew. I always told Aikan or sent someone to tell him before I went out."

Cailean looked at Aikan. The older man shifted uncomfortably. "You had more important things to worry about, my lord. I personally checked the security of each passage."

"Lord Cailean, Dalrian and I will search the wall for suitable entrances," Yion interrupted smoothly. "Should we find any, we will report at once."

Cailean scowled, then nodded. "Go. Be careful."

"We shall." Yion bowed, then caught Dalrian's arm and pulled the Tathren after him, removing him from the range of Cailean's fuming.

Cailean turned to Shiolto, voice sharp. "Did you know of

these additional entrances to my keep?"

"Um… I knew Dalrian didn't tend to leave by the main gate, sir." Shiolto looked like a mouse trying to edge away from a hungry cat. "I didn't know you didn't know, sir."

"And you, Torqual? Did you know?"

"During the rotation of posts, I guarded those entrances at times, sir," Torqual answered. "And, as he said, Aikan regularly checked that we manned our posts and remained on guard during the siege."

Cailean said nothing else, only paced like an angry wolf in a cage. Lyan had nothing to say to ease the tense silence. He rested Equinox across his lap and closed his eyes to catch what little rest he could.

"Protect us from discovery, if you can," he thought to the Spear.

As Lyan started to doze, he wondered if he only imagined amusement—a response in which he could all but hear Equinox answer, *"Why don't you try asking me to do something difficult?"*

Lyan woke when Dalrian returned.

"Where's Yion?" Cailean asked. He sounded calmer and less angry than before. Lyan blinked away sleep and rubbed his eyes.

"He's keeping watch on the entrance we found, sir," Dalrian said. "Two guards are posted at it, but they look bored. I'm surprised Yion found the door—I missed the gap completely. The guards came on duty not long before I headed back here, so the watch shouldn't change again soon. They let out a couple of hunters, and I don't expect they're going to be back soon either."

"You want to break in now, in the morning?" Shiolto asked.

"They'll lock the door at night," Dalrian said. "Yion thinks we should go now."

Eyes turned to Cailean. He looked over the group, then nodded. "Leave the horses here. We're going."

4

Fear us.
If our weapons you take, fear our hands.
If our hands you take, fear our feet.
If our lives you take, fear our spirits.
We do not live, we do not die,
But to take what you hold dear.
We are the shadows, creeping ever closer.
We are elves.
Fear us.

The closer they drew to the looming stone fortress, the more oppressive the structure grew. Dalrian led at a pace barely faster than a crawl, paralleling the wall. The undergrowth had been cleared from the base of the walls, and the group clung to the minimal shelter of the brush line. Lyan struggled not to tangle Equinox in the undergrowth, and envied the comfortable ease with which Cailean carried Solstice. Insects buzzed and droned around them, disturbed by the intruders' passage. Lyan fought the urge to slap at them or wave them away from his face. On occasion, he glimpsed figures on the walls above, and each time a patrol passed, the group froze, ducking low to the ground. An insect crept under the brown bandanna Lyan had tied to cover his red hair, and he scratched his scalp, feeling the itchy prickle of its crawl. A dew-laden spider web caught him in the face, leaving Lyan spitting away strands.

Dalrian paused, looking around, then up. He gestured for the others to follow, then bolted across the stretch of open ground to the wall's base. Lyan clutched Equinox, finally freeing the Spear from a tangle of ground-crawling vines. He watched the Tathrens cross the gap until only he remained.

Don't let the guards notice me, he pleaded desperately. Lyan cast a look up for any movement, then sprinted to the wall, heart pounding and ankle throbbing. At any instant, he expected to hear an alarm from above. He was sure everyone could hear the rapid thudding of his heart. But no alarm rose, and after several tense moments, Dalrian started moving again.

A dip in the ground and an alcove in the wall proved to be a doorway low enough that anyone taller than a child would have to duck. The wooden door was painted the same color and pattern as the stones, and if it hadn't been standing slightly ajar, Lyan would have missed it. Yion leaned against the wall, searching for threats and absently rubbing the shallow divot in his forehead. He nodded to Cailean and the rest of the group.

"Where are the guards?" Cailean asked in a low voice.

"They will not wake, Lord Cailean," Yion answered. The mercenary pulled the door open and stepped inside.

Cailean's expression darkened. "You killed them?"

Yion paused and looked back at Cailean with the same calm air he always projected. "Lord Cailean, if we are to rescue elves, then best that those within the keep believe the rescuers are elves as well. The elves of Malgor Forest would not have been satisfied with merely incapacitating those who stood in their path. As well, if the men are loyal to Ewart, they are by definition traitors to you."

An uncomfortable silence fell over the group. Yion walked into the passage with a nod for them to follow. Lyan followed Cailean and Aikan, wincing as Equinox scraped against the low ceiling. He tried to shift the Spear's position enough to keep it from banging, though the shake of his hands didn't help him hold the weapon steady.

Lyan couldn't stand straight in the narrow stone passage, bumping his head against the ceiling even though he ducked. Scuffs marked the floor where muddy feet had tracked often enough to grind the dirt into the pores of the rock.

Shiolto, behind Lyan, whispered, "Somehow, I expected getting inside to be harder."

"I think getting out will be the difficult part," Torqual responded.

"Then perhaps someone should think more about how to use his Spear for something useful and less about how to bang it against every stone in this tunnel," Aikan said. The older man probably intended the words to be spoken under his breath, but the tunnel carried sound well enough that even the other humans heard him.

Lyan flushed angrily and shifted his hold on Equinox. Shiolto put a hand on his shoulder and whispered, "Not here."

Lyan took a deep breath, reminding himself that this was one of the worst possible places for him to lose his temper at Aikan. *Equinox, is there an easier way for me to carry you, or at least, a way I can make less noise?*

A touch of amusement in his mind, then several words ran through Lyan's mind. He whispered them aloud.

"What did you say, Lyan?" Cailean asked.

"Nothing," he answered quickly. Lyan straightened a little, and winced as the butt of Equinox scraped on the floor. But the Spear made no noise against the stones. Lyan's step faltered for a moment, then he kept walking. *Thank you.*

Yion motioned for silence, then moved ahead of the group. Lyan listened, straining to hear hints of what might lie ahead. He jumped when voices spoke, the tunnel carrying the guards' words as clearly as if they stood in front of Lyan.

"No sign of elves yet, eh?"

A nasal voice answered with a laugh. "Not a hint. Maybe Cap'n Horst was right, without their leader they're nothing. Just a bunch of starving savages."

"Getting what they deserve," agreed the other with a chuckle.

You call us savages? Lyan gripped Equinox. *You laugh about elves starving in the forest and you mock prisoners being tortured within your stone fortress. You're worse than Vynzent. At least he had a goal behind his torture.* He closed his eyes and prayed to his gods. *I don't know if you can hear me inside a Tathren fortress, but please, watch over and guide us to the prisoners.*

The nasal voice spoke. "Hey, look, they're going to bring one out."

"Really? I wondered why no one opened the gates yet. Think we can see from here?" Metal rattled as someone took a few steps. "Damn, barely. What do you think? Anyone going to notice if we get a better angle?"

The nasal voice didn't answer. Lyan heard the other guard turn. "What's wrong, Lak? Hear something?"

"Yeah. Come over here for a sec." The nasal voice sounded off to Lyan, though he couldn't say why—some inflection to the voice sounded wrong.

"What is it?" More movement ahead, just outside the tunnel. Then, silence.

Yion reappeared moments later. "The way is clear. Shall we continue?"

"Yion, what did you do?" Cailean asked, voice tight.

"I have learned tricks to imitating voices, my lord. We must take care. A crowd gathers in the courtyard."

"For what?" Dalrian asked.

Yion's expression grew grim. "I believe they intend to bring a prisoner from the [illegible], and raise no alarm when you step from the passage."

Even with the mercenary's vague warning, Lyan started and grabbed Equinox when he discovered a guard standing at either side of the tunnel exit as he ducked out of it. Yion rested a hand on his shoulder.

"Be at ease. Their absence would be noticed, so here they stay. They will not wake."

Neither man leaning against the wall breathed. Lyan shivered and looked to Yion. "Yion, can I ask you something?"

Yion smiled faintly. "Do you intend to ask about Kithr's suspicions of my nature? I do not follow the path of the assassin."

Lyan wanted to believe him, but it bothered him that Yion both knew the suspicion Kithr had once revealed to Lyan and anticipated the question. "Then how?"

Yion spoke quietly in a language not Tathren. Lyan couldn't identify the tongue, though his enchanted ear cuff translated it. "I am a humble servant of my god, he who chose to bestow his blessings upon me, an undeserving soul, and free me from the shackles of my past. The skills of my former life, however, still cling to me, and they have proven useful for better purposes than they were first intended." He spoke in Tathren again. "Come. Time waits not for us."

The tunnel opened into a short, narrow alley between the wall and a stone building. Lyan heard voices rising and falling in excited conversation. He edged down the alley and peered around the corner. A crowd stood gathered around a raised platform, though no one stood on the platform. A pair of wooden posts rose from it, but he didn't see anything of extreme interest about them.

Cailean joined Lyan. "I've heard tales of previous Spearbearers of Solstice who could hide entire armies from sight. Can Equinox do such things?"

Lyan looked at the Spear, and an answer came. He spoke loud enough for all his companions to hear as they gathered at the alley's edge. "Not exactly unseen, but we can be… unnoticed. People will see us, but we'll become unworthy of attention—uninteresting, not even worth remembering. We still have to be careful. If we try to draw attention, we will succeed, and the magic isn't flawless. It'll get us through the crowd, but I don't know if it'll get us into the dungeon unnoticed."

"Any help is better than trying to go through that crowd by stealth," Cailean said. His voice grew softer, for Lyan only to hear. "If I could, I would, but—"

"I know, Cailean," Lyan said. He gripped Equinox. Warmth ran through the Spear. Lyan sensed magic wrap around them like a soft blanket, not smothering or stifling.

Not without misgivings, Lyan stepped from shelter and walked toward the crowd. His companions scrambled after him. Lyan glanced up to the wall. A sentry passed on his rounds. The man cast a look toward the crowd, but paid the intruders no heed. Lyan let out a breath.

We can do this.

As he neared the crowd, the sensation of something *wrong* slammed into his mind. Lyan staggered, head whipping around in search of the source. He saw only an empty, open space, then the fortress wall.

Cailean caught him, voice tight and worried. "What's wrong?"

"Do you feel that?" Lyan asked. "Please tell me you do."

"Feel what?" Cailean asked. "I don't… maybe? Something in the back of my head."

Lyan shook his head sharply. "Something's here. Something's hidden. Something…"

"Equinox is telling you something?" Cailean prompted.

"Yes." Lyan closed his eyes and moved toward the sense of wrongness. One hand reached out, searching for anything, and found stone. Opening his eyes, Lyan didn't see anything before him, but felt smooth stones. He touched Equinox to the surface, and saw a ripple shimmer over the surface of the illusion.

"Uh, Lyan? What're you doing?" Dalrian asked.

"Something *is* here," Lyan said again, more confident. "Something hidden." He traced Equinox along the edge of the structure until he found a door. Lyan tested the knob, but it didn't budge. On impulse, he retrieved Patch's key from his pocket and tried it in the lock, expecting nothing.

To his surprise, the key clicked, and the door opened. He stepped inside without a second thought.

Softly glowing elven lamps lit the interior of the single large room. The air smelled of spices, incense, and blood. A tapestry hanging on one wall drew Lyan's gaze—a star chart all but identical to one that had hung in his teacher's home. He stepped toward it, then stopped, looking down at a table littered with calculations. He knew what they were: an attempt to solve the riddle of the stars and locate Equinox. Alongside the calculations, he saw detailed diagrams of what he guessed to be some sort of stronghold.

"Lyan, what are you thinking? You have no idea what protections or alarms you might disturb in here," Cailean hissed, catching his arm.

"I think we found one of your enemy's lairs," Lyan answered. "Are these familiar to you, Cailean?" He gestured at the diagrams.

Cailean looked, then his face grew hard, admonitions to Lyan forgotten. "They are. Someone made a very thorough examination of my keep and all its entrances." He cast a look over his shoulder at his men, perhaps thinking once more about Lyan's implication of treachery within his ranks.

Cailean's men filed nervously inside, casting looks around the room. Yion lingered just inside the door. "This place is profane," he said, shuddering.

The prickling sensation in Lyan's head directed his attention to the back of the room. A section of the floor lay empty of tables or workbenches, with only a shrine in the far corner. He frowned, wondering at the placement of a shrine here, and trying to guess what gods it honored. Carvings ringed the flat stone altar, the details too small to distinguish from a distance. The etching atop the altar depicted a pair of crossed spears, their outlines highlighted in rusty red. Sealed jars clustered in the corners. Lyan walked toward the shrine.

His foot hit a line drawn on the floor, and a jolt of power, swift and sharp, threw him back. Lyan yelped in surprise and pain as he hit the ground. His companions scrambled to him. "What happened?"

"Protection," Lyan managed. "Wards around that shrine." He panted for breath. He'd last felt such a sensation when he rested his hand on Solstice—a painful warning. "I'm all right."

Torqual helped him stand. "Better not try that again," he said.

Lyan's mouth moved in a small, wry smile. "I won't." He looked toward the shrine again, then turned to Cailean. "You said your enemy is a mage. I am not sure he is. Or if he is, that's not all he is."

Cailean's brow wrinkled in a deep frown. "Oh?"

Lyan licked his lips. "Elder Brenhan puts wards around Heartshrine Village to protect us from danger. He can because he is a priest of our gods. If this is your enemy's lair, and he crafted these wards and the shrine, he's not a mage. He's a priest."

"A *priest?*" Aikan repeated. "What god would condone this?"

"Murdo," Lyan whispered, hesitant even to speak the name. "I think this is the work of a priest of the Mad God." Murdo, the only mortal to ever have claimed both Spears of the Stars and complete the ritual at the Altar of the Heavens. The only mortal known to have wielded the powers of a god.

The Tathrens stared at Lyan, shocked wordless. Even Aikan fell silent, mouth agape. Finally the older man shook his head. "I cannot believe even Ewart would sink so far as to—"

"Oh gods," Shiolto whispered from his spot by the door, voice choked. "Lyan?"

"What?" Lyan turned from the shrine and moved to see what had arrested Shiolto's attention. Then he saw, and his breath caught in his throat, the shrine to the Mad God dimming in importance to the scene unfolding outside. He stepped from the hidden building, drawn almost against his will by the sight.

The platform no longer stood empty. The chains fixed to the two wooden posts were locked around the wrists and ankles of an elf, restraining him spread-eagle between them. The prisoner had been stripped to the waist, and blood streaked his raw skin. He was more gaunt than the warriors in the forest, ribs clearly showing. His eyes burned with rage as he twisted against the chains to look over his tormentors.

People cheered when a man climbed onto the platform. The elf fixed a baleful glare on the smirking human. Lyan shuddered and closed his eyes when the man uncoiled a whip.

"Let them hear you scream, elf."

The whip cracked, drawing a choked cry of pain from the prisoner, to the cheers and mockery of the crowd. Someone rested a hand on Lyan's shoulder. His heart skipped a beat. Opening his eyes, he saw that his companions stood around him.

"Do we have to watch this, Lord Cailean?" Shiolto asked in a strained, tight voice.

"When he is returned to the dungeon, we shall have the

best opportunity to follow," Yion said. "But we need not wait here." The mercenary quickly scanned the surroundings and made for an outbuilding.

"You will all rot."

Lyan had turned to follow Yion, but those words, spoken in Elven, stopped him in his tracks. He looked back to the prisoner, who panted for breath after another strike of the whip. Blood dripped from the prisoner's mouth as he continued. "Everything you touch will crumble and die. Blight and locust will devour your crops. Your women will be consumed to die screaming in agony as wasting takes them. Your brats will be eaten alive by disease before your eyes." He screamed as the whip tore across his back again, ripping into skin.

Like a miasma, power gathered in response to the elf's curse, drawn to the blood—not the blood running down his back, but that willingly shed where the prisoner had bitten into his lip. Lyan felt a blight spreading around the courtyard, wanting only a little more strength to take hold.

"Lyan?" He distantly heard Cailean say his name. "Lyan, don't. You don't want to watch this."

"Stop it," Lyan whispered. "Stop it. That's enough. Stop."

"Lyan?" Cailean caught his arm and pulled him toward the rest of their group.

Don't do this. Lyan's gaze fixed on the prisoner. *Do not lay a blood curse on this land. Do not end your life for this.*

The prisoner's head jerked up, and the gathering curse faltered a moment. His eyes tore over the crowd, but never settled on Lyan. He found strength to raise his voice a little above the hoarse whisper. "Who dares? You think you can stop me? Save your filthy land? Kill me, then. Kill me, and see what power you give my curse," the prisoner panted in Elven.

Curse this land, and you curse your own people as well as the Tathrens. The Tathrens can find other ways to get food, but your camp?

You'll condemn them to starve? I don't want to see you dead. I want you alive and free.

Cailean had pulled Lyan back far enough that he couldn't hear the elf's words any longer. The Tathren said something, but Lyan wasn't listening. The curse hung over them, waiting for the final bloodshed to give it life. By the torturer's sneer, he intended to beat the prisoner to death for the jeering crowd.

That's enough. Stop. That's enough! Lyan desperately fixed his gaze onto the torturer. *You've satisfied your lust for blood. It's enough. You're done. Stop. It's enough.*

The torturer flicked his whip next to the prisoner's face, in front of the elf's eye, and laughed at the elf's reflexive flinch and jerk back. Then he coiled the whip, smirking in satisfaction, and signaled to the guards.

"Take him below."

A few in the crowd groaned in disappointment, but on the whole, the onlookers seemed satisfied with the spectacle they'd witnessed. Lyan took a deep breath and sagged back against the closest wall.

"Lyan, what in the Mad God's Pits? You did something, didn't you?" Cailean insisted in a low voice. The Tathren lord stood in front of him, worry written on his face.

"He intended to lay a blood curse," Lyan whispered. "And he has enough magic to do it. I couldn't let him. I think he expected to be beaten to death."

"I admit, I expected the same thing," Cailean responded. "You influenced the situation somehow, didn't you?"

Lyan just nodded. He blinked several times, clearing his gaze. "This is our chance to follow."

Cailean steadied him and nodded. "Let's go."

The elven prisoner had been pulled down and his arms chained to a pole, allowing the guards to carry him between them without getting in his reach. Lyan counted ten guards just to move one beaten, starving prisoner from the courtyard to the dungeon.

It seemed excessive only until the elf lashed out with chained feet, catching a guard who'd stepped too close. Before Lyan quite saw what happened, the elf had the leg chain wrapped around the guard's neck to choke him. The guard gurgled as he grabbed at the chain.

The other guards hit the prisoner with clubs until the elf couldn't keep the chain drawn tight. The entangled guard struggled free and staggered back, coughing and gagging. One of his fellows pulled him further back.

"Idiot! Don't you have any sense? Trying to get yourself killed?"

Ever since meeting Cailean and his men, I've known elves have a certain reputation among the Tathrens. But not until now did I understand that it's a reputation our warriors worked hard to build and fully intend to maintain.

Though barely conscious, the prisoner managed to lift his head, lips curled in a bloody, wicked smile. "One day, Tathren. Just wait."

The guards glared, but none moved close enough to hit him again. They dragged the elf forward, and he moved his feet in a vague attempt at walking. Cailean looked at Lyan with a question, and Lyan nodded, taking a chance. Ten guards and one prisoner… it might be enough that another seven people could somehow be overlooked.

Shiolto and Dalrian looked as nervous as Lyan felt when they followed the guards into the main building. Yion had regained to his usual calm. Tension radiated from Aikan, expecting a trap to snap shut at any moment, or expecting hordes of elves to swarm down and attack. Torqual studied the fortifications with a soldier's gaze, or at least, with the look Kithr might. Cailean's face was expressionless and difficult to read.

The guards moved through the building with purpose. Others scattered from their path and away from the prisoner. Lyan's gaze swept the interior as they trailed the guards. Inlaid colored stones formed mosaics on the stone floor. The guards showed no concern over the blood their prisoner trailed on the colorful floor, and when Lyan glanced back, he saw a servant already had a bucket of water to wash the stones. No one gave Lyan or his group a second look, not even when they followed the guards and the prisoner into a room with a dozen more guards. The guards in the room looked up in surprise, and Lyan's heart stopped for a moment. But the men looked at the prisoner, not at them.

"Bringing him back? I thought Essen planned on killing him today."

One of the men carrying the prisoner chuckled. "Yeah, I thought so too, but I guess he screamed pretty enough that Essen decided to keep him around another day. Going to let us in?"

The man who'd spoken opened the heavy wooden door, revealing a stairway leading down. The prisoner's escort started down. The guard at the door scowled toward Lyan, though his gaze never quite settled on Lyan's face.

"Come on, hurry it up. They're all chained up down there. Scared of a few elves?"

Lyan shivered. Cailean took the lead, marching down the stairs like he had every right to be there. Lyan hurried after, and heard the others follow. The door slammed shut behind them, making Lyan jump with a wince. The air stank of wastes and rot, making Lyan quickly raise a hand to cover nose and mouth.

"Well, what do you know, elf? You get to enjoy Lord Ewart's finest hospitality for another day," a guard laughed.

The prisoner said nothing in response. Lyan followed Cailean to the bottom of the stairs. Another door stood before them, opening into a larger room. Cailean paused, drew a deep breath, and then grimaced at the smell. With a shudder, the Tathren lord stepped inside.

Lyan had heard of dungeons as places filled with small

cells where prisoners were locked away. The lord of this keep followed a different style to his prison. Cages hung from the ceiling, and some sat on the floor, but few solid walls blocked sight. In the center of the room, fiery coals smoldered in a pit, casting light and shadows to all corners. The chains hanging over the pit were empty, to Lyan's relief. Other implements of torture, however, held victims, their limbs stretched tight or bound at unnatural angles. The guards dragged their prisoner to an empty cage and shoved him in, still chained to the pole.

The leader of the guards turned. "And you thought we were going to kill your man, didn't you, 'Captain'?"

Lyan followed the Tathren's mocking gaze to the first elf he could identify. Nylas hung from the ceiling by chained wrists near the middle of the room, where he had a clear view of any tortures being inflicted. Thick shackles anchored his legs to the floor. Like the other prisoners, Nylas had been stripped to the waist. His face was lean, and he was thin, though not as gaunt as the other prisoners. Unlike the others, he bore no fresh wound, only a map of old scars. The glow of the fire highlighted the red hues of his hair, though Lyan remembered it being browner, darker than his own. No light, however, could warm the icy blue eyes Nylas fixed on the human.

Nylas spoke, voice as cold as his eyes. "I will see your head impaled over our gates, Tathren." Not a threat—a promise.

"You'll rot away in here long after we've killed the rest of your so-called warriors. You'll watch every one of them die screaming in agony. Our lord will keep you here until you've sunk so far into madness that you don't even remember your own name." The guard sneered and turned on his heels. "Move out."

The other guards hastened to obey. Lyan scrambled away from the doorway, tensely waiting for the Tathrens to take notice of them. But the guards withdrew quickly. For all their bravado, they feared the elves. The prisoners were chained, bound, starved, and tortured, yet armed, armored, unrestrained humans kept a wary distance. It seemed laughable, but Lyan could find no humor. These elves had earned their reputation with blood.

The door slammed shut with a force that [illegible], but with the guards' departure, Lyan started to breathe a sigh of relief. Then Nylas's cold, hard gaze fixed directly on him. Spell or no spell, Nylas saw him. The icy eyes narrowed, and he spoke again in Tathren. "What dark corner of my mind did you wander into and go mad, mage, to think dredging up *this* phantom would gain you anything? Do you even know what face you wear?"

"Lyan?" Cailean whispered.

"Cailean, right now, I don't think any power in this world would prevent these elves from noticing Tathrens in their midst," Lyan responded quietly. He never took his eyes off Nylas as he stepped away from the wall. "It's the same face I've worn my whole life, Nylas. That of Lyan of Heartshrine Village."

The other elves started to shift and move, those who could, and more venomous eyes found Lyan and his Tathren companions. Nylas spoke again.

"Lyan, the fool of the village. What idiocy made you think you should drag him from my memory—a useless, weak *stargazer*?" He jerked against his chains.

Lyan's hands clenched. The words cut sharply, the mockery he'd learned to live with in youth. "Yes, the 'master of falling out of trees,' wasn't it?" He spoke in Elven, and walked closer to Nylas—far closer than any Tathren guard had dared. "But I never told anyone the real folly that earned me *that* title. *You* told me I had to steal an egg from the nest of the silver-wing eagle."

Nylas's eyes narrowed.

Lyan spoke in a low voice. "You did, because you didn't want to deal with a younger cousin who idolized you. You told me anyone who wanted to join you and those boys who followed you had to bring a silver-wing eagle's egg. I knew you were lying. I knew that before I snuck off to do what you thought no one would be stupid enough to attempt." He stood before Nylas, white-knuckle grip on Equinox. "A broken leg, a broken arm, a sprained wrist—those were the worst of it, though gods know I should have lost a few fingers to the bird for robbing her nest." Lyan held Nylas's icy gaze. "But I got that damned egg, and I got it to you without a single crack, and I never said a word to the adults who questioned me about what drove me to make the attempt in the first place. Think about that next time you call me 'weak', Nylas."

"Then I'll simply call you an idiot. What in the names of our fallen would bring *Lyan* here?"

Lyan raised Equinox. Nylas didn't flinch, but the other elves tensed, as if they had any means of stopping Lyan from striking Nylas. Lyan swept the Spear over his head, striking the chains binding Nylas's arms. Equinox cut through the metal as easily as through fresh bread.

Of any act Lyan could have taken, that one caught Nylas by surprise. He fell to the floor with a clatter of chains. Nylas sprang to his feet with surprising speed, the first emotion other than hate glimmering in his eyes: the faintest hint of confusion. He had thought he had the truth, but now doubt entered his certainty.

Nylas looked at Lyan with narrow eyes. Chains still held his legs, but he could move. "I could kill you where you stand."

Lyan swallowed the lump in his throat, but answered. "You could try, if you want to attempt to become a kin-slayer. Patch said you don't kill your own people, but she might have been wrong."

Nylas grew abruptly still and tense, a response echoed by the other elves. "What do you know of her, mage?"

"Those who remain in your camp sent us here, Nylas. We

agreed to free the elven prisoners in this keep in exchange for passage through the forest."

Nylas's eyes flickered away from Lyan long enough to take in Lyan's companions, standing well out of reach at the back wall. Lyan didn't turn. He could feel Aileen's stare boring bore holes in the back of his head. Nylas spoke. "Tathrens who enter my forest don't leave alive."

"They do when they come as companions to the Spearbearer of Equinox," Lyan said in a voice as cold as Nylas's.

He could hear the drip of water and the ragged breathing of prisoners who refused to give voice to their pain. No one moved. In the stillness, Lyan felt the weight of eyes on him. Nylas broke the silence.

"You dare to claim that *you*, the useless stargazer, have claimed a Spear of the Stars. Not even a warrior, but a book-rotted *astrologer*."

Lyan's jaw tightened. "I dare to tell you we have no right to Solstice, and we never did. I bear Equinox. I solved the riddle to find the shrine, and I succeeded in the Trials, then was chosen by the Spear itself." He stepped closer, until he stood within easy arm's reach of Nylas. "I hold one of the most powerful weapons known to us. I didn't *have* to agree to go with your men when they attacked us in the forest. I *chose* to, and I *chose* to agree when they proposed that we free the prisoners from this keep. I thought I would be aiding my kin and my people, but now I wonder if I was wrong." He looked over the prisoners, then back to Nylas, speaking loud enough that none could mistake his words. "There is no helping those Lost to Eilidh Wood."

"You dare," Nylas hissed, rage burning in his eyes.

Lyan braced himself, anticipating the rage turning to murderous intent at any moment. "Then prove me wrong. I am here, in the company of *Tathrens*, to free you. You can try to kill me—the Spearbearer, or you can accept our help. What will you do?"

Nylas's fingers curled like claws, and he caught hold of Lyan's shirt, pulling Lyan face-to-face with him. Lyan smelled sweat and unbathed flesh, but no fresh blood on Nylas. Nylas's icy blue eyes bore into Lyan's for a heartbeat that hung like an eternity, then he released his grip. Nylas looked slowly around the dungeon, to his men. Finally he spoke in Tathren. "We will accept *your* help, Lyan. Only yours. These 'companions' you claim will not be touched, but we acknowledge nothing of them or from them."

"I wouldn't have gotten here without them, but if that's the resolution you can abide by, that will free you without shedding your blood or ours, fine." Lyan took a step back and held Equinox lengthwise before him. "Then you don't owe any debt to the Tathrens. Only to me."

Nylas's hands clenched in fists. He closed his eyes, drawing a slow breath that betrayed fury. The elves of Eilidh Wood rarely counted debts among each other. It implied distrust. To elves who were counted as Lost to Eilidh Wood—the exiles and those who had fallen from the ways that the elves held sacred, to them, the elves of Eilidh Wood counted debts.

"You dare call us Lost, then you claim debt against us?" another elf demanded from his cage, slamming a fist against the bars.

"Silence!" Nylas ordered. He opened his eyes to stare hard at Lyan as he rested his hands on the Spear's shaft. "For the release of my men and a safe return to our camp, I will be in debt to Lyan of Heartshrine Village, Spearbearer of Equinox. If you have lied, and either of those titles does not apply to you, then there is no debt, and I will kill you."

Lyan didn't flinch from Nylas. "I know."

5

Hope in the night
Dream for the day
Of shadow and light
And unbroken way

Lyan didn't waste time looking for a key. Equinox cut through the chains at Nylas's ankles, giving the elven captain free movement. He didn't expect any thanks from Nylas, and he got none. Nylas's icy glare didn't even lessen. His doubts wouldn't be easily put aside, nor his smoldering anger at Lyan's accusations. His eyes flashed to Cailean and his men, then back to Lyan. Without a word, Nylas walked to the nearest of his men, an elf with a long burn down the side of his face, locked in a cage. The ends of the chains rattled as Nylas moved.

His tone was brusque. "Physon. Can you walk?"

The other straightened painfully. "I can kill Tathrens."

Nylas's eyes narrowed. "Of course you can. That's not what I asked."

"Yes, Captain."

"Good." The look Nylas gave Lyan required no words.

Why do you ask that? What would you do if he said no? Leave him here? Lyan touched Equinox to the cage door, and saw a brief flash of blue-white fire in the keyhole. Liquefied metal dripped to the floor as the lock melted. Physon carefully pushed at the door, and it swung open. He looked toward Cailean, then to Nylas. Nylas shook his head, and Physon's lip curled in a brief sneer, nearly a snarl.

Nylas moved to the next elf. He moved slowly, and Lyan knew he must be in pain, but Nylas didn't let it show on his face. Compared to the others, he hadn't been physically tortured beyond being left hanging in chains, and Lyan guessed he didn't want to let his men see him hurting.

Or maybe he thinks showing pain is "weak", and he won't act "weak".

Lyan freed the second elf, then caught Nylas's shoulder before Nylas could move on. Nylas spun, one hand clenching to strike at anyone who dared such an affront as to lay a hand on him without permission, but he held back, only narrowing his eyes at Lyan. "What?"

"I don't have to do this one at a time, Nylas. If I can trust you and your men to do as you've said and not attempt to harm my companions, I can release them all at once." Leaving elves trapped in their suffering sickened him.

"You doubt my word?" Nylas asked in a low, dangerous voice.

"I have just as much faith in your word as you do in mine," Lyan countered.

"Do you ever know when to shut your mouth?" Nylas's eyes narrowed.

"Obviously not, since I still suffer under the delusion that I can actually talk sense into you," Lyan snapped. "Now, do we keep doing this the slow way or not?"

"I accepted your terms, provisional on you being who you

claim to be. Until you prove you are not, we will all abide by those terms." Nylas looked from Lyan around the room. "Your Tathrens do not exist, so far as we are concerned. They are nothing, neither threat nor enemy. So long as you are who you claim to be." He spoke as much to his men as to Lyan. *He's willing to consider I might be who I claim. Otherwise he would already have killed me for that insult.*

Lyan drew a deep breath and focused on Equinox. A hundred answers raced through his mind, all possible ways of releasing the prisoners. Lyan gripped the Spear to steady himself. *Simple. A simple way that won't draw the guards upstairs.*

The spell was elven in origin, or at least, the words to cast it were Elven. "Let that which binds be undone, that which restrains be broken, those who are in chains be set free."

Nylas drew a quick, sharp, surprised breath. Cages opened, chains fell from the limbs of those caught in their hold. Then Nylas looked at the manacles still around his own wrists and ankles, and he fixed his gaze on Lyan again.

Lyan met his gaze. "They aren't restraining you."

"You think not? Idiot mooncalf."

Lyan's jaw tensed, but he kept his voice even. "I'll thank you not to insult the moon like that, Nylas. I'm sure any child of hers has far more sense than I."

Nylas paused a moment, taken aback. He didn't respond, only moved to his men, helping those who needed the aid to get to their feet. He stopped before one soldier who had managed to push himself up to sit on the angled table where he'd been bound with limbs stretched tight. Nylas looked at the elf and said simply, "You won't walk."

The other didn't deny the assessment. Lyan saw his feet and knew why. The elf's feet were black and swollen, misshapen with broken or crushed bones. Pain lined his pale, drawn face. "Then find me a weapon, sir."

"Why—" Lyan started to ask, before understanding sunk

in. He looked sharply at Nylas. "You're not leaving anyone behind!"

"And who do *you* suggest carry a cripple?" demanded the injured elf, anger giving his voice strength. "You?"

"Reeze is not the only cripple here," Nylas said, voice flat. "Regardless of how you got in, do you really expect to walk back out without causing a stir?"

"Do you care so little about your own men that you'll leave them behind to die?" Lyan burst.

Lyan didn't see the blow coming, but expected it. Nylas hit hard. Lyan crumpled to the floor. Chains rattled as Nylas grabbed him by the shirt and lifted Lyan up to his face. "You know *nothing*," he hissed. "I would rather carve out my own heart than leave my men here. I do not abandon them, and they know it. They are willing to see their lives end in battle against our enemies. They know we are not going to get through Tathren guards if half my men are unable to fight because they're carrying those who can't stand. So, tell me, 'Lyan', do you and your Spear have some means of making the lame walk?"

"If you don't let go of me, you may never find out." Lyan locked gazes with Nylas, and they glared at each other. Finally Nylas released Lyan's shirt, letting him back down to the ground.

The elves stirred, angry eyes fixing behind Lyan as he heard steps on the stone. Lyan turned to see Cailean approaching. The Tathren lord stopped when he saw he had Lyan's attention. Lyan said nothing to Nylas, but walked with Cailean back to the far wall where the rest of their group stood.

Aikan trembled with anger. "There is no reason we should be freeing these bloodthirsty savages."

"Elven ears are very keen, Aikan. Keep your voice down," Lyan replied. "How much of what Nylas said did you understand?"

"He's kept mostly to speaking in Tathren," Cailean answered in a low voice. "He switches to Elven sometimes, but mostly we've understood. I did hear that not everyone can walk. Those left behind will kill as many guards as they can before they fall."

Lyan nodded.

Cailean gazed at Lyan, then motioned for him to follow as he opened the door to the stairs and moved into the short hallway, creating at least an illusion of privacy. The Tathren spoke softly. "Can Equinox create a way to get everyone out, Lyan?"

"I don't know," Lyan admitted. "When I ask questions like that, there are so many possibilities I can barely think, or figure out what any of them are or do." He paused as Equinox thrust a barrage of sensations at him. "I think… not easily."

"You don't have stories? Legends?"

"I know a tale where a Bearer of Solstice uses the Spear to move people from one spot to another like the door at the shrine did, but that isn't much help."

"Why not?" Cailean asked.

"From what little I can tell, the Spears don't share abilities. Solstice can do things Equinox cannot, and Equinox can do things Solstice cannot. They may be able to reach the same ends, but not by the same ways."

"That's not what I meant, Lyan," Cailean said. "Equinox is not the only Spear here."

"No." Lyan shook his head. "If you use Solstice—"

"I'll manage," Cailean said.

"You'll be unconscious and surrounded by elves who invaded your land to take the very Spear you're talking about using!" Lyan argued. "I don't trust Nylas's word nearly *that* much."

"Lyan. We agree we can't leave anyone behind, right?"

Lyan nodded reluctantly.

"Can you tell me a better way?"

I can't let Cailean do this! If he tries to transport us outside the keep, he won't be able to do anything, not even defend himself. Isn't there some other way? Some way that won't drain him and announce to Nylas and all his men that Cailean carries Solstice?

A thought pressed into his mind as Equinox offered an alternative. Lyan stopped. *They don't have to know Cailean did it. If they think it my doing… Can I give Cailean strength and offset the curse's effects?*

He looked at Cailean. "I have a plan that could work, if you're willing."

"Tell me." Cailean met his gaze evenly.

"You use Solstice, as you offered. Equinox will give you my strength so the curse won't drain you. As far as Nylas and his men know, the magic would appear to be my doing and the work of Equinox."

Cailean stiffened. "That would put the brunt of the curse's effects on you, Lyan."

"Exactly." Lyan held Cailean's gaze. "I'm the one who becomes weak and exhausted. I'm the one who shows all the signs of working powerful magic, giving them no reason to suspect you."

"You have no idea how dangerous what you're suggesting is, Lyan."

"It's a danger you're willing to take for people who would gladly kill you regardless of Solstice. So it's one that I'll take for my own people."

Cailean nodded finally. "All right. I don't like it, but if you're sure."

"I'm sure."

When they returned to the prison, Lyan saw the elves had scoured the dungeon for weapons. Their captors left little, but even poles and chains became deadly in elven hands. The elves divided into two groups: the walking wounded and those whose legs and feet had been too mutilated to stand. Even some who kept their feet did so by sheer determination. Lyan saw bloody footprints left by a pale-faced elf who limped past clutching a wooden pole in one hand; rough bandages wrapped the other.

Nylas faced Lyan. "Well?"

"We're not leaving anyone here," Lyan said, unbending. "Whether they can walk or not."

Doubt met his words. Watching Nylas's men, Lyan didn't know how some could move without screaming. He looked away from the fresh burns and lash marks he saw all around. Near Lyan, Shiolto shifted uncomfortably, wanting to help the injured. Lyan rested a hand on his arm and shook his head.

"Let's see this miracle you claim you can work," Nylas sneered.

"Gather together." Lyan walked to the middle of the room, where Nylas had been chained.

Cailean followed close, and the rest followed. The elves surrounded them. Even Torqual stood stiffer, wary and uncomfortable. Yion still radiated calm.

Thinking back to the implication of Yion's words to him at the passage, Lyan couldn't help but wonder if some of Yion's calm came from an assurance that he could kill even a band of raging elven warriors if he needed to. Lyan tried not to ponder the thought too long.

A new distraction came, but not an encouraging one. Somewhere up the dark stairs, the door creaked open. Nylas spoke, voice dead calm. "If you expect your miracle to work, Lyan, you should do it before the torturers arrive. They're on their way now, the same time as they always come."

Lyan shot a look of alarm to Cailean, icy fear running through him. "You could have mentioned that sooner, Nylas."

The elves held their weapons, eager for a fight. It would be only the start of a battle that would leave this keep red with blood. The door above groaned shut. Lyan gripped Equinox, palms damp with sweat. Cailean drew a deep breath, eyes closed.

Give him the strength he needs.

Lyan couldn't feel the magic Solstice began working, but he did feel Equinox respond. As if a pile of stones had suddenly been slung onto his shoulders, Lyan staggered. He panted for breath as if he ran uphill pushing a boulder, or swam endless circles, unable to find shore.

At his silent command, his earring didn't translate his words. Lyan whispered in an archaic language, certain the words would be indistinguishable from spellcasting to those who heard. "Hurry. Please hurry. And please, if any gods are listening, please let this work."

The weakness grew worse, and still nothing happened. Lyan clung to Equinox, but even hanging onto the Spear felt like trying to carry lead weights.

The door at the bottom of the stairs opened, and a moment of stunned silence followed. Lyan didn't look to see the disbelief on the faces of the Tathren torturers. He heard it clearly enough in their voices.

"The prisoners are loose! Guards! To arms!"

All around Lyan, the elves tensed, ready to attack. Lyan spoke sharply in Elven, voice thick and strained. "Move and you'll die a meaningless, unnecessary death at Tathren hands."

"Hold position," Nylas ordered.

Guards poured down the stairs with battle shouts. Lyan sagged against Equinox as an endless Tathrens hoard charged, too exhausted to do more than watch. Elves bared their teeth, ready for battle.

Lyan's stomach dropped to his toes as the world lurched. Vertigo assailed him and sounds became a blurred chaos of noise. He heard someone shriek, and didn't think it himself. Lyan squeezed his eyes shut against the bottomless, empty void into which he fell until finally the spinning stopped and sound returned—his own rapid panting for breath and a cricket's uncertain, querying chirp.

He opened his eyes. Balance abandoned him. He staggered and tripped. Lyan gasped in pain as his ankle twisted. He grabbed desperately for any support.

Hands caught him and lowered him to the ground. A voice whispered in his ear. "Sit down. Mooncalf."

Firmly seated on solid ground, Lyan blinked rapidly. Nylas stepped back, arms now folded across his chest as if he hadn't stopped Lyan from falling on his face. Looking past him, Lyan saw that most of the elves lay sprawled on the ground, or sat with expressions as dazed as his. Tall grass grew all around them, and the midday sun shone down. Raising a hand to shield his eyes against the light, Lyan searched the landscape for the looming stone monstrosity, but saw no keep. Lyan closed his eyes and dropped back on the ground.

"You certainly have a sense for the dramatic," Nylas said.

Lyan peeled one eye open to look at his cousin. "Could have mentioned… schedule… little sooner."

"Why? Either you could do what you claimed, or you couldn't. One way or the other, we would have left the dungeon. It simply would have taken longer if you'd failed." A long pause followed, then Nylas spoke in a low voice. "I am in your debt. No doubt you and your 'companions' will be parting ways with us now."

Lyan found energy enough to shake his head. "To forest… with you."

"Why?" Nylas demanded.

"Your men insisted… leave someone… with them."

Nylas's mouth curled in a sneer. "You were fool enough to leave a Tathren in my camp? You won't get him back."

"Didn't leave… Tathren," Lyan answered. "Kithr stayed."

Nylas stiffened. "Kithr is here, and he left *you* alone with *Tathrens*?"

"He thought it better than leaving me alone with your men." Lyan closed his eye.

Nylas shook him, making Lyan wince. "You don't sleep until I know where we are." He lifted Lyan to sit again, though Lyan slumped with the boneless sag of a dead weight. "Where did you take us?"

Opening an eye again took most of Lyan's fading determination, and he could barely focus. He couldn't answer Nylas.

"Let him be, elf. Lyan just saved your life and the lives of all your men at the expense of most of his strength." Cailean spoke, voice sharp and protective. "He needs rest. And I believe the dark spot on the horizon is Malgor Forest."

Nylas looked in the direction Cailean indicated, but he addressed his words to Lyan. "Closer to the forest than the keep, then. We need to leave before the soldiers come hunting."

"Just stick me on a horse," Lyan said.

"So next you'll conjure horses? Good. I could use some food," Nylas responded.

"Not food. Gifts from Ohrlan. And Shadowstar." Lyan blinked and tried again to focus, but he knew it a losing battle. He spoke again, but not to Nylas. "Shadowstar. Find us. Bring the other horses."

Nylas lowered him back to the ground, and Lyan gratefully anticipated sleep. Before it found him, he heard Nylas speak to Cailean in a low, angry voice, meant for no one else to hear.

"I don't know what business you think you have with Lyan or what he's doing in your company. But know this, Tathren dog: if you allow any harm to come to him, I will hunt you down, gut you alive, and strangle you with your own entrails."

"If I let harm come to Lyan, I assure you that you won't be the first in line to bring me slow and painful death," Cailean responded.

"Don't dismiss me, *Tathren*!"

"I don't," Cailean responded grimly. "But to carry out that threat, you would have to reach me before either Kithr or my own men."

If Nylas said more, the words flowed past Lucan, not even reaching his dreams as the darkness of sleep swallowed him whole.

6

Guiding star, lead us home
Bring us safely to our rest
Guiding star, forever roam
Guide us ever through your test

The scent of food wafted past Lyan's nose, rousing a groggy mumble. His stomach growled, and he wondered fuzzily whether hunger made it worth the effort to open his eyes.

He heard Dalrian chuckle. "If this didn't get a response, I was going to wonder if you'd ever wake up, Lyan."

"Huh?" Lyan blinked, opening his eyes a little. He smelled moisture in the air and heard the soft patter of light rainfall hitting something just overhead. "Morning already?"

"More like mid-afternoon," Dalrian answered. "Careful sitting up—the shelter's keeping the rain off you, but it's not sturdy."

Lyan blinked again, finally recognizing the obstruction between him and the rain—live grass stalks woven together closely enough that only an occasional raindrop slipped through. He reached up to touch the grass. When his fingers brushed the stalks, they unraveled, returning to their natural state.

Nylas's work.

Lyan clumsily sat, every muscle in his body throbbing. Even with the overcast sky, the light stabbed in his eyes, and moving made his head pound. His right hand ached, and he realized he still clutched Equinox as if the Spear would be wrested from him. He peeled stiff fingers loose.

Dalrian handed him a trencher of thick stew. "Eat. I can hear your stomach from here."

Still little more than half awake, Lyan devoured the stew. He nearly burned his tongue, but his stomach quieted.

Lyan grew aware of eyes on him. He looked up and around. Cailean, Aikan, Torqual, Yion, Shiolto, and Dalrian all sat near. Nylas's soldiers kept watch on Tathrens, Lyan, and the land around them. Tall grass rose over their heads, shielding them from patrols that might be searching for them. Beyond the elves, Shadowstar and the other horses grazed, unbothered by the rain.

"Anyone else eaten?" Lyan asked, rubbing gritty eyes. He could see the elves had bandaged their more serious wounds, but their gazes didn't tell him whether or not they resented his meal.

"Everyone's eaten," Dalrian said. "The elves hunted and brought meat for the stew. We tried to wake you earlier, but you didn't even stir. Lo… Cailean said to let you alone."

"Still rather be asleep." Lyan paused, frowning. "I thought… didn't I say to put me on a horse and keep going?"

"You did." Nylas spoke from behind him. Lyan jumped. "Apparently, you failed to inform Shadowstar of this plan, Lyan."

Lyan shifted around to face his cousin. Nylas scowled down at him, arms folded across his chest. Freedom from the Tathren dungeon hadn't softened his disposition in the least.

"Sorry. Shadowstar was stubborn? And you at least believe that's Shadowstar?"

Nylas's scowl deepened. "There's little chance I could mistake that damned beast for anything else, Lyan. As Shadowstar has shown a marked preference for only one person, I am forced to accept that you are the fool you claim to be."

"Wait. How would he recognize Shadowstar?" Shiolto asked. "How long has it been since he saw you, Lyan?"

"Not since he left for the war," Lyan answered. "But Shadowstar has been not exactly my horse, but has answered my call since my youth."

Nylas cuffed him, making Lyan's ears ring. "You still insist on calling that creature a horse?"

Lyan rubbed his throbbing head. "What? Shadowstar *is* a horse."

Nylas crouched down to eye-level with Lyan, speaking in a tone he would use with a slow-witted child. "Tell me you at least know how long a horse lives, mooncalf."

Lyan thought. "Fewer years than a human?"

"And Shadowstar has lived how many?"

"More than I have," Lyan answered.

"And you're nearly a hundred and fifty. Yet you still call that creature a horse?" Nylas pressed.

"Well, not an *ordinary* horse," Lyan allowed.

"The guardian spirit of Appret Plains is not an ordinary horse." Nylas snorted scornfully. "And Equinox is not an ordinary weapon." He stood. "Get up. We've lingered here too long."

Lyan picked up Equinox and started to get his feet under him. When weight settled on his left ankle, he drew a sharp breath and stumbled.

Cailean jumped to his feet and steadied Lyan. "What's wrong?"

Lyan straightened and braced himself with the Spear.

"I'm all right. Thanks. Just twisted my ankle again when we arrived here." He sucked in several deep breaths. "I'll be all right. Just need a moment."

"Don't make me have to explain to Kithr why he shouldn't kill me for letting you get hurt. Be careful, Lyan."

Lyan smiled faintly at Cailean. "Don't worry. I'm fine, and I'm sure it'll feel a little better by the time we reach the forest." Though the pain wasn't as sharp as the first time he'd injured his ankle in Eilidh Wood—the event that had precipitated his first meeting with Cailean and his men—this fresh aggravation promised to leave him limping for a few days.

Shadowstar looked up at the movement of the elves, and the stallion trotted to Lyan, brushing past Nylas's men and ignoring their resentful looks. Lyan rubbed Shadowstar's nose. "You could have let Nylas toss me over your back and go, you know."

Shadowstar snorted and tossed his head. Shiolto spoke quietly. "I doubt they'll admit it, but the elves needed the rest too, Lyan."

"Did they let you help?"

"I didn't try. I set out the bandages and herbs I have, though, and they used them. Their leader there—Nylas, right?"

Lyan nodded.

"Nylas never talked directly to us. He just made sure he spoke our language if he wanted us to hear, and he addressed a lot of comments to Shadowstar." Shiolto hesitated. "Um… guardian spirit of Appret Plains?"

Lyan shifted uncomfortably.

Shiolto forced a smile and patted Lyan on the shoulder. "Don't worry about it. We'd better get the other horses."

The rest of the horses hadn't followed Shadowstar into their midst, but watched the elves warily. Cailean spoke with Aikan quietly. Aikan looked less than pleased, but finally nodded. Cailean turned to Lyan, and waited until Lyan had settled onto Shadowstar's back.

"Lyan, would you please extend to your people my invitation to ride? Some might find it easier."

Lyan admired the care with which Cailean chose his words, avoiding the implication that some of the tortured elves couldn't walk. "Of course." Turning to Nylas, Lyan asked in Elven, "Do I need to repeat Cailean's offer? I know you heard him."

"We will accept *your* offer," Nylas said, pointedly ignoring Cailean. "It will simplify matters."

At Lyan's nod, the Tathrens retrieved their mounts and the two packhorses. All the animals distrusted the elves, but with soothing, were convinced to stand still. Shadowstar kept watch over the proceedings, Lyan on his back.

Shiolto, Dalrian, Torqual, and Yion unloaded gear from the horses. Torqual handed Aikan and Cailean their packs. Aikan scowled, but didn't object, though he did fuss with the ties on his bag, adjusting them to his liking.

Shiolto tripped, dropping his bag with a curse. Lyan looked quickly at the elves, but none stood close enough to have tripped the human. Torqual offered Shiolto a hand.

"Okay?"

"Yeah, I'm fine." Shiolto smiled and wiped mud from his pants, embarrassed.

Yion and Torqual helped him collect the items that had spilled from his bag, and Shiolto laced the bag shut and swung it over his shoulder. Lyan walked Shadowstar to Aikan and Cailean.

"Shadowstar and I can carry your bags," he said, looking more to Aikan than Cailean.

"Then take Lord Cailean's," Aikan said, forgetting to omit the honorific.

Cailean handed Lyan one bag of supplies, then looked pointedly at the older man.

"I do not need help," Aikan snapped, "nor do I need any elf poking through my belongings."

Lyan remembered the Forests of Cossette, when he'd noticed someone had searched his bags, and he wondered if that had been Aikan. He spoke in a low voice. "When we start moving, Nylas and his men are going to move as fast as they can, to prove they can. Anyone who straggles, they'll leave behind. Especially Tathrens. Allow me to help, Aikan. Please."

Aikan eyed him with suspicion. "Helping us rather than your own people?"

Lyan spoke low. "They may be elves, but they are not my people. They are Lost to Eilidh Wood."

Aikan gazed at Lyan, then handed him the heavier bags without a word. Lyan secured it with Cailean's. Shadowstar shifted restlessly, and Lyan patted the stallion's neck.

The elves who couldn't walk were helped onto the horses, faces pale with pain but fixed in masks of grim determination. Feet had been bandaged, limbs splinted. Lyan's gaze moved over Nylas's men, stomach twisting at the wounds they hadn't yet bandaged. The elf who had been flogged in the courtyard sensed Lyan's eyes on his raw back and turned to meet his gaze. Despite the fresh beating, he walked.

"You interrupted my curse, didn't you?"

"Yes," Lyan answered.

"And you used the Spear to stop the Tathren from killing me."

"Yes," Lyan said again. "I wasn't going to watch him beat you to death."

"Why not?"

Lyan gave the only answer he thought the other might accept. "For the same reason I interrupted your curse: because you didn't have to die that day, and because a life should be worth more than that kind of death."

"Not for the sake of the Tathren brats who would have starved?"

"I know better than to think appealing to anything to do with Tathrens would matter to you. Though I could argue that your own people are the most likely to starve if famine strikes. Especially the young ones." He thought of Patch and the other half-Tathren children he'd seen.

"We survive," the other elf said.

"Just like you survived. Are you unhappy to still be alive?" Lyan asked.

"I did not ask your help, and I owe you nothing for your interference in the courtyard."

"I never claimed you owed me for it. Count it however you choose," Lyan told him.

"Move out," Nylas ordered.

The rain trailed off as they rode, and the clouds gradually broke apart. Lyan stole glances at the sky, but kept his eyes more often on their path. Keenly aware Nylas watched him, Lyan refused to give his cousin more reason to mock him. The elves marched in silence at a pace that discouraged conversation. The Tathrens kept the pace, but their gear's weight took a toll on them.

After a silent march, they reached Malgor Forest late in the afternoon. The horses balked at entering, but Lyan let Shadowstar walk beside Nylas, and the other horses reluctantly followed the stallion. Nylas barely glanced at Lyan. As he advanced, brambles and thorns curled back, clearing a path for the elves, and not striking at Cailean or his men.

Lyan heard a birdcall from the trees ahead, answered by a similar call from an elf behind Lyan. His hand closed around Equinox and tension ran up his spine, but he didn't raise the Spear. As long as Nylas's men held to their side of the agreement, he shouldn't be worried.

But he wasn't willing to assume he could trust anyone who dwelt in this place.

Feet and hooves crunched through dry leaves, and in the trees above them, Lyan heard other feet moving along the branches. Sooner than he expected, they faced the bramble wall of the elven camp. The wall opened. For the first time, Lyan saw traces of relief in the elves around him.

Inside the wall, other elven warriors stood armed and waiting, no more willing to assume this wasn't a Tathren trick than Lyan was to assume he could trust Nylas.

"Stand down," Nylas ordered in Elven, frosty glare raking the camp. "What in the Mad God's Pits were you thinking to send a *stargazer* to free us from a Tathren dungeon?" He waited. "Well?"

"Welcome back, Captain." Patch slipped around a pair of warriors and gazed at Nylas. "Lyan insisted he and his companions are not part of the war, and that the war is over. We couldn't judge what we should do with them in your absence."

"So you decided to send him to get me?" Nylas demanded. He closed his eyes and let out a deep breath. "Very well. Patch reaching such a conclusion I can understand. The rest of you, however." He growled in anger, opening his eyes and looking around the camp again. "Where is Kithr? Lyan said he's here."

"He's below, Captain," Milosh said.

Nylas set off across the camp in a swift stalk.

"Captain? What about… them?"

Nylas spun to glare at his men. "Lyan, Spearbearer of Equinox, is responsible for freeing those held in the Tathren dungeon. His companions do not exist. And *you* sent the wielder of our sacred weapon alone into a *Tathren* stronghold!"

Milosh had no response to that. A protest that he hadn't known Lyan carried Equinox was unlikely to assuage Nylas's anger. Milosh silently bowed his head as Nylas stormed into the tunnels.

The elves helped their companions off the horses. One of the elves of the camp eyed the closest horse with a decidedly hungry look. Shadowstar snorted a warning, and the elf backed away, casting a dark look at the stallion. Lyan slid from the saddle, gingerly testing his weight on his ankle. He freed Equinox from its bindings and used the Spear to support himself. Shadowstar nuzzled his hair, and Lyan patted the stallion on the nose.

"Watch over things for me, okay?"

Shadowstar tossed his head in agreement. Lyan looked to Cailean. The Tathren lord returned his bags to his saddle and reassured his mount all was well. Cailean didn't even glance over. "You don't need my permission, Lyan. Find Kithr so we can be on our way."

"Right." Lyan moved toward the tunnel Nylas had entered. He walked slowly, trying not to limp.

Patch joined him. Lyan glanced at her with surprise. She met his gaze. "I would speak with you."

"All right," Lyan answered. He reached into his pocket and pulled out the key. "I want to thank you for this. It helped."

Patch folded Lyan's fingers around the key once again. "Keep it. I think you might need it more than I."

She didn't say anything more until they entered the tunnels. Then, she caught his arm and pulled him into a nearby storeroom. Patch studied Lyan as he sat on a crate. "Your Tathren friend carries Solstice, doesn't he?"

"Why do you ask?" Lyan asked warily.

She pointed at Equinox. "I noticed similarities between your weapons. The Captain said you carry Equinox. We have been taught of the two Spears, and that we are here in search of Solstice, which the Tathrens have. Your friend's Spear has the same aura as yours, and if you carry Equinox, his must be Solstice."

"Then why are you asking, if you already know?"

"To see how you respond," she said.

"I protect my friends," Lyan told her. "And the bearer of

Solstice is my friend. So, since I've acknowledged that secret to you, tell me something in return, if you will."

"What is it?"

"Do you think you're Nylas's daughter?"

She frowned. "Why do you want to know?"

"If you are, then we're kin—family. Nylas is my cousin, so, if you're his child, we are cousins as well."

"Kin," she repeated thoughtfully. "No one knows if I'm the Captain's child, not even him."

"So, you have no one who claims you as theirs," Lyan said, sadness gripping his chest. In Eilidh Wood, even an orphan would be claimed by someone, whether or not any blood relation existed. "Do you want a family?"

Her sharp eyes searched him for mockery. "Would you dare to claim a child born of a Tathren as your kin?"

"Why shouldn't I?" Lyan asked.

The simple answer surprised Patch. "You're odd."

"So I've been told."

"What is a stargazer? They all call you a stargazer, and say it with some mockery, but at the same time, respect."

If she heard respect toward him from Nylas's men, Lyan did not. "I'm an astrologer. I read the stars to predict future events. I can look for major events, or use someone's signs to look for their individual fortunes. A person's signs are a combination of the constellations of their naming day with constellations specific to them." He sighed. "But I can't read anyone's fortunes now."

"Why not?"

"An enchantment covers the night sky with clouds," Lyan said. "I can't see the stars at night."

"This is important to elves? The reading of stars?" Patch asked. "I've never heard of it being done here."

"It is important to us—or it should be, at least," Lyan answered.

She nodded solemnly. "When the sky clears, I will find you. Then you will find and read my stars, cousin."

It was a demand and a test in one. Lyan bowed to her. "It will be my honor to read your fortune, cousin."

Her lips curved in a smile. "It is a promise, then. I will watch for the clearing of the stars, Cousin Lyan Stargazer." She stood.

Lyan pushed to his feet. "And when the sky clears, I will watch for you, Cousin Patch Warborn. Until then, be safe."

"Be victorious, and I will be safer." She smiled again. "You'd better get your friend before he and the Captain come to blows."

7

Bring light unto the Lost
Find those who lose their way
For those who fall must know the cost
That ever after they shall pay

Lyan limped down the tunnel, more willing to acknowledge the pain in his ankle now that he walked alone. He wanted little more than to get Kithr and leave, but he slowed when he heard Nylas's voice rise in anger from the room where their group had been held.

"Then why in the names of our fallen didn't you stop this idiocy?"

Kithr answered, voice as icy as Nylas's. "Why didn't *I* stop Lyan from leaving Eilidh Wood with the Tathrens? Why didn't *I* turn him back? What, am I Lyan's Keeper? I have the right to choose what he can do?"

"You claim to be his friend. Or at least, you did last I heard," Nylas replied.

An angry hiss from Kithr, and the sound of movement. "If I were not, I wouldn't be here now, Nylas. You ask why I didn't stop him. You should first ask how long it took before Lyan chose to acknowledge that I'd followed him."

Nylas snorted. "As if he even knew you were there."

"He knew." Kithr's voice was cold. "He knew he was followed. He always has. Didn't you realize that? He may not recognize what he senses, or be able to identify the source, but Lyan knows when he's being followed."

"A talent like that would have been trained, if it existed in Lyan," Nylas said, dismissive.

"But it wasn't," Kithr cut in sharply. "It was ignored. Just like his skill with animals was ignored. *You* made a weed sprout out of season, and your talent immediately got you attention and trainers. Lyan *bonded* with *Shadowstar*, and we *all* know what that horse really is, and yet *every one* of us—not just you and me, but our whole damned *village*—ignored his talents, letting them develop wild and untrained, while at the same time deriding his one skill we *do* acknowledge!"

"And what use is there to staring at the stars, Kithr?" Nylas scoffed.

"How would you know? You never look at them," Kithr countered. Lyan listened, uncomfortable with thinking about what Kithr had said. He felt a strange disquiet at Kithr arguing with Nylas about the stars using much the same words as Lyan had directed against Kithr. Kithr continued. "If I were Lyan, I would tell you to look up and tell me what you see."

Nylas laughed sharply. "What do I see when I look up? Rocks and dirt, Kithr, that's what I see."

"Exactly. And that answer would prove Lyan's point without you ever understanding what that point is." Kithr spat. "But you gave up on the stars well before the end of the war. I remember, the apprentice astrologer to Sandalwood Village served among your men. Three days after you openly derided the stars and star reading as worthless, he was dead. I have to wonder, was that chance, or did your words send him to his end?"

To Nylas, who took such pride in his devotion to his men, there was little greater insult. "You dare accuse me?"

"Yes, I do," Kithr snapped. "And I'll tell you I'd rather leave Lyan alone in the company of his *Tathrens* than leave him in the reach of you or your minions, winterborn blooddrinker. At least the Tathrens appreciate his skills."

Lyan heard a hiss of metal as Nylas drew a blade. "Those words border on treason, Kithr."

"The war is *over*, Nylas." Lyan stepped into the doorway and fixed a dark gaze on his cousin.

Both Nylas and Kithr started. Kithr took a look at Lyan's face and muttered a curse. "Oh, yes, then there's his uncanny knack for walking in on conversations you didn't intend him to hear."

Nylas turned from Kithr to face Lyan. He must have armed himself before visiting Kithr, because he'd borne no weapons when they reached the elven camp. The manacles still hung from his wrists and ankles. Nylas looked Lyan up and down with disdain. "Look at this, Kithr. Is *this* what you want to be?"

Kithr's hands clenched in fists. "Having seen what you've become, yes, I'll take Lyan over that any day."

"What we've become, Kithr? We haven't become anything. What we haven't done is walk away, like *you* did."

"You can't even see the corrupted wretch you are," Kithr said. "Not until you're forced to come face-to-face with someone who isn't drowning in bloodthirst and hate. Tell me, do you remember enough of what it means to be an elf of Eilidh Wood to give the children of your camp playthings other than your trophies?"

Lyan flinched.

Nylas saw, and laughed harshly. "What, Lyan? You didn't enjoy the gifts Kithr brought back?"

Kithr stood on the verge of hitting Nylas. Much as Lyan longed to do the same, a fistfight now wouldn't help anything and might endanger the rest of his friends. Not to mention Nylas had an unsheathed sword. Lyan limped forward and touched Equinox against Kithr's arm. Kithr said nothing, but lowered his hand.

Lyan drew a deep breath and tried to keep his voice even, with marginal success. "No, Nylas, I didn't. Not that you'd care. All you want is battle. You want to fight and kill, and you don't care who your opponent is. You'll attack Kithr, who fought alongside you, or me, who has never sought battle, without a second thought. You demand to know why I'm here, in Tather, but you never pause in your derision long enough to listen to my answer!" Lyan slammed the butt of Equinox against the rock floor. The ground trembled and dust shuddered from the ceiling, causing Nylas to cast an alarmed look up. "You don't care if I have a reason, so long as you can continue a war against a people who don't want to keep fighting you. Cailean and his men barely trust Kithr. They weren't sure they could trust me. And the reason for that, Nylas, is *you*. The Tathrens don't know why the war started; they just know that nearly every elf they meet wants to kill them, and they haven't done anything to earn that blind hate. You want your war, Nylas? Fine. Keep fighting it. It'll never end until they finally cut you down. And when you fall, no one will pick up your banner. No one will care. You're already Lost to us."

Nylas shook with rage. "Get your head out of the clouds, Lyan, and look from your precious stars long enough to see the world as it really is. This war won't end with *words*."

Lyan's jaw tightened. "Look away from the stars? I don't have much choice in that right now. Look up sometime, Nylas. There are no stars. You're perpetuating a grudge against Tathrens, while outside these holes where you hide, a mortal uses the power of *Murdo* to defy the Thunderer in order to gain possession of *both* Spears! While *you* crawl blind in the darkness, seeing light only long enough to sate your thirst for blood, a Tathren is standing and fighting to stop someone from taking hold of the power that could free the Mad God. You want your war? Keep it! But don't try to tell me that I am the fool.

Neither Nylas nor Kithr spoke as Lyan spun away and stormed from the room. He didn't look back.

Lyan didn't get far before he had to stop, leaning heavily against the wall and bracing himself with Equinox. Sweat beaded his forehead, and he sucked in gulps of air, waiting for his ankle to throb less before he tried to continue. Blood rushed in his ears.

He jumped when someone rested a hand on his shoulder, biting back a yelp as he jolted his ankle.

"What did you do this time, Lyan?" Kithr asked, steadying him. "That damned ankle will never heal right if you keep abusing it. Here, lean on me."

"I'll be all right. Just twisted it after we got Nylas and his men out."

"Lyan. This isn't a place where you want to look injured. They're no better than a pack of starving wolves, ready to take on any prey they think weak. They might hesitate about attacking their own, but you aren't one of them."

"And I'm weak." It rankled.

"In their eyes," Kithr said. "Equinox or not, those who live in holes and in dungeons have no use for stars and signs, nor for books or lore. You've already said what they are."

Lyan nodded, leaning on Kithr's offered shoulder. "I guess it's safe to assume you won't regret leaving." He tried to make light of his words.

Kithr's look at him held no humor. "Did you think I would?"

Lyan drew a deep breath. "The thought crossed my mind

that you'd prefer the company of fellow warriors over that of a mooncalf stargazer and the descendants of your enemies."

Kithr said nothing for a long moment, helping Lyan limp up the passage. Lyan couldn't read his expression. When Kithr spoke, his voice was quiet, with hints, Lyan thought, of regret, even shame. "I'm not like them, Lyan. I am not." He glanced around, judging whether they were alone, and stopped. "I see what I was, though." Kithr shook his head. "Being among them while you and the Tathrens freed Nylas and his minions, I have the thinnest idea of what you felt, the first time you faced me when I came home."

Lyan shuddered. He didn't often have nightmares about it anymore, but he remembered all too well the pride and satisfaction on Kithr's face when he had presented his collection of heads.

Kithr flinched as if he'd been struck. "I was wrong, Lyan, and you're right. You were right then, and you're right now. They're Lost to us, and when death takes them, they'll go unmourned. I'll take the company of your Tathrens over Nylas's minions, and welcome it. Are you ready? The air reeks in this charnel pit, and as little as I want to have these winterborn blooddrinkers at our backs, I prefer it to staying here a heartbeat longer than I have to."

Lyan couldn't help but press a little. "You trust Cailean?"

"No," Kithr answered flatly. "But I trust Nylas and his minions even less. Your Tathrens hold their illusion of civility and seem unlikely to tear you to shreds at the slightest provocation." Kithr fixed a stern look on Lyan. "And have no doubt, you have provoked Nylas. He hates the accusations you've laid on him, and he hates them more because they come from you."

Lyan drew a deep breath. Stale air and the odor of dirt and stone closed around him. The weight of the stone pressed in, smothering his senses. He shut his eyes, as if that could block out the terrifying thought of living like this, trapped underground like a tomb. "I want out of here."

"We're almost there," Kithr assured him. "Can you walk from here?"

Lyan straightened and opened his eyes. "I can." He looked at his friend. "Kithr, once we're outside, there's one thing I must do. It'll anger them, but I still must do it, and I need you to trust me."

"All right." Kithr looked concerned, but didn't argue.

Twilight drew on to night when they stepped outside. Cailean and his men waited on their horses, all gear packed in place. Cailean's eyes betrayed heartfelt relief to see Lyan, eager to be away from the hostile eyes of elves who longed to shed Tathren blood. Aikan sat stiff, as hostile to the elves as they were to him. Yion alone was at ease, as if immune to the forest's seething anger. Shadowstar trotted to Lyan, followed by Kithr's horse. The stallion knelt unasked, and Lyan stepped into the saddle.

He felt the weight of eyes as he settled Equinox into its resting place. Warriors stood silent, half-hidden by shadows, though whether the shadows were those of the forest or those within each of them, Lyan couldn't be sure. Expressionless faces and dark eyes followed him. Nylas stood near the wall, opening a path through the bramble wall. Lyan wasn't surprised, certain the tunnels had more than one exit. Lyan didn't let his gaze linger on his cousin. Nylas might take eye contact as a challenge.

Instead, Lyan walked Shadowstar into the center of the camp. He tilted his head back and turned his eyes to the dark sky above. "As astrologer of Heartshrine Village, I am duty-bound to ask, are there any among you who wish their fortunes read? Who wish to know the readings of the stars?"

From the corner of his eye, Lyan saw Kithr stiffen, understanding. He sensed Patch frown at him for making an offer she knew he couldn't fulfill.

Self-conscious, embarrassed shuffling moved from the shadows. A handful of elves stepped forward. They shot one another nervous, thin smiles. After a moment, more followed with glares daring anyone to scoff. Lyan flinched inwardly, but steeled himself. "There are. I'm sorry."

His response and genuine sympathy confused them. They looked at him in bewilderment.

"Look up," Lyan instructed. The warriors looked at one another, puzzled, then glanced upward. They made the action look unfamiliar and unnatural. After a moment, they actually turned their eyes to the sky.

"You see?" Lyan asked. He doubted they did, but continued. "The stars are hidden. These clouds cover them every night, masking them. I can't see the stars to read them. I asked, because it's my duty, though I had doubts that anyone here still cared for our ancient traditions such as the telling of fortunes."

The elf closest to Lyan had been one freed from the dungeon. A long burn scar marred his face, barely missing the left eye. He came from Heartshrine Village, and though Lyan couldn't put a name to him, he remembered the other's constellations immediately. "What do you mean by this, Lyan?"

"A mortal is responsible for this—a mortal blessed by the Mad God, seeking something only the stars can reveal. That is the enemy *we* fight. If it is your fortune you wish to know, look for the stars. When they shine in the night again, you'll know we've succeeded. If you should choose to seek your home again, I'll read your signs. I would if I could now, but..." Lyan gestured helplessly toward the shrouded sky. "I am sorry."

The elves stood in silence. Lyan didn't look at their faces. When Shadowstar stepped forward, they shifted aside to allow the stallion to pass.

Kithr nodded to Cailean, and the Tathren lord gestured for his men to follow. At the camp's edge, Shadowstar paused before the opening in the wall. Lyan looked down at Nylas, who glared at him in a mix of anger and pain.

"That was cruel, stargazer."

He knew it. But he refused to bow to Nylas. "It was truth, bloodlord."

Nylas stiffened at the name. "You dare."

"I dare walk away from a war that doesn't matter anymore, and I dare to tell you so. Keep fighting the enemy you've chosen. My battle isn't yours."

With that dismissal of Nylas and his warriors, Lyan nudged Shadowstar with his heels. The stallion snorted and walked from the camp. Lyan glanced over a shoulder. Nylas stood in silence, watching him go. Then, almost reluctantly, the gaunt elf raised his eyes to look to the sky and the stars he'd never realized were gone from sight.

8

Secrets lie
Where men don't speak
Secrets lie
Where keepers fear to seek

Eerie stillness hung over the night-shrouded forest. Not even crickets stirred the silence when Cailean asked, "As we prepared to leave, what did you say, Lyan? When they all gathered around you?"

Kithr answered. "Lyan proved that revenge need not appear malicious to be cruel."

The Tathrens looked first at Kithr, then at Lyan in surprise. "Cruel? Lyan?" Shiolto asked.

Lyan shifted uncomfortably. "It *was* cruel."

"And no less than they deserved," Kithr said sharply, knowing Lyan already second-guessed himself.

"I have difficulty imagining Lyan intentionally being cruel," Cailean said, pushing a branch away from his face. "Say something in anger, maybe, but cruel? What happened?"

"I did my duty as an astrologer—I offered to read their

fortunes in the stars," Lyan answered quietly. "Then I made them see why I couldn't."

The Tathren lord looked puzzled. "And that was cruel?"

"Yes," Lyan said. "It forced them to remember who and what they were before this place, this war. It made them remember when such things mattered, and made them wonder how long it's been since the stars vanished—how long since they last turned their eyes to the sky." He looked to Kithr. "I didn't expect so many to accept my offer. Two, maybe three. Was I wrong, Kithr? Are they not all Lost?"

"Yes, they are," Kithr said. "They turned their backs to Eilidh Wood and forgot their first duty. They are Lost, Lyan. Never think otherwise. The difference is that now they know they're Lost, and it's by their own choice." His voice was harsh and his eyes hard. "Believe me. I know."

In quiet Elven, Lyan said, "You know even the Lost can sometimes find their way again."

"Only those who want to, Lyan." Kithr's eyes raked the dark, angry forest, a glare that challenged anything to present a hostile face. The forest recognized the warning and sullenly let them pass.

We've finished what needed to be done here. What path do we take now? Lyan let his hand rest on Equinox, and the Spear glowed with light strong enough to illuminate the area around them. He let his eyes adjust and followed the Spear's prompting.

Shadowstar snorted but didn't object when Lyan turned him off the path they followed and toward a bramble-choked track. The stallion raised a hoof over a twisting thorn vines. It shifted with a dry crackle, not unlike a hiss. Lyan gazed at the brambles. "We completed our side of the agreement and earned our passage. Let us through."

The vine barely slithered out of the way as Shadowstar stomped a fore-hoof down. Kithr eyed the narrow path dubiously. "This way, Lyan?"

"Yes, this way. We need to follow this trail."

Cailean's expression mirrored Kithr's, but he turned his reluctant horse to follow. "You've led us true this far. I'm not going to ignore our guide now. Certainly not here."

A moment of silence from Kithr, then he said, "You're less a fool than I thought, Tathren."

Cailean raised an eyebrow at the closest thing to a complement Kithr had said to him. He considered his response, then simply inclined his head in a nod. "Thank you."

"Don't get used to it." Kithr followed Cailean.

Lyan heard unhappy snorts from the other horses as they followed the trail that reluctantly opened no wider than necessary for a single horse and rider. Shadowstar snapped at a thorny vine that dangled too near Lyan, and it withdrew sullenly. Lyan glanced over his shoulder to be sure his companions followed safely.

The horses trailed one another as close as they could. The riders were more occupied with keeping their mounts calm than with studying the path. Shadowstar needed no calming, giving Lyan far too many opportunities to see the skeletons half-hidden and trapped in the brambles surrounding them. A shiver ran down his spine.

When the trail curved away to the right, Lyan drew Shadowstar to a halt and glowered at the wall of thorns ahead, ignoring the more inviting path. "I'm not playing this game, Nylas. Let us through, or we will turn around and return to your camp."

In response, he heard brambles close behind their group. Dalrian's horse whinnied in distress and alarm as thorns nicked her rump. "Uh, Lyan," Dalrian said uneasily.

Lyan pulled Equinox free from the saddle. The Spear's light chased away night's shadows, bathing them all in a glow like moonlight. Lyan glared at the forest and spoke.

"Bloodlord."

He felt the stillness of the forest all the way to his bones.

Even Shadowstar tossed his head and shifted. Lyan tensed when a vine brushed his arm, but no thorns dug into his skin. To his surprise, the whisper of Patch's voice touch his mind.

"The Captain is angry with you. He doesn't want to let you out. But you have a promise to keep, and you can't do that within our forest. I'll open your path."

"Thank you," Lyan said softly. "Be careful."

"The Captain won't stop me, though he knows what I do, cousin. You be careful. You have a promise to keep."

"And I will," Lyan answered solemnly.

The vine slid from his arm, and the brambles slowly peeled back ahead of Lyan. Shadowstar sniffed, then advanced.

"Lyan?" asked Kithr.

"Patch is letting us through," Lyan said. "Come on."

"Ah." Kithr's gaze said more words waited until they were away from the forest and its listening ears. Lyan didn't need to hear Kithr to know he'd acted recklessly in insulting Nylas again.

Aside from crackling, shifting brambles, the forest remained still and silent. When the trees thinned, the brambles loosened their chokehold on the trail and released the party. The weary horses plodded, barely able to rouse relief at the less oppressive air. Patch said no farewell as the path closed behind them.

Cailean rubbed bloodshot eyes. "Should we stop here?"

"Not until we're beyond the forest," Kithr said. "Lyan. Too much light."

"Sorry." At his bidding, the glow from Equinox faded away. Lyan blinked, waiting for his eyes to adjust.

Shadowstar continued walking, followed by the rest of the

horses. The stallion moved just beyond the forest edge and stopped.

Kithr glanced around. "Good enough. Get some rest. I'll take watch."

"I shall take a turn at watch as well," Yion said.

Even in the filtered moonlight, Lyan could sense Kithr's scowl. "I've rested. You haven't. Sleep. Now."

Lyan smiled wearily. He had neither energy nor desire to argue with Kithr. He slid from Shadowstar's back and steadied himself with Equinox. He considered pulling his bedding from the saddle, then decided retrieving it more effort than it was worth. He laid down near Shadowstar's hooves and fell into exhausted sleep.

Dark vines slithered through his dreams like poisonous serpents, blood dripping from savage thorns. Lyan struggled to hold them at bay, but could only protect a tiny pocket around himself. All around, voices called to him for help. Some he recognized, others he couldn't identify. Lyan struggled to reach them, but no matter how he tried, he could never drive the attacking vines back far enough to find even one of the people he heard. And above everything else, he heard cold laughter, mocking his efforts.

Lyan woke shuddering, muzzily slapping away dew-laden stalks of grass. The sun had just begun its slow creep into the sky. Weariness still clung to him. Finding no vines attacked him, Lyan pushed up to sit.

"Are you all right?" Kithr asked. Lyan saw his friend sitting a little ways from the horses, turning from his watch to look at Lyan.

"Bad dream," Lyan answered.

Kithr nodded. "I guessed as much. You tossed a lot."

Lyan rubbed his eyes. "You've been up all night."

"I slept in Nylas's camp. You still look ready to collapse."

"I'm not getting any more sleep now." Lyan shivered.

Kithr nodded. His gaze moved back to the land. "We

shouldn't linger here in any case. I think there's a village near —I've seen a little smoke." He smiled grimly. "If they're that close, they'll have no liking for elves and won't care if we're not with Nylas."

Lyan had nothing to say to that. Instead he asked, "Did Thon take a watch?"

Kithr shook his head. "He didn't argue when I told him to sleep. Have you noticed that at every camp, he paces the perimeter before he sleeps? He did that here too."

"Maybe he's warding it," Lyan responded, still tired and not quite paying attention.

"I think you're right," Kithr said.

"Huh?" Lyan blinked.

"I said, I think it's quite possible your mercenary *is* establishing some manner of protective wards around our camps. And once again, I wonder who and what he is."

"Then ask him yourself," Lyan said. "Because next time you start wondering about him, I'd rather *you* get his answer."

Kithr gave Lyan a questioning look.

"Your first suspicion came up when I spoke with him on our way to free Nylas. And when I question someone about *your* suspicion that they are an assassin, I really don't like getting an answer of 'not anymore'."

Kithr stiffened. "He said that?"

"Not in quite those words. He said he'd put aside his former life, but some of the skills from it are still of use to him now. Or something to that effect."

If Kithr intended to say more, he held silent as the Tathrens stirred. Shiolto and Dalrian passed around dried jerky for a meal while Torqual saddled the horses.

Cailean took the lead when they rode. Shiolto cast a look over his shoulder and shivered. "Glad to be seeing the last of this forest. I wasn't sure we were ever going to make it out."

"Especially after whatever our ever-helpful guide said last night when he declined to follow the path," Aikan said.

"If I'd followed the path when it turned, we would still be in Malgor Forest, Aikan," Lyan said sharply.

"As we would if the half-Tathren girl hadn't opened the path," Aikan retorted. "What *did* you say to close our way?"

"I called Nylas a bloodlord," Lyan said. The earring didn't translate the last word from Elven, and Aikan clearly didn't understand its meaning.

"The closest equivalent in Tathren is 'master of blood'," Kithr said. "Our name for one of the Mad God's demons—one said to torture and kill its victims, then bathe in their blood to gain strength and life. Lords of winterborn blooddrinkers. Another demon, one that does exactly what its name suggests. To call an elf either is a deadly insult. To call Nylas either is no less than he deserves."

Aikan's eyes narrowed. "And worth possibly trapping us?"

"If Patch hadn't opened the path, Equinox would have," Lyan said. "I had no intention of staying there."

Dalrian looked over his shoulder to assure himself that no elves of Malgor Forest lurked at his back. "I'm surprised none of the elves bothered us in the camp when Nylas went to find Kithr, or after you did, Lyan."

"When we freed them, Nylas agreed that for purposes of both debt and targets, none of you exist to them," Lyan said. "He said it again before he went to find Kithr—they all heard."

"I know, but when he wasn't there to enforce it?" Dalrian said.

"Nylas has been captain of that band for longer than any of you have been alive," Kithr said. "He's never been known for lenience. When he gives an order, he expects it to be obeyed completely. Anything less, and his punishments are immediate, decisive, and brutal. That should be explanation enough for his minions fearing to disobey him even when faced with Tathrens."

He wasn't always like that. Lyan didn't say anything as they rode, though he looked back over his shoulder even after the forest had disappeared from sight. *He is my last living family, and Nylas is Lost.*

He caught himself. *No, Nylas isn't the last family I have. Blood kin or not, I have another cousin: Patch. She doesn't know many of the ways of Lilian Wood, but she's not Lost.*

"Cailean, how far are we from your home?" Lyan asked.

"About eight days' ride north." Cailean's expression darkened. "Where Ewart has been doing as he pleases in my absence."

"Are you going to find the men who remained to fight?" Lyan asked.

"If we can," Cailean answered. "I have an idea where to look for them."

While they rode, Lyan wrapped a bandana around his head, covering his ears, and noticed Kithr doing the same. Here, in this land especially, anyone who recognized them as elves would consider them enemies.

Close to midday, as they started looking for a place to pause, they encountered a boy herding sheep. The boy saw the riders and immediately drove his flock away from them. Cailean tried to show they meant no harm and changed direction.

"Must be a town near," Cailean said. "Let's keep moving. We can take a break later."

Lyan suppressed a groan. Much as he wanted to get out of the saddle and stretch his legs, he didn't want to face a village of suspicious Tathrens. His ankle ached, but he tried to ignore that along with the rest of his discomfort.

The boy watched them ride past, not relenting in his suspicious guard until they were far enough away to not be a threat. Lyan silently wished him well and hoped he could protect his flock from whatever dangers might threaten.

Kithr studied the land. His expression was difficult to read, but Lyan could guess he was remembering the last time he'd been in Tather. Lyan saw Kithr's lips move as he whispered something, but the words were too soft to hear.

"Kithr."

Both Kithr and Lyan turned when Torqual spoke his name. Kithr eyed the soldier. "What?"

"Willing to spar when we camp tonight?"

Kithr considered, then nodded. "I'll take the practice at fighting Tathrens again." He looked to Cailean. "This Ewart. His men *are* Tathrens, aren't they?"

Yion answered before Cailean. "The majority are, and mainly untrained as soldiers. They are mercenaries with loyalty to coin only."

"Interesting description, coming from a mercenary," Kithr said coolly.

"My loyalty is not to coin, but to my god, Kithr. I accept the title of mercenary because a foreigner in any land must name some trade, and it suits my skills." Yion smiled, unperturbed.

"Who's your god, and why *are* you here?" Kithr demanded.

"When my god wishes himself known, he will reveal himself. As to my reasons, my answer has not changed since Lyan asked the same question. If you did not believe my words then, you have little reason to believe them now."

Cailean cleared his throat. "Ewart's forces?"

"Your pardon, Lord Cailean," Yion apologized. "The bulk of his forces are desperate men willing to take any work for pay. Those in command keep order by force and fear, but are effective and knowledgeable of tactics. Ewart's information on your fortifications and strengths was surprisingly thorough."

Cailean stiffened, reminded of the diagrams found in Ewart's keep. "I see."

～

They rode through the day with only a brief stop to rest. When they made camp, Lyan ached through and through. As he helped, he noticed what Kithr had mentioned—Yion walked the camp's perimeter in the guise of performing other tasks. It brought to mind something Venycia had said when she visited their camp in the form of a bear to heal him after he escaped Vynzent. "The protections on this camp are meant only to keep out those who would enter with harmful intent."

He also recalled the brief exchange between Venycia and Yion as they left the Shrine. Yion had passed on greetings from her uncle.

Could that mean Venycia's uncle is Yion's god? She never told me who her father is.

"Hey, Lyan, want to give me a hand with dinner?" Shiolto asked.

"Huh? Oh, sorry. Of course. What can I do?" The more immediate need for food distracted Lyan from his wandering thoughts.

Kithr and Torqual began sparring. Lyan watched briefly. Kithr quickly fell into old habits, and Torqual could predict him more often than not. That didn't always *help* Torqual, though. Kithr was fast.

Lyan dumped the last handful of chopped roots into the stew pot. "Anything else, Shiolto?"

"Just need some spices." Shiolto opened his pack and sorted through it. As he pulled out the spice bag, a folded sheet of parchment fell from the bag. Shiolto frowned, giving the parchment a puzzled look. "What's this?"

He set aside the spices and picked up the parchment. When he unfolded it, his expression remained bewildered. Shiolto held it to Lyan. "Is this yours?"

Shiolto held the parchment upside down. It looked like a missive. Lyan didn't try to decipher the unfamiliar Tathren words. He shook his head. "It isn't mine."

Shiolto folded it again. "Must be Lord Cailean's, then. I

guess it got mixed up and fell out of a bag when we shifted things off the horses. Add a handful of spice to the stew, would you? I'll give this back to Lord Cailean."

"You don't read, Shiolto?" Lyan asked. In Eilidh Wood, every child learned to read and write.

Shiolto laughed. "Who, me? No, that's stuff for lords, not the likes of me and Dalrian. I'll be right back."

Lyan stirred the spices into the stew while Shiolto waited for Cailean to finish studying the map. Kithr and Torqual finished their sparring match in relative good humor. Aikan sorted through his bags in search of something.

The older man went through his bags a second time, still not finding whatever he sought. Aikan pushed stiffly to his feet and walked to Lyan, scowling.

Lyan gave him a questioning look. "What is it, Aikan?"

"You were the last person aside from me to have my bags. What did you take, and where is it?"

Lyan blinked, surprised. "I didn't take anything—I never opened the bags you had Shadowstar carry."

Aikan's eyes narrowed. "Don't lie to me, elf."

"I'm not lying," Lyan said. "What are you missing?"

"A letter, perhaps?" Cailean asked. His voice was colder than Lyan had ever heard.

Aikan stiffened and turned to face Cailean. Cailean's expression was a mask of thinly restrained rage. In one hand he held Solstice, in the other, the parchment Shiolto had found. Cailean held the parchment toward Aikan like an accusation.

"*This* letter, perhaps?"

Color drained from Aikan's face and his eyes widened in fear and guilt. He stood rooted to the spot. When he opened his mouth, no words came out but a whispered, horrified, "No."

9

The past comes to light
For wrong or for right
And secrets wake
For faith to shake

All eyes fixed on Cailean. He closed the distance between himself and the unmoving Aikan. Lyan stood and scrambled back several steps. Shaking with anger, Cailean leveled Solstice at Aikan.

Aikan found his voice. "M… my lord?"

"Am I?" Cailean demanded, voice cold and hard. His hand crumpled the parchment. "This says otherwise."

"Lord Cailean?" Shiolto asked uncertainly behind Cailean, eyes darting between the two men as he wondered how a piece of parchment could inspire such rage.

"Lord Cailean, it's not—" Aikan began faintly.

"It's not *what*, Aikan? It's not an invitation from my enemy? It's not a promise of reward? It's not a betrayal?" Solstice didn't waver, pointing at Aikan's throat.

Aikan swallowed hard. "My lord, I—"

"You what? You can explain? Then do. By all means, do

explain how this doesn't prove you a traitor and oath-breaker. How *loyal* you are. *Explain*, Aikan, why you carry words of thanks and praise from my enemy—a message Solstice says reeks of magic." Cailean's eyes never wavered. His voice dropped dangerously low. "A message by which he can follow our every move."

Lyan hadn't thought Aikan could grow paler. The man proved him wrong. Aikan shook his head as if to deny Cailean's words, stumbling back a step.

"Answer me!" Cailean shouted. He hurled the crumpled parchment at Aikan's feet.

No one else moved, watching in silence as Aikan sank to his knees, head bowed. Slowly, he picked up the parchment and unfolded it, spreading it open on the ground before him. Aikan stared at the missive and spoke.

"Two nights before Ewart's final strike, when I retired to my room for the night, I found a sealed letter tucked under my door. It addressed me by my full name, using the titles my family once held. Opening it, I found a missive I thought could only be a perverted joke. The author claimed to be Ewart, and he claimed he could restore my family to their original status with our former titles and lands, in exchange for my loyalty. If I were interested, he bid me come to the west gate at the third mark of the night." Aikan let out a shaking breath. "I thought it a cruel jest, and I determined to find the one responsible and see them punished. I thought about bringing the letter to you, Lord Cailean, but the hour was already late, and you slept little enough as it was. I decided not to disturb you over someone's idea of amusement. I know well enough that I'm not the most well-liked with your men, my lord."

Cailean's cold eyes narrowed. "And no one questioned you going out in the middle of the night?"

"It wasn't the first time I'd done so since the siege began, my lord. I often chose unexpected times to check posts and be sure those on watch remained alert. The guards were attentive, and I checked the west gate thoroughly. I decided the inventor of this joke had done so simply to deny me some sleep, and prepared to retire to my room, when mist surrounded me. Everything grew silent, and I couldn't see anything, not even the keep. I called to the guards, but no one answered until Ewart appeared."

"In my keep," Cailean said tightly.

"I don't know, my lord. I can't say for sure whether I *was* still in your keep," Aikan said. "I could see nothing through the mist until I saw Ewart. He thanked me for accepting his invitation, and I couldn't say anything. I certainly couldn't say I had thought his letter a trick. I found enough words to ask what he wanted from me.

"'Your loyalty,' he said. 'I'll take this place and everyone in it, with or without your help. But it need not cost unnecessary lives. I will gladly spare those who I can, and I will generously reward all those who pledge themselves to me. Think on it, Aikan. The lands unjustly stripped from your family. The honors stolen from you. All that the elves destroyed can be restored to you, and with it, riches enough to fulfill your dreams. I know what you long for, and I know how to grant it to you.'

"I told him my loyalty lay with you, Lord Cailean. He laughed. 'The Dev'gilla family holds a sacred gift, the very source of their power and influence. They could have used it to restore your family to their rightful place, yet they have not. They have been content to use you as servants, vassals, far less than your noble birthright. With that power, I will change all that. I will correct their neglect. You have but to serve me.'"

Aikan closed his eyes. "He didn't demand an answer from me. All he asked was that I return his invitation. I did, thinking myself glad to be rid of it, not sure why I'd brought it with me. When it left my hand, the mist vanished and Ewart with it. The guards acted as if nothing had happened.

"I returned to my room and tried to sleep, but I couldn't stop thinking about Ewart's words. At one point I rose and dressed, intending to tell you what happened, my lord, but…" Aikan didn't look up. "Without the letter, I had no proof, and I was less and less certain of what I'd seen. If Ewart had magic available to him, he might have known if I'd gone to you, my lord. I thought if he remained determined to win me to his side, I had a chance to learn his plans, deceive him…" Aikan trailed off.

"Entertaining the enemy's offer in secret for *my* sake?" Cailean said with scorn. "So his promises of riches and reward had *no* consideration in your decision?"

Aikan didn't answer.

Cailean sneered. "Instead, you pretended nothing happened, and went on with your business. What token of good faith *did* Ewart give you when you returned his invitation?"

Aikan started. "My lord?"

"Don't treat me like a fool, Aikan. He gave you something as a pledge so you couldn't dismiss the meeting as a dream," Cailean said. "You *had* proof."

"I…" Aikan's shoulders slumped. "A gold coin, my lord. I found it in my hand when the mist vanished."

"Gold?" Both Shiolto and Dalrian sat up straighter.

"And you kept it with you," Cailean said, a statement rather than a question.

"I couldn't leave it in my room, my lord. It bore Ewart's mark. And I hesitated to show you for the same reason, Lord Cailean. A gold coin bearing the mark of the enemy besieging our walls…"

"So, instead, you knowingly carried a token given you by my enemy as you walked my walls, showing him every step of my defenses. Every gap. Every barricade, every point of supply."

Aikan's expression was stricken. "No! My lord, I didn't…"

"Didn't you?" Cailean spat. "I won't ask why you kept the coin. I don't have to. A gold coin. Is that the price of your loyalty, Aikan?"

Aikan shook his head in silent answer.

"Just where *were* you when the fog rolled in and Ewart's men took my walls?" Cailean demanded.

"In my room, Lord Cailean. I heard the alarm and was about to find you when Ewart entered. Not in fog and mist, but in the flesh, inside your keep, into my room. The guards in the hall lay dead. Any alarm I called would have gone unheard." Aikan paused a moment, then continued. "Ewart asked if I'd considered his offer, and if I was ready to swear into his service. He reminded me what he had to offer me. Lands and titles, riches. I was tempted, my lord. I… I cannot deny that. I'd been tempted since he first spoke of it. But then Ewart said he would restore my family's honor." Aikan drew a deep breath and finally raised his eyes to Cailean's. "Ewart might promise to restore lands and wealth to me, but he could never restore the honor I would sacrifice if I accepted him as my lord. When my grandfather was destitute, only your grandfather, Lord Cailean, spoke for him before the rest of the lords, to give him more time. When our family still could not pay the war taxes from a land ravaged, the fields stripped and burned by the elves, the men dead or conscripted, the women and children starving, our family stripped of land and title, our name made a mockery, your grandfather intervened once again. He gave shelter and made a place for a dispossessed lord in the midst of war when most struggled to feed those already in their service. I could not dishonor my ancestors or my daughter by betraying that legacy and turning my back on the debt of life my family owes to yours, my lord." Aikan didn't look away. "I refused Ewart, my lord."

"I should believe he simply *accepted* your refusal?" Cailean demanded. Aikan opened his mouth, but Cailean didn't give him a chance to respond. "While *I* struggled in the trap laid by his mage, *you* courted Ewart's promises of riches and rewards! And what about *this*?" He stabbed Solstice into the parchment at Aikan's feet. "What does it say? 'I will not forget your service to me, nor will I fail to fulfill my promise to you. For all you have done, your reward will be all the greater.' Are *those* words written to someone who *refused* Ewart's offer?"

Aikan started to say something, but bit back those words and chose others. "I found the missive in my bag after we fled the keep, my lord. I… I meant to show it to you, to tell you."

"You did? When? When you could stand gloating over me to reveal how you'd betrayed me to Murdo?"

Aikan blanched. "No, my lord! There was no time when we were pursued, and then in Eilidh Wood…" Aikan's voice trailed off and he bowed his head.

"So I should believe you? After you went to such lengths to hide these things, I should believe you now?" Cailean snapped.

Aikan didn't answer. He flinched when Cailean slammed Solstice into the ground next to him.

Cailean's eyes raked over the group. "All right, I'll accept this tale you've spun if you've managed to convince one, just *one*, person here of your innocence." He glared at his men, letting the silence stretch. "Well? Dalrian? Torqual? What about you, Shiolto?"

The Tathrens shifted uncomfortably, looking anywhere but at Aikan or Cailean.

"No one?" Cailean scoffed. "You couldn't convince a single person, Aikan? No one will speak for you?"

"I will."

Aikan's head jerked up, mouth falling open as his eyes, like all others in the camp, turned to Lyan with disbelief.

"*You*, Lyan?" Cailean demanded. "*You* believe him?"

"I believe Aikan's loyalty to you, Cailean, and I believe he isn't a follower of Murdo." Even as he spoke, Lyan asked himself why he raised his voice in defense of the Tathren who'd made himself a constant thorn in Lyan's foot through the entire journey.

"Based on what?" Cailean gestured at the kneeling Aikan. "This story he would have us accept?"

"Based on his actions and reactions. Based on the outrage he felt that a bear, sacred to your god Ahebban, who hates elves, healed me. Based on Solstice allowing Aikan to pick up the Spear when you, unconscious, dropped it after the ambush on our way to Toirni's shrine." Lyan found the thinnest of smiles. "Based on the offense he takes every time I don't call you by your title. I don't believe Aikan intentionally betrayed you, Cailean."

"So he *unintentionally* kept my enemy's gold and *unintentionally* refused to tell me, or to reject Ewart's offer?" Cailean's eyes narrowed, angry. He jerked Solstice from the earth.

The forgotten stew bubbled and hissed as it boiled out of the pot and into the fire. Lyan heard it, but didn't move to rescue the food. Cailean's furious gaze moved from Lyan back to Aikan. "I trusted you, Aikan. I believed you when you swore you would never even *think* of following Ewart. You must have congratulated yourself on what a fool I have been."

"That's not true, Lord Cailean," Aikan said softly.

"Get out of my sight," Cailean hissed. His entire body shook with rage.

"My lord!" Aikan pleaded.

"Leave my camp!" Cailean roared, making everyone jump. "Go—before I strike you down where you stand."

Head bowed, Aikan climbed to his feet with slow, stiff movements. His cloak slid from his shoulders to the ground, and he didn't pick it up.

Lyan tried to find his voice. *This isn't right.*

No one spoke or moved as Aikan slowly walked to the camp's edge. The older man took nothing—not even gear or horse. He hesitated and looked back to Cailean. "My lord…"

"You have no right to call me that," Cailean said coldly.

Aikan's shoulders slumped and his head hung. With no more words, he walked from the camp, crushed and defeated, unable to bear the burden. Lyan watched until the night swallowed the steward.

No one spoke, and no one moved until finally Shiolto rescued the pot from the fire and attempted to salvage the stew. Cailean speared the letter left crumpled on the ground. He stared at the parchment with angry eyes, then fed it to the fire. Lyan moved to his bedroll and sat.

I've spent so long suspecting Aikan. Yet, when the accusation came, I defended him. Was I wrong before, or wrong now? He looked into the darkness, though Aikan was gone from sight. *Were you the traitor among us, Aikan? Or did Cailean just banish a loyal man?*

10

When darkness falls,
Then shadows prey.
When darkness falls,
Then wise men pray.

Lyan woke from restless sleep before dawn, but he wasn't the first. Cailean paced around the camp, sometimes sitting by the fire pit to stir the coals, but never still for long. At a loss for what to do, he soon wandered again. Aikan's gear sat in a neat stack near the horses, and Cailean alternated between staring at it and avoiding it.

Lyan pulled a blanket around his shoulders against the brisk early morning air—the only time of day when it felt cool. He stood, wincing as his ankle protested, and walked to Cailean.

"He didn't take anything with him." Cailean looked once again to Aikan's bags.

Lyan didn't say anything.

"Lyan, I have a request for you. If you decline, I'll understand."

"What is it, Cailean?" Lyan asked.

Cailean looked to the ground as he spoke in a whisper. "Would you and Kithr find Aikan?"

"Cailean?"

Guilt lined Cailean's face. "I shouldn't have said what I did. If he told the truth… I heard him, but I didn't listen. If he wasn't lying. If he didn't betray me. If Ewart made sure that last message reached Aikan just so he could create division—" He trailed off. "Aikan has been part of my family's house since before my birth. He's always been there. He doesn't deserve… Please, Lyan, will you try to find him?"

Lyan hesitated a moment. Then he remembered the slumped, defeated man who had obeyed his lord's final command, walking away, broken. "We will, Cailean."

"Thank you," Cailean whispered.

"How will we find you again, when we do?" Lyan asked.

"I'll tell Kithr where to meet us. I suspect he knows this area well enough."

"All right."

Cailean resumed his restless pacing, but he seemed a little more at ease, some small weight lifted from him. Lyan laced his shirt and rolled his bedding.

"I heard my name," Kithr said in Elven. "What does your Tathren lord want now?"

"He asked if we would find Aikan," Lyan answered in the same. He expected argument, or at least sarcasm from his friend.

Kithr, however, just nodded. "You agreed?"

"I did."

"Then we'll leave after we eat. The old man's on foot. He could only go so far. But food first. Last night's dinner was wretched."

The stew had been barely edible, burned and overcooked. "Dinner would have sat poorly even if it hadn't been," Lyan responded.

Kithr nodded. "True. So, my name came up?"

"Cailean can tell you where we should regroup once we find Aikan. I don't know the land; it's not much help if he tells me."

"Ah." Kithr headed to Cailean. The Tathren lord looked surprised, but Kithr spoke in a low voice, and Cailean nodded, then retrieved a map.

The air in camp was uncomfortable, Aikan's absence a hole no one wanted to mention, but none could ignore. Few words were exchanged during the morning tasks. Breakfast was edible, though it sat like a lump in Lyan's stomach.

When they broke camp, Cailean packed Aikan's bags onto the older man's horse. The mare looked around as the group mounted, searching for her rider. She tossed her head, but followed when Cailean tied her reins to his saddle.

Cailean nodded to Lyan and Kithr. "I'll see you in the place I told Kithr."

Kithr nodded silently.

"What?" Shiolto asked, startled. "Lord Cailean? Lyan and Kithr aren't coming with us?"

"I asked them to take care of something for me," Cailean replied. "They'll meet us later."

"Oh. Be careful, Lyan," Shiolto said.

Lyan smiled, as if their task was a minor matter. "We will." He climbed into the saddle and nodded to Kithr.

Without further farewell, Kithr turned his horse and rode south, while Cailean and his men headed north. Lyan looked after Cailean a moment as Shadowstar followed Kithr.

"Do you think they'll be all right?" Lyan asked.

"The Tathrens know their own land," Kithr said. "Better than I do now. There isn't much we can do to help them, Lyan."

Lyan nodded, walking Shadowstar up beside Kithr's horse. The land appeared uninhabited, but both elves checked that their heads were covered and their distinctive ears hidden. Kithr gradually adjusted their course, circling back to the camp they'd left once he was certain Cailean's group had gone. Kithr studied the tracks and turned his horse northward.

"The old man didn't try to hide," Kithr commented. "I don't even have to dismount to trail him."

"Kithr?" Lyan started to ask.

"I don't know, Lyan."

"Huh?"

"You're going to ask if I think the old man's a traitor or not, and if you were right to defend him last night. I don't know. But I know you're the only one who could have done so."

Lyan frowned. "I don't understand."

"Cailean put his men in a bad spot when he asked if anyone believed the old man. Obviously, he didn't want an answer favoring Aikan. They're all Cailean's men—he told them to choose between him or a story they might or might not believe. None of them were going to speak up. Keeping their mouths shut was the only sensible thing to do. That left you or me. I wasn't going to. I wasn't sure if you would, but you acted like an elf of Eilidh Wood ought to, despite not liking the old man. Whether you were right or wrong about him, I don't know."

Lyan heard the shift in Kithr's tone when he spoke of how an elf should act. "Kithr, you're an elf of Eilidh Wood as well." Even seeing no one near them, he shifted, nervous saying those words in Tather.

"I'm not Lost like Nylas and his minions, but I used to be, Lyan." Kithr's eyes stayed fixed on whatever trail he followed. "I'm not going to speak for a Tathren who obviously hates me."

Lyan didn't want to hear anything more Kithr might say on the subject of the Lost. "If Aikan isn't the traitor, and there is one in the group, who would you suspect?"

"You think one of Cailean's men is a traitor?"

Lyan nodded.

"Intuition?"

"Something the pooka said," Lyan answered. "I know, it could have been lying, but there have been other things as well, though I don't know who was responsible."

"Hmmm." Kithr considered. "The timing of events feels wrong for the mercenary. So, if I'm not going to suspect Yion for the moment, I would say the horse-tender's brother. Dalrian."

Lyan started. "Dalrian? Why?"

"He knows paths in and out of his keep and no one would think twice about him going out. His attitude and reactions to certain things raise my suspicion."

"But why would he? And what about Shiolto? You suspect him too?" A chill of fear ran down Lyan's spine. He began to regret having asked.

Kithr shook his head. "No. I think the horse-tender's loyalty is genuine. But he is the reason I suspect his brother. Dalrian is the sort of man who'll do whatever he thinks he must to protect his brother. I believe he would betray their lord in exchange for a promise of safety."

"Shiolto said neither of them knows how to read. How could Dalrian be responsible for messages?" Lyan argued.

"Knowing how to read when everyone thinks you can't offers many opportunities to a spy," Kithr countered. "But he wouldn't have to know how to read or write if he simply carried messages."

"How would the letter have gotten from Aikan's bag into Shiolto's?" Lyan didn't like how much sense he found in Kithr's suspicion.

"I heard mention of bags being moved from horses?" Kithr asked.

"Oh. After we'd escaped with Nylas and his men, Cailean ordered the gear taken from the horses so the elves who couldn't walk could ride," Lyan said.

"At which point someone who knew what to look for could have taken something from one bag and put it in another. And if not then, they would have had another opportunity when packing the horses again in Nylas's camp. An ideal time to switch things around. If Dalrian stole the parchment from Aikan then, would you think twice if sometime later, he found an excuse to open his brother's bag?"

"Why plant it on Shiolto, though?" Lyan asked. "Why not 'find' it himself?"

"Some suspicion naturally falls on the person who finds damning evidence so conveniently," Kithr said. "So, Shiolto made the best person. First, he's predictable. Give him something he can't read, and he'll naturally assume it belongs to his lord. Second, he has the air of a genuine, honest, loyal man, and everyone likes him. Suspicion sticks to him about as well as water to oiled leather. Put the evidence in the hands of the person who everyone trusts and let him innocently deliver it where you need it to go. Then, when the accusations begin, simply say nothing. Let your plan unfold, and a man who isn't entirely innocent, but might not be a traitor, takes the blame."

"And you really think Dalrian could betray Cailean?" Lyan asked.

"He seems more likely than my other suspicion," Kithr answered.

"I hesitate to ask. Who's your other suspect?"

"The Tathren lord himself."

Lyan sat up straight. "What?" he burst in disbelief. "*Cailean?*"

Kithr nodded. "An elaborate trap, in which the one person who appears to have been the most wronged and have the most to lose is, in fact, the enemy."

"No. Cailean is not serving the Mad God," Lyan said sharply.

"You have proof?" Kithr countered.

"Equinox."

Kithr frowned, not understanding.

"Equinox trusts Cailean, and above anyone else, I believe the Spears would recognize if a Spearbearer followed the Mad God. Solstice could recognize Equinox would think me a suitable Spearbearer before *I* had *any* thought of taking the Elven Spear."

Kithr nodded slowly. "All right. Based on the judgment of a Spear of the Stars, I withdraw my suspicions of the Tathren lord." He frowned at the ground.

"What's wrong?" Lyan asked.

"The old man must have walked all night. I'd expect to see some sign of him stopping to sleep by now. Well, he's turned north, so I'd guess he's heading toward familiar territory."

"Are we catching up?" Lyan asked.

"We are, but we might not find him today. If he keeps this up, we'll find him passed out from exhaustion. Might simplify things if that happens."

Shadowstar stepped over something, and Lyan looked down to see rotting wooden handles attached to a rusted harrow. He looked around in surprise, but saw no other indications that this area had once been inhabited except perhaps for the stalks of grain growing wild amid the grass.

"Was this a farm?" he asked.

"Probably," Kithr answered. "Likely abandoned during the war, and so far unclaimed because of the distance from any defenses. A farm out here would be easy prey to marauders, Tathren or elven."

"Do you think elves other than Nylas and his band remain in Tather?" Lyan asked.

"If you can still call them elves. If they remained in Tather, they *are* Lost. Some are probably little better than animals."

Kithr didn't say more, but Lyan could hear the words he didn't speak. *Rabid animals, fit only to be put down.* Lyan shivered.

When the afternoon grew late, Kithr turned from the

tracking and found shelter for a camp. Lyan didn't like stopping so early, but he didn't argue.

Kithr saw Lyan's expression and restless pacing. "We don't want to camp in the open in this land. These might be the only trees for half a day's ride. We'll stop here for the night, then catch up with the old man tomorrow."

"I didn't say anything," Lyan said.

"You didn't have to," Kithr replied, tying his horse to a study branch. "No fire tonight." He wiped sweat from his neck. "Not that we need one. Days are too hot and nights are too stuffy."

"It's the clouds," Lyan said. "Night can't cool off."

"All the more reason to kill the Tathren responsible," Kithr said. "What's his name? Ewart?"

"Ewart is cousin to Cailean's father, and the ostensible leader of the attack. The mage… priest is named Porephyn, and I think he drove Ewart to attack and try to take Solstice."

"And both suspected followers of the Mad God." Kithr sat and leaned back. "Gods only know, Lyan, when you decide to find something more interesting than quiet life in our village, you don't hold back."

"Kithr." Lyan sat facing his friend.

Kithr waved a hand. "I know. I know, it wasn't your plan when you left the village. It wasn't my plan to do anything but knock sense into you and drag you back home. Shows what we know about the gods' intentions for us, doesn't it?" He sighed. "I certainly didn't think I'd be back here."

"I'm sorry for bringing you back into Tather, Kithr," Lyan said. "But we're here, and once we're done, we can go back home again and let things return to…" He almost said "normal". Then he looked at the Spear he carried. "Let things quiet down again," he finished instead.

"Right. And you can make trips to the Shrine to woo a lovely elven woman who can turn into a bear," Kithr said.

Lyan turned bright red. "I… wha… Kithr!"

His friend just chuckled.

Embarrassed, Lyan opened his pack and found one of his books. He read until the sun set, and Kithr didn't disturb him.

"Wake me for a turn on watch," Lyan told Kithr when he lay down to sleep.

"I will," Kithr promised.

~

Night passed without incident, and the two elves set out again in the morning. Dew lay heavy on the grass, and the stalks bent and bowed as the horses walked, leaving a trail Lyan hoped would fade as the grass dried. He had few questions Kithr could answer. Instead, Lyan turned his eyes to the blue sky.

Partway through the morning, Kithr dismounted to search the ground. He muttered curses under his breath.

"Kithr, what's wrong?" Lyan asked.

"Lost the old man's trail. I thought I had it, but—" Kithr shook his head. "Come on, I need to backtrack."

Lyan caught the reins of Kithr's horse and followed as Kithr walked. The sun continued its relentless course across the sky, and Lyan tried not to dwell on the time or the knowledge that Aikan moved further from them. He fretted, anxious and exposed, wishing for the company of Cailean and his men.

Finally, Kithr made a sound of satisfaction. "There! I was careless—the old man changed his course and I missed it. First turn he's made from his straight line. Wonder where he's headed." He swung back into the saddle. "We'll catch him soon. Before the end of the day, I expect."

Kithr's voice didn't hold the confidence his words proclaimed. Lyan watched him. "You're worried."

Kithr shook his head. "Just cautious. I see a few other

tracks. Might be patrols or other people in the area. We'll avoid them."

But what will we do if Aikan did not do the same? If he runs into other people, what will he do? Who will he tell them he is?

Kithr called a halt after midday to rest the horses. Lyan dug jerky from his bag and shared it with Kithr.

"Are we gaining on Aikan?"

"I think so." Worry creased Kithr's brow. "Lyan, do you have any sense that we're being followed?"

"Followed?" Lyan blinked in surprise. He thought a moment. "A general feeling of 'I don't like it here' and 'Something's making my skin crawl,' but nothing specific like 'We're being followed'." He hadn't been consciously aware of the sensations, but they explained his unease at the delay while Kithr backtracked, and when they stopped early the night before. "What about you?"

"The same, and I don't like it." Kithr took bow and quiver from his saddle.

Lyan clutched Equinox. Kithr's tense stance said he expected battle at any moment, and that, more than anything, fanned fear in Lyan. Dark clouds flowed over the sun, blotting out the light, and Lyan glanced up in surprise. He wondered how he missed signs of a gathering storm, but now a chill wind whipped through the grass. Shadowstar and Kithr's horse both snorted uneasily, pawing the ground and stamping their hooves.

"I really don't like this, Kithr," Lyan said, clutching Equinox.

"Neither do I." Kithr sidled back toward his horse.

Lightning ripped across the sky. Thunder shook the ground, leaving Lyan's ears ringing. With the storm's first strike came something unnatural. It chilled Lyan to the bone and froze him where he stood.

Both Kithr's horse and Shadowstar reared with whinnies

of fear, then bolted. Lyan's mouth opened, but no sound came out. *Shadowstar, fleeing? What is this? This isn't right.*

The first icy drops of rain pelted down. Lyan's eyes caught movement, indistinct shapes flowing toward them. Kithr's arm shook as he raised his bow and took aim. An arrow flew from the string, and passed straight through the center of his target without effect. Lyan read the same desperate terror that he felt in Kithr's fumble with another arrow and rapid draw. The second arrow had no more effect than the first.

Kithr panted for breath. "Go!" he ordered, shoving Lyan away from him.

Lyan stumbled, clutching Equinox. He wanted to run, but his legs, like blocks of ice, refused to move as the shapes oozed forward like living pools of ink. Kithr didn't waste any more arrows, but drew his sword.

"Go!" Kithr repeated. Fear made his voice sharp. "I'll watch your back."

"Run," taunted a whisper through the air. "Yes, run."

Lyan managed several steps back, gripping the Spear in white-knuckled hands. Two forms drew themselves into shapes resembling large dogs—lean, wiry, muscled bodies with sharp, pointed heads and alert ears. Their eyes glowed red, and lips curled back to show gleaming white fangs, the only spots of color on otherwise unrelenting black bodies.

The other two shapes took on humanoid forms, and Lyan couldn't say which, dog or humanoid, stirred deeper terror in him, freezing him where he stood and turning his thoughts to senseless babbling. One of the humanoid shapes looked directly at Lyan. Its eyes glowed red, like those of the dogs, and its hungry grin revealed a mouthful of teeth, jagged as glass shards. A long black robe hid its body, but its head looked like that of a mummified corpse—desiccated skin stretched too tight across the skull, beginning to peel away. Thin strands of pale hair spotted the scalp. In its bony hands, the thing held a harvester's scythe.

"By the gods," Kithr whispered.

Four sets of glowing red eyes fixed on him. A dry, dusty voice rasped from one of the robed figures, sending ice down Lyan's spine. "Men rise, and men fall."

The other continued. "Gods rise, and gods fall."

They spoke the last lines in unison, the words rattling like the last breath of a dying man. "Lord Murdo takes them all. So sing the reapers."

Reapers. These are reapers. These are what terrified Vynzent and his men so much that I had a chance to slip free of them. Terror held Lyan like a vice as the two reapers and their dogs advanced on Kithr. Kithr stood as unmoving as Lyan. One scythe swept out in a lazy arc, opening a slash across Kithr's arm.

Kithr cried in pain, but it broke him free of the paralyzing fear radiating from the reapers. He raised his blade to block a second swing, grimacing as the force of the seemingly effortless attack knocked him back. Kithr gripped his sword with both hands, shifting his stance to brace himself in the slick grass. He cast one look over his shoulder to Lyan.

"I said *go*, blight it!"

"It won't help." The words came in the softest whisper from Lyan's lips, lost in the gusting wind. *Don't just stand here! Help Kithr! Come on, Lyan, don't stand like a fool and watch them cut him down!*

His body wouldn't obey his mind's frantic orders. Kithr blocked another swing, but even Lyan could see the reapers merely toyed with him. A scythe ripped across Kithr's back, too quick for him to dodge. The dogs lunged as one, sinking fangs into Kithr and dragging him to the ground. Kithr screamed as ragged teeth tore through cloth and skin.

The reapers laughed—horrible, hollow laughs. Together, they bent over Kithr. One tore the sword from Kithr's hand and knelt, pinning Kithr's arm under its knees. Lyan smelled blood, and Kithr screamed in agony, thrashing against the creatures that effortlessly held him to the ground.

One reaper raised its head to look again at Lyan, blood dripping from its mouth. A black tongue darted out to lick its lips, then it returned its attention to Kithr, confident Lyan could neither react nor flee. Lyan heard flesh tear, and Kithr screamed again, spasming.

No. No! Lyan's hands gripped Equinox so tight he expected something to break.

His eyes opened wide as one thought forced through the terror. Lyan tore his eyes from the reapers to stare at the Spear. Equinox, Spear of the Stars. *I'm such a fool.*

"Help me," Lyan whispered.

The Spear might have been waiting, as if Lyan finally opened a door in his mind blocking Equinox out. Heat shattered the icy fear that pinned him to the spot, and knowledge flooded his mind, too much to comprehend at once.

"Give me some way to save Kithr!"

Equinox pressed unfamiliar words into Lyan's mind. He shouted them before he realized he spoke. Lightning burned across the sky. The reapers raised their heads as one, glowing eyes fixing on Lyan. One dog snarled, crouched, and sprang at him.

Equinox glowed in Lyan's hands. The drenching downpour should have made a billowing cloud of dust impossible, yet one rose before Lyan, choking the air momentarily. Lyan tensed, expecting the dog to slam into him.

He sensed a presence in the cloud before him. The dog yelped in surprise and pain.

The dust dispersed. Lyan blinked rapidly, and shook wet, muddy hair from his eyes, to find himself staring at a back. It was a muscular back, with a massive pair of draconic wings settling against bronze skin. A slender feline tail twitched lazily back and forth, nearly brushing Lyan's leg. The owner of back, wings, and tail stood two heads taller than Lyan.

He was also, as best Lyan could tell from behind him, naked.

Unconcerned by his nudity, the newcomer gripped the dog by its throat. He spoke in a deep voice that Lyan felt in his bones, tone heavy with disgust. "Reapers."

Toned arms twisted. The dog gave a strangled yelp before its neck snapped audibly. The winged newcomer tossed aside the limp, broken dog and stepped toward the reapers.

One reaper screeched in rage, lunging at him. "Men rise and men fall."

A casual flick of the winged man's wrist sent a lance of blue light into the reaper. Lyan's hair stood on end at the strength of the magic. "Maybe so," the winged man said, "but there won't be any more singing from *you*."

The other reaper and its dog abandoned Kithr, backing away with hisses and snarls.

"Do you think I'm going to let you run, reaper?" The winged man gestured, and blue fire burst from the ground in a wall behind reaper and dog. He advanced like a stalking feline closing on its prey, tail twitching in predatory anticipation. "Murdo won't even be able to *find* your blackened soul to question you."

A coil of fire lashed out from the wall to snatch the dog's hind legs. The dog yowled, thrashing as the coil dragged it into the blaze. The stench of burning hair filled the air before flames consumed the creature.

The reaper screamed, glowing eyes maddened with fury and pain. "Gods... rise...," it rasped.

"And reapers fall." Shimmering blades sprang like claws from the winged man's fingertips. He slashed through the reaper, shredding its body and severing its head.

Finally, the winged man turned to face Lyan, piercing amber eyes studying the elf. "So, that damned Spear found itself a new Bearer. Well, at least you summoned me for something halfway interesting."

Overhead, the storm clouds broke apart and the rain cut off as if it had never been. The first golden shafts of sunlight fell on the man, gleaming on impossibly dry bronze skin. Shivering, soaked to the skin, Lyan dully repeated, "Summoned?" He couldn't deny what his instincts told him, nor what his eyes did. He'd seen this tall, winged figure before. Never in the flesh, but cast in gold in a temple hidden in the depths of the Forests of Cossette. The twist of his mouth could be a smile or a sneer, the eyes could be mocking or promising vengeance on enemies. But cold metal had failed to capture the dark amusement in the god's expression. Lyan licked suddenly dry lips and whispered, "Nachyne."

11

Mortals and gods
Earth and sky
Ever seeking, ever searching
Let dreams and prayers fly

The god of monsters sketched a bow. Despite the storm that had raged moments before, he stood dry, not a single dark hair out of place. "The one and only. And you, Spearbearer?"

Kithr gasped and jerked, tearing Lyan's mind from the question before he could answer. He bolted past Nachyne to his friend. Kithr's eyes were closed, breath quick and shallow, pale face beaded with sweat. Blood ran, especially on his chest and abdomen—jagged wounds torn by jagged teeth, as if the reapers had been eating him alive. Remembering the blood-spattered face of the reaper as it looked at him, Lyan's bile rose. He choked it back down.

"I am impressed he's still alive. A reaper's bite poisons their victims even if the unfortunate escapes their feeding." Nachyne followed Lyan, looking down at Kithr. "I suppose you want me to heal him."

Lyan's head jerked up. "Can you?"

"Yes."

"Then heal Kithr. Please." Desperation and fear made Lyan ignore the presumption and sheer idiocy of demanding anything of a god—the "please" little more than an afterthought. Each breath Kithr took grew more labored, and his skin's pallor grew worse.

Nachyne crouched beside Kithr across from Lyan and held a hand over the bleeding elf. A yellow-green glow bloomed under his palm, the unhealthy color spreading to settle over Kithr. Kithr jerked and cried out, his voice a thin sound. Lyan's jaw tensed and his hands tightened around Equinox.

Nachyne didn't look up. "I'm forcing his body to mend faster than is natural, and burning the poison from his body. Neither are pleasant, but necessary if he's going to live. He should live. He won't remember this pain."

Lyan forced himself to relax. "Why are you telling me this?"

"Because you obviously have no idea what's going on. Because I have no desire to give that damned Spear another taste of my blood. Because the lords of the dead would get very irate if I had to intrude on their domain to bring your friend's soul back to his body."

Lyan tried to make sense of the god's words. For the first time, he noticed a wicked scar on Nachyne's side—an old, long-healed wound, but the only mar on Nachyne's otherwise flawless body. Lyan opened his mouth, but didn't speak.

"Ask your questions. They won't distract me," Nachyne said.

"How many questions do I get?" Lyan asked uncertainly.

"As many as you want."

That sounded unusually generous for the god of monsters, not known for benevolence to those outside his domain. Or to those within his domain, for that matter. "Why?"

"Because you're the Spearbearer of Equinox."

"What does that have to do with you?" Lyan asked.

Nachyne made a face of distaste. "I suppose I might as well get this particular humiliation out of the way now, rather than have you drag it out one question at a time. The third— no—fourth Spearbearer of Equinox after Murdo. She thought highly of her skills and ability to wield the Spear's powers. At the height of her arrogance, she issued a challenge to me. I accepted, and we fought."

Lyan blinked. "A Spearbearer challenged a god?"

Nachyne grimaced. "To my continuing regret, her opinion of her skills was justified."

Lyan paled and looked at the Spear in his hands. *A Spearbearer challenged a god to combat, and won? How? To what end?*

"As a result, I'm bound to that damned Spear, at the call of whatever bearer it chooses to adopt. Despite my desire that the 'incident' be erased from mortal memory entirely, Equinox has an unpleasant habit of prompting its wielder to draw on all possible solutions." Bitter anger colored the god's voice, but it didn't show on his face when he stood. Kithr gave a final, fierce jerk, then fell still. A moment passed, then Lyan saw him draw the steady, even breaths of deep sleep. "Your friend will wake hungry and sore tomorrow morning. So, what title am I supposed to call you, Spearbearer?"

"Title?" Belatedly, Lyan remembered Nachyne's earlier question. "My name's Lyan, and that's my preference. Just Lyan." His thoughts still raced and tumbled. *I knew Guardians of the Spear who failed the Trials became bound to serve the Spear and its bearer, but a god? Equinox can bind even a god?*

"Just Lyan. Hmm. Lyan the Just? No, too pretentious for you. No titles at all?" Nachyne mused.

"The elves of Eilidh Wood don't hold to many titles beyond 'Elder', and I'm no village elder," Lyan answered.

"That never stopped previous Spearbearers from finding honorifics that suited their fancies," Nachyne said. He crossed his arms over bare chest and studied Lyan as if thinking what to attach to the elf's name.

"Some of my friends call me Lyan Stargazer when they feel a need to call me by more than just my name," Lyan allowed, not wanting to know what title the god of monsters might find amusing to impart.

"An astrologer?" Nachyne raised an eyebrow. "An interesting choice by Equinox."

"Why?" Lyan asked, feeling his defensive ire stir, ready to defend his worth and that of reading the stars.

"Don't think I'm ignorant of an astrologer's skills, Just Lyan Stargazer," Nachyne told him. "Most Spearbearers have been warriors of one sort or another since the *last* astrologer who became Spearbearer." His eyes narrowed. "That didn't turn out so well."

"What do you mean?" Lyan asked, surprised. "Who was the last astrologer to become Spearbearer?"

"Murdo." Nachyne spat the name with distaste.

Lyan stiffened. "The Mad God? An astrologer?"

"He was. I'm sure he'd love to be one still, but in his prison, there are no stars." Nachyne smiled grimly.

Lyan nodded quickly, the course of the conversation uncomfortable. He looked around for Shadowstar and Kithr's horse. Not seeing either, he murmured, "Shadowstar, please find Kithr's horse and come back."

He finally realized he was shivering, and remembered his own clothes were soaked through, as were Kithr's. He looked around for dry wood, but didn't see any good tinder to build a fire. Nachyne stood by, arms crossed, watching with a mildly interested and slightly amused expression. Lyan turned to the god.

"I'm sorry to be asking something so mundane, but could you start a campfire or something for us?"

"Simple, mundane, mortal concerns." Nachyne gestured casually, and a deep blue flame burst to life on a clear patch of ground, the size of a moderate campfire. The wet ground hissed and steamed around it. The heat drew Lyan, and he finally stopped shivering. Nachyne studied him again. "How long have you carried Equinox, Just Lyan Stargazer?"

Lyan paused and thought. "Less than a month."

"You don't know how to use it. No one's taught you?"

"Who am I going to ask?" Lyan answered. "The Guardians of Equinox have never used the Spear, and the previous bearers are dead. Cailean's given me some help, but he has his own troubles, and doesn't know a great deal more than I do."

"Cailean?" Nachyne asked.

"Spearbearer of Solstice, Lord Cailean Dev'gilla, Earl of Ihvako."

"Ah, that's right," Nachyne said. "The Tathrens have been passing Solstice through the family line." He considered Lyan. "I'm surprised an elf of Eilidh Wood would discuss Spears with a Tathren, knowing Ahebban hasn't budged a breath in his grudge against Soldarr."

"Cailean is my friend, and I wouldn't have found Equinox without him," Lyan said sharply.

"Just commenting, not criticizing." Nachyne waved a hand in what could have been apology.

Lyan set Equinox on the ground and rubbed his hands together to warm them. Then he looked at Nachyne and asked, "Aren't you… cold?"

"I'm not limited by the constraints of mortals. Why?"

"Because you're naked," Lyan said.

"So?"

"So would you *please* put on some sort of clothing?"

Nachyne raised an eyebrow, then laughed. "Ah, it's been a while. I had forgotten about mortals and their little taboo about nudity."

"Yes, well, there's only so much divine glory I want to see," Lyan muttered.

Nachyne produced a length of vivid green cloth—it looked like silk—from the air and wrapped it around his waist, holding it in place with a silver belt. "Enough to satisfy mortal sensibilities?"

"Not really, but it's an improvement," Lyan answered.

Nachyne smirked. He settled across the fire from Lyan, assured of his superiority over lesser beings. "So, what else, Just Lyan Stargazer?"

The title was going to get tiring, Lyan knew. But he didn't comment on it. "I'm not going to be going anywhere until Kithr wakes and our horses come back."

"You expect horses to return on their own after a reaper attack?" Nachyne laughed.

"Shadowstar will. I called him. He'll come back."

"Shadowstar?" Nachyne raised an eyebrow in surprise.

"Shadowstar is—," Lyan began.

Nachyne cut him off with a wave of his hand. "Favorite stallion of the Horselord's own herd, guardian of Appret Plains. Rare that he chooses to bond with a mortal. If he has, you're right, he'll return."

"I didn't know you knew of Shadowstar," Lyan said.

Nachyne shrugged. "Tried to steal that stallion once. It didn't turn out well."

Lyan made a choked sound. "You? Steal Shadowstar?"

"*Tried*," Nachyne repeated. "The Horselord wasn't terribly happy with me about it."

"And I thought myself a scholar," Lyan said. "I've never heard of that, or of you and Equinox."

"Of course you haven't," Nachyne said, voice suddenly cool, reminding Lyan he spoke to a god. "The incident between the Horselord and me had no bearing on mortals. As for the Spear..." His eyes narrowed. "A few attempted to record that humiliation. I have found every writing of it and burned the words from the pages. The mortals should consider themselves lucky I didn't burn their heads from their shoulders. You will find no record of *that. Ever.*"

Lyan nodded. A chill ran down his spine, followed by reassurance from Equinox—Nachyne could not harm him or take any act of retribution against the Spearbearer of Equinox.

He glanced at the Spear. *"Thanks, but all in all, I'm still not reassured to know I can summon a god whether the god likes the idea or not. I don't like knowing I can demand the obedience of the Guardians. I don't want to force my will on anyone."*

"Do you mind if I ask you something else?" Lyan asked.

"You can ask," Nachyne said, tone implying that it didn't matter whether or not he minded.

"I know I *can* ask, but do you *mind* if I do?"

The god's expression lightened and he quirked an eyebrow in amusement. "I suppose I don't mind. Ask."

"Those reapers. Someone had to summon them from the Mad God's prison, didn't they?"

Nachyne nodded gravely.

"Do you know, or can you tell, who did that?"

Nachyne looked toward the scorched ground where the reapers had died. "No, I can't tell what mortal was foolish enough to force open a way into the realm where we caged Murdo. Whoever it was had to be a devout follower of Murdo, willing to make all the necessary sacrifices." Nachyne looked at Lyan. "Even we gods couldn't defy all the principles of exchange when we sealed access to his prison. Those followers who escaped us learned they could pull minions from Murdo's realm for a limited time by offering lives in exchange."

Lyan shifted uneasily. "How do you mean?"

Nachyne gestured toward the scorched earth. "To summon one reaper, for example, the summoner must sacrifice five people in exchange. Three are ritually tortured and killed." His expression grew more grim. "The other two are drawn alive into Murdo's realm when the reaper and its hound step through the opened portal."

Lyan paled. *Ten people died horrible deaths to bring these things here to attack us?* He shuddered, hand closing tight around Equinox. "If that... but wouldn't someone be able to summon Murdo?"

"If someone sacrificed every living creature between the two seas, they could still not let Murdo slip free of his prison, even for a moment," Nachyne told him. "Fortunately, few of his followers are strong enough to endure his touch on their mind long enough for him to speak through them. Even if he does, his powers are limited. The host will die a hideous death shortly after."

If the god intended his words to discourage further questions, he succeeded. Lyan sat and tried not to think too deeply on Nachyne's words. He looked to Kithr, now sleeping, then to the horizon, where the sun sank into dusk.

Lyan heard approaching hooves. He tensed and looked around for enemies, but was relieved to see Shadowstar approach. Kithr's mount followed behind. The stallion stopped at the camp's edge, eyeing Nachyne with suspicion. Lyan walked to Shadowstar and rubbed the stallion's nose.

"It's all right, Shadowstar. Nachyne helped us, and he's not here for any other reason."

Shadowstar snorted, deigned to enter the camp, and ignored the god of monsters. Nachyne chuckled. "I see you haven't forgotten me either."

The stallion snorted. Lyan rummaged through his saddlebags and found food. "Do you eat?" he asked Nachyne.

"When I want to," Nachyne answered. "Unlike mortals, I rarely *need* to eat, much less sleep." He waved toward the fire. "So, eat, sleep, whatever it is you need to do."

Lyan hesitated, but only for a moment. He realized how exhausted he was, and it took him little time to decide food could wait until morning. "I'll eat when Kithr wakes. Would you mind watching the camp while I sleep?"

"Of course, of course. Sleep deeply, Just Lyan Stargazer."

"Thank you. That won't be a problem." Lyan pushed out his bedroll and lay down. His eyes closed, and sleep came.

Chasing the trail
A dreamer was lost
And into travail
His lot was crossed

Lyan woke just before dawn, startled from sleep by a sound. He blinked blearily, confused to see a winged man sitting in a casual slouch, back against a rock. Memories caught up with Lyan a moment later.

Before Lyan even sat, Nachyne spoke. "Your friend's still asleep. He's been stirring, though. Might wake soon." When the god of monsters spoke, Lyan felt it in his bones.

"Thank you." Lyan sat and rubbed sleep from his eyes. As he pulled on a fresher shirt, Nachyne watched with an amused smile. Not sure where the humor lay, Lyan looked at him. "What?"

"Mortals are entertaining," Nachyne responded. "Fighting reapers one day, the next looking as if a newborn cub could best them."

"Entertaining. Thanks," Lyan muttered.

"You should be glad. I could hold far less kind opinions of

mortals." Nachyne's tone didn't change, but Lyan heard the ice under it, if only for a moment.

Lyan just nodded.

The fire Nachyne had started still burned, hot blue flames consuming no fuel. Lyan found dry rations in his bag and heated water in two mugs. He looked back to the god of monsters. "Do you want anything to eat or drink?" Hastily, Lyan added, "I know you don't *need* anything, but would you *like* some?"

Nachyne waved a dismissive hand. "No need." Some sense of tension eased in the air, and Lyan thought that, even though he declined, Nachyne was pleased the offer had been made in the first place.

While tea steeped in the mugs, Kithr groaned and tossed. Lyan left the mugs and moved to his friend's side. "Kithr? It's all right, you're safe."

Perhaps the words reached Kithr, perhaps Lyan's voice was enough to calm the restless sleep. Kithr stilled. Then his eyelids fluttered. "Ugh. Wha…"

Lyan found a smile. "Eloquent as ever, my friend."

Kithr's eyes snapped open and he jerked up, one hand fumbling for a weapon. Lyan held up his empty hands. "Kithr. We're safe. It's all right."

"Those things. Where?"

"They're gone, Kithr. They're dead," Lyan said.

"Dead?" Kithr's hand moved to his own chest, running over the shredded cloth of his shirt. "They are dead? Not us?"

Lyan nodded. "Yes."

"What were those monsters?"

"Reapers," Nachyne said. "Don't insult monsters by numbering spawn of Murdo in the same category."

Kithr jumped, looking sharply to the unfamiliar voice. "Who in Murdo's Pits are you?"

Nachyne stood, wings spreading, then folding against his back. "I'm one of the ones who put Murdo *in* those pits."

"Kithr, that's Nachyne," Lyan said softly. "He killed the reapers and saved your life."

Kithr stiffened, staring at the god. "Nachyne? God of monsters?" Once again his hand moved toward his waist in search of a weapon.

Nachyne smirked, amused. "You're lucky to be alive, mortal. You nearly had your guts eaten by reapers. And now you think you can face a god?"

Kithr tensed. "Does the god of monsters just conveniently drop in on a whim? Why are you here? What do you want?"

"Coincidence? Not at all," Nachyne replied. "For the rest of your answers, I direct you to Just Lyan Stargazer. In fact, Spearbearer, now that you're awake, and your friend is awake and the picture of health, I'll take my leave." He paused very briefly—just long enough that Lyan could have objected if he'd wished.

Lyan stood and bowed. "Thank you, Nachyne."

The god's eyes twinkled with amusement. "You're off to a better start than some. This should be interesting, Just Lyan. Until we meet again."

Nachyne's wings lifted him from the ground and raising a great cloud of dust. The cloud enveloped Nachyne, then, with a boom of thunder, the god was gone. Kithr's horse started and whinnied at the noise, but Shadowstar ignored Nachyne's departure just as he'd ignored Nachyne's presence.

"Lyan," Kithr said slowly, "what in rot and ash is going on? A god. Not even one of our gods, or, ancients forbid, a god of *this* land, but the god of monsters? What are you doing?" He paled. "You didn't make some kind of bargain with him, did you?"

Lyan offered Kithr tea. The fire still burned, but not as vigorously as it had. Lyan watched the dying blue flames. "Long ago, a Spearbearer of Equinox challenged Nachyne to combat. Nachyne accepted. And… he lost."

Kithr had started to drink the tea, and he spat it out in disbelief. "*What?*"

"The god of monsters was defeated by a mortal Spearbearer, and as a result is bound to the Spear, and a Spearbearer of Equinox can summon him," Lyan said softly.

"You're telling me that a mortal with just *one*—not even both, but just *one* Spear had the power to challenge and beat a *god?*" Kithr demanded.

Lyan nodded. "That's what Nachyne told me."

"You believe him?"

"What god would make up a story that humiliating, Kithr?" Lyan asked. He looked from the fire to Equinox. "I believe he told the truth. I don't think he *could* lie to me if he wanted to."

"The Spears have that much power? If someone can do that with just one, with both…" Kithr trailed off.

"With both, a mortal could be powerful enough that it would take all the gods to stop him," Lyan finished. "And they don't want to have to do so ever again." He offered Kithr food.

Kithr devoured it. Lyan's stomach complained, but he took advantage of Kithr's distraction to give him half of his own portion as well. Remembering the hunger he'd felt after Venycia healed him, Lyan knew his friend needed the food more. Kithr wiped his fingers on the remains of his shirt and looked down at his chest. New pink scars ran over his skin in jagged patterns.

"They were eating me alive. Weren't they?" Kithr shuddered. "I could hear them whispering in my head." He closed his eyes.

"Are you all right, Kithr?" Lyan asked, worried.

"I'm fine, I'll be fine." Kithr opened his eyes. "And we need to keep going. If those *things* found the old man before they came after us… well, if that's the case, he can at least have a decent burial."

Aikan. Did the reapers attack him? What about Cailean and the others? "Can you still find Aikan's trail, Kithr?"

"I'll try. The storm washed away tracks. But I think I know where he's going."

"You do?" Lyan sat up straighter. "Where?"

"Now that I've seen more of this area, I have a better sense of where we are. There's a keep a couple more days' travel—one our forces avoided rather than try to besiege. Seems to me the old man is heading home."

"To Cailean's keep? Why? It's under Ewart's control," Lyan said, startled.

"I can think of two possibilities," Kithr said. "First, he's fooled you with his apparent contrition, and he really is a traitor going back to his master. Or, second, his story was true, he's loyal to his lord, and he's entering enemy territory to try to resolve unfinished business. If the second, he's likely to get himself killed."

"We need to find him before he gets there in either case." Lyan jumped to his feet.

"Yes." Kithr stood more slowly, and walked to his horse. Searching through his bags, he found a fresh shirt and tossed the shredded, blood-stiff rags into the fire. Flames devoured the cloth immediately. As Lyan and Kithr mounted the horses, the blue flames flickered and died.

Kithr was unusually subdued, even as they started riding. Lyan watched him, and broke the silence. "What's wrong?"

"The reapers. Those demons. I always believed that, even in the face of the Mad God's minions, I could fight and defeat them." Kithr shuddered. "Faced with reality, I could do *nothing*. I just *stood* there, too afraid to move. What kind of warrior can I call myself when I cower like a green novice before the enemy?" His hands clenched in fists. "I *still* can't think of those black robes, that skeletal face, those teeth, without my hands starting to shake!" He growled in frustration and anger.

Lyan shuddered and gripped Equinox. An answer crept into his mind as he desperately sought reassurance for his friend. "It's not your fault, Kithr. The reapers… you felt it. Before we even saw them, we both felt the aura of fear they project. That would terrify anyone, Kithr. Even you. Even Nylas would have cowered from them. Kithr, *Shadowstar* bolted. It's a reaper's nature, not your fault." He watched Kithr and saw his friend listening. Lyan pressed on. "Now we know. We've felt it, and we know what it means." He paused again. "There aren't many people who can say they've felt the fear a reaper exudes and lived to tell the tale."

Kithr raised his head, and his eyes gleamed. "And if I feel it again, I'll know what it is—a cowardly demon's way of hiding from those who would kill it."

Lyan nodded. Then he smiled faintly. "But let's not go trying to find more just to test our resolve, okay?"

Kithr started, then nodded with a chuckle. "Don't worry about me seeking them out, Lyan. Once is sufficient for this lifetime."

Lyan's thoughts roamed as they rode. *Why did the reapers attack us? Did they come specifically for us? Or for me?* Lyan looked at Equinox. *For the Spearbearer? Would they have killed me? Would they have killed Kithr in front of me, then taken me captive to their summoner?* He shivered at the thought. *What about Cailean? Is he safe?*

Another thought occurred to him, and Lyan started. "Kithr, I don't think Aikan is the traitor."

"You've mentioned that already. What brings it up now?" Kithr responded.

"The reapers. Someone had to summon them and send them out. If they were sent to kill or capture us, their summoner had to know we were separated from Cailean and his men. Aikan wouldn't know that, and wouldn't be able to pass that information on."

Kithr considered, then nodded. "All right, makes sense. So we're back to agreeing that Cailean has some traitor in his company, whichever of them it is. Whether Dalrian, Shiolto, or, I suppose, Torqual."

"You don't think Torqual's a possibility?" Lyan asked.

"He's a warrior," Kithr responded, as if that alone removed Torqual from suspicion.

"All right, so you don't suspect him because of all of them, you kind of trust him."

Kithr scowled. "He's Tathren. Of course I don't trust him. But I feel more of a sense of something in common with him than with the others."

"You trust him, you just won't admit it," Lyan said.

"Bah."

They rode through the day with few pauses, pushing the horses to make up lost ground. Aikan's tracks remained absent, washed away by the rain, but Kithr was confident he knew the man's destination, and Lyan trusted Kithr's instincts.

During the night, Lyan slept restlessly, plagued by half-remembered dreams. During his turn on watch, he saw that Kithr also slept poorly.

We don't want to admit, either of us, how badly the reapers have frightened us. Lyan gripped Equinox. *And they aren't the worst Murdo has to offer. Those were only a small taste of the minions he has at his disposal.*

In the morning, Lyan didn't mention his nightmares, nor did he ask about Kithr's. Neither spoke much. Weariness hung over them like a gloomy fog.

Mid-morning, they entered a forest. As the undergrowth gave way beneath the leafy canopy, Kithr jumped to the ground, and his expression turned to surprise.

"Tracks. The old man's, I think, though I can't say for sure." He followed the trail a little way, then freed a scrap of cloth from a bramble. "It was him—this came off his shirt.

And in a hurry. Running. Why?" Kithr continued walking, leading his horse. He froze.

"What is it?" Lyan craned his head, trying to see what Kithr had spotted.

"Horses. They came from the left. He must have been trying to avoid them." Kithr shook his head. "Looks like they caught up. Six horses, I'd say. Circled around him." He passed his reins to Lyan and walked the area. Lyan saw the trampled earth, and hoof tracks in the once damp soil. "I don't see blood, so he's probably alive. I'd say the old man didn't want to be found, though."

A chill ran down Lyan's spine. "Someone's taken Aikan prisoner?"

"That's my guess, but I can't say for sure. The horses continued north. For now, at least, they're also riding toward the keep." Kithr swung back into the saddle. "Let's go. We're a day behind them. If they aren't pushing, we can gain time— find out who they are and why they want the old man."

Lyan nodded, kneeing Shadowstar after Kithr. The stallion snorted and stepped into a trot. "How large is this forest?"

"Large enough. Hunting preserve for the lord of the land if he feels like taking an expedition away from home for a few nights. I understand it's punishable by death for the peasants to hunt any animals from it."

"Meaning, you've hunted here before," Lyan said.

Kithr just shrugged. "We had to eat. And it made the Tathrens mad. But I don't know the area well. We weren't here for long."

Like the Forests of Cossette, this forest was indifferent to elven presence under its boughs, neither welcoming nor rejecting them. Kithr focused on the trail he followed, and Lyan held back other questions to avoid being a distraction.

The trees grew closer together. Kithr watched the tracks and muttered a curse. "How in the Mad God's Pits did they get their animals through here? Magic?" He jumped to the ground. "Wait here, Lyan. I'm going to scout ahead."

"Be careful," Lyan said uneasily.

"Of course." Kithr slung his bow over his shoulder and moved ahead, barely making noise as he walked. In a few moments, he had vanished into the forest's shadows.

Lyan tried not to fidget. Shadowstar caught the restlessness, pawing the ground and nibbling at leaves and grass, constantly shifting his weight. Finally, Lyan heard Kithr's voice.

"Lyan. Come here—quietly."

He slid to the ground, holding Equinox. Shadowstar snorted. Lyan patted the stallion's nose. "It's all right. I'll be right back. We're not going to leave you here."

Shadowstar snorted again, but settled. Lyan walked toward Kithr's voice, trying to move as quietly as his friend, and knew he did a poor job. Speaking in a loud whisper, he asked, "Kithr, where are you?"

"Over here."

Kithr's voice came from the left. Lyan corrected course. As he did, a shiver ran down Lyan's spine, becoming the sense he finally recognized as the awareness of being watched.

"Kithr?" he asked warily. His eyes searched the forest. "Where are you?"

Moisture gathered in the air—not a storm, but a heavy mist with no source and no discernible cause. From somewhere far to his right, Lyan heard Kithr's voice—a curse he knew had to be Kithr, and a call of "Lyan! Where are you?"

Something used Kithr's voice to trick me. His eyes narrowed. *I don't know how it found me, or how it got here. I thought we'd lost it when the portal took us from the Shrine of Equinox to Tather. But I know what it is. The pooka.*

1 3

Hand, foot, and throat
Bind the beast by three
Bind, but do not gloat
For such a creature still is free

Mist thickened around Lyan. He gripped Equinox and called, "Kithr! Pooka!"

A wave of vertigo washed over Lyan. Though he was sure he stood still, trees moved around him as rapidly as if he galloped on horseback.

I walked blindly into its trap, and now the pooka is separating me from Kithr.

He didn't know where the pooka intended to take him, but he had no intentions of finding out. He drove Equinox head-first into the ground. "Enough!"

A pulse from the Spear banished the mist, and the world stopped spinning. Lyan stood in an unfamiliar part of the forest, surrounded by trees and silence.

"I know you're here. Come out," Lyan ordered.

A shadow flowed from tree to tree. "Ah, little elf, you've gained a new toy, have you? And who would have thought it?"

"*I* would," Lyan responded coolly. "I don't have time for your games."

"You have nowhere to run this time, little elf, and no ally lurking in wait. Your Tathren 'friends' are in chains—every one of them. The other elf stalks real... the pooka whispered from the forest.

Lyan tensed and pulled Equinox free of the ground. "Where are Cailean and his men? Where is Aikan?"

"You'll be with them soon enough. You've run as far as you can go, little elf. Will you stand and fight, try to prove yourself capable of winning the challenge I issued at our first conversation, or will you admit defeat?"

"Surrender? To you? Never!"

Lyan saw the pooka step around a tree. It wore the form of a black-haired human male dressed in dark silk shirt and trousers. The red eyes narrowed on Lyan, then the man became a black horse. The pooka reared and charged Lyan. Lyan raised Equinox and, accepting the first answer the Spear pressed into his thoughts, shouted several short, sharp words in a command. Dust swirled, and a form materialized beside him.

The pooka scrambled in a frantic effort to stop, glowing eyes wide in sudden fear. Only then did Lyan realize the significance of what he'd just done.

Nachyne's massive wings folded against his back as he stepped forward. The god of monsters fixed an icy gaze on the pooka. A monster belonging to Nachyne's domain. The pooka skidded to a halt at Nachyne's feet. The black horse awkwardly knelt, head bowed.

Nachyne turned his glare to Lyan. "You interrupt a bottle of absinth finer than any vintage a mere mortal could endure for *this*?" He spun back to the quivering, kneeling pooka. "And you. You dare."

The ground trembled at the anger in Nachyne's voice. Lyan wanted to cower, however much Equinox assured him the god could not and would not turn that anger onto Lyan. More than anything, Lyan wanted to turn time back a few precious moments and use some alternative, any alternative other than summoning Nachyne here, now, against the pooka. But that was beyond even the power of Equinox.

"*Honored and glorious Lord Nachyne.*" The pooka's voice whispered in Lyan's mind and, presumably, in Nachyne's.

"You *dare* attack the bearer of a Spear of the Stars. You *dare* defy my laws." Nachyne's gaze remained fixed on the black horse at his feet.

"*My lord, I begged you to release me from the binding placed on me by the mortal who hunts the Spears.*" A hint of defiance colored the pooka's words.

"You will be silent before me." Nachyne's voice chilled the air. "You were careless and stupid enough to let yourself be bound. Then you asked me to free you. You said nothing of Spears or Spearbearers."

"*The mortal who bound me would not permit——,*" the pooka began.

"I said you will be *silent* before me." Nachyne raised his hand. A sharp gesture sent the pooka flying back to slam into a tree.

The black horse shrieked in pain. Nachyne's power swept the pooka into another tree, drawing a second cry.

Lyan looked away. "Nachyne, is this necessary?"

"This pathetic excuse for a monster belongs to me, Spearbearer. Over matters of my domain, you have no say. This wretch broke my laws. Do not think you have any right to interfere." The god's power jerked the pooka into the air, and Nachyne stepped toward it. "Especially not when the wretch proves incapable of following one simple command."

The pooka trembled, eyes wide as Nachyne held its gaze trapped in his own. The god spoke slowly and deliberately. "You will be silent before me. Each failure will result in further punishment. And you have not yet succeeded."

Nachyne raised a hand. Coils of fire wound around the pooka's body. Lyan smelled burning hair. The pooka jerked in pain and hung helpless in the air, unable escape the flame. The faintest sound of agony escaped the black horse.

Nachyne's eyes narrowed. Cords whipped out of the air, wrapping around the pooka's thrashing limbs, pulling tight and pinning them still. One cord began to draw the pooka's right foreleg at an unnatural angle. The pooka's eyes widened in fear and pain. It struggled, as if it had any hope of escaping its god. Lyan turned away, but he couldn't close his ears. The snap of breaking bone filled his hearing, made all the louder by the absence of other sounds—most especially, the absence of any cry of pain from the pooka.

Lyan looked back. The pooka's sides heaved as it struggled for breath, eyes rolled back in its head. The coils of fire and the cords vanished, and Nachyne let the pooka fall with a thump to the dirt.

"Take human form," the god ordered.

The pooka raised its head with great effort, and its shape changed with a slowness painful to watch. Its black hair hung loose and tangled, and its skin sallow. It still wore the gaudy finery Lyan had seen before, but dirt and blood stained torn cloth. Its right arm lay bent in a place no bone should bend. The pooka struggled to its knees and crawled to Nachyne's feet.

"So, you want to be released from your bonds to the mortal who caught you," Nachyne said to the cowering figure.

The pooka gave a faint nod.

The god turned his head an inch. "Lyan, come here."

Lyan approached Nachyne and the pooka. The pooka didn't look up. A trickle of blood ran from its mouth where it bit into its lip to hold back the agonized cries. Lyan looked uneasily at Nachyne. "Yes?"

"You know how to bind a pooka?" the god said.

"Yes," Lyan answered with trepidation.

"Good. Bind this wretch."

The pooka didn't move, but it trembled a little more. Lyan almost refused.

But isn't this what I've intended to do since it first challenged me? Lyan drew his knife.

"The traditional method would be to pull out its hair," Nachyne commented in a deceptively mild tone.

A fresh trickle of blood ran from the pooka's lip as it bit down harder. Lyan looked at the god of monsters. "Do you *really* want to wait all day while I do, Nachyne? No? Then I'll use the knife."

"If you insist." Nachyne crossed his arms and waited.

Lyan cut the pooka's hair close to the scalp, leaving uneven black stubble. The pooka didn't move.

I never thought I'd even think this, but I'm sorry. When I claimed I could bind you at our first meeting outside Eilidh Wood, I never imagined I would do so by bringing your god's wrath down on you.

Lyan sheathed his knife and divided the long hair into three twisted cords. The first he used to secure the pooka's ankles, but he hesitated on the second. The pooka's broken arm hung limp, and forcing the creature to move it seemed an unnecessary cruelty on top of everything else.

Nachyne spoke with thinly disguised impatience. "Bind the wretch's arms behind his back."

The pooka moved. Wavering without the support of its good arm, it lifted its broken limb with the uninjured one and shifted it to rest behind its back. Lyan tied the pooka's wrists with as much care as he could, unable to overlook the tremors of pain that shook the monster.

To complete the binding, Lyan wrapped the final cord loosely around the pooka's neck. As Lyan stepped back, Nachyne snapped his fingers. Lyan started, drawing a sharp breath when his rude cord twisted and transformed. Where the ropes of hair had bound the pooka's limbs together and ringed its neck, instead seamless bands of black metal circled its wrists, ankles, and neck. They provided no visible restraint, not pinning the pooka's limbs or impeding movement, but the pooka shuddered and squeezed its eyes shut.

What did Nachyne do? Nothing I've ever read mentioned anything like this being part of a simple binding.

Nachyne gazed at his creature with icy eyes. "You belong to Lyan, Spearbearer of Equinox. Any bonds that held you before are broken. No mortal but Lyan has or ever will have command over you. You are a free creature no longer."

Lyan's eyes opened wide, along with his mouth, wanting to protest, but no words came. Nachyne glared at Lyan, his eyes dark and angry.

"If there's nothing else, Spearbearer, I'll be leaving now."

Lyan tried to speak again, and still no words came. He shook his head in answer. The god cast the pooka a final, disgusted look, then took wing and vanished.

Lyan looked at the kneeling pooka. "You, um, you may speak."

"What is your will, master?" The pooka's voice was thin with pain, and its body still trembled.

Lyan struggled to collect his wits. "Your arm first."

The pooka moved its broken arm to rest in its lap, face pale and tears of pain in its eyes. "What is your will, master?"

"How long does it take you to heal broken bones?" Lyan asked. He searched the forest floor for thick sticks to use in a splint.

"Healing naturally, almost half a moon to return to full strength, master. If you order it to be whole sooner, it will be sooner."

Lyan stopped in his tracks and stared at the pooka in disbelief. "If I order your arm to heal faster, it will?"

"If you will that I be whole sooner, I have ways of forcing it to heal faster, master."

"At what cost?" Lyan asked cautiously.

"I can force creatures of Lord Nachyne's domain that are

weaker than I to give me from their essences. If you will it, I could be whole by tomorrow's dawn."

Leaving how many other creatures dead and drained? Lyan didn't ask the question aloud. Instead, he splinted the pooka's arm and fashioned a sling, unapologetically using the pooka's ruined shirt for materials. The pooka looked at splint and sling in bemusement, then shot Lyan a questioning look.

"If you're anything like us mere mortals, keeping it supported and still will help it heal," Lyan said. "And it might hurt less."

"Yes master," the pooka said quietly.

Uncomfortable and awkward, Lyan turned away from the pooka that had, only a little while ago, been attacking him. He looked around the forest in a half-hearted hope Kithr would appear. "Which way back to Kithr and the horses?"

The pooka raised a trembling hand to point. "The other side of the forest, master. But I don't know that the other elf will be there. He probably tried to follow the false trail. I can't be sure; he is skilled at evading attempts to locate him."

"What about Cailean and his men?"

"Ambushed by men in the service of the master of the keep and taken prisoner, as was the man you followed. They are either on their way to or already at the keep, master. I was ordered to capture you and bring you there as well."

Lyan stiffened. "Cailean's been taken prisoner? But how would Ewart know—" He looked sharply at the pooka. "How did he know? Who told him? Who betrayed Cailean?"

The pooka studied the splint on its broken arm, shifting its weight and not meeting Lyan's eyes. "I don't know, master."

Lyan blinked. "What do you mean, you don't know? You told me long ago you knew the traitor's identity, when you taunted me with the knowledge that there *was* a traitor!"

The pooka reluctantly raised its head to meet Lyan's gaze. "I lied, master. I know one of them is a traitor, but when I claimed to know who, I lied."

Lyan didn't know whether to rage or give in to hysterical laughter. He sank down and sat on the ground, head in his hands. The pooka watched him silently. After a moment, Lyan collected himself and stood again. "Are you fit to walk?"

"In human form, yes, master."

Lyan drew a deep breath and let it out slowly. "I need to find Kithr."

Without a word, the pooka followed Lyan when he started walking. Having it so close at his back made Lyan's skin crawl. However much his rational mind claimed the monster could not do him harm, his instincts rejected the idea of trusting it. Lyan remembered all too well his flight from the pooka in the Forests of Cossette.

His thoughts turned to Nachyne. Lyan shivered at the memory of the god's anger. *I've really made a mess. And I don't even know the best way to find Kithr.*

"Then you're either a fool or willfully ignorant," the pooka said sharply.

Lyan spun around. "What?"

The pooka's baleful gaze met his, showing a creature somewhat recovered from pain and shock, and far less than resigned to its loss of freedom. "What is it you carry? A glorified walking staff, or one of the most powerful weapons to be found on this world? You moan and complain that you can't find your friend while you ignore the power you earned the right to bear? Disgusting."

Lyan bristled. "And how am I supposed to know how to use the Spear, when there's no one to teach me?"

"The same way previous Spearbearers have, *master*," the pooka spat. "By *using* it. Are you truly a coward? Is the Spear of the Stars nothing more than a decoration for your wall? You *have* it. *Use* it. Use it or be used by it."

"I *do* use Equinox," Lyan snapped.

The pooka sneered. "Badly. You've discovered a few tricks,

but you don't know when to use them." Its eyes narrowed. "Or when not to use them, *master*."

Lyan flinched.

"You don't even have the wits to shield your mind! Announce your thoughts to any being that cares to listen! How can I *not* hear what you're thinking when you all but shout it?"

Lyan's grip tightened on Equinox. *My thoughts are my own, not for anyone else to hear!*

Equinox responded—Lyan felt the touch of the Spear's power. He was sure he also felt impatience from Equinox, as if the Spear agreed with the pooka and felt irritation at Lyan's hesitation to call on its power. Lyan drew a deep breath and forced a calm, steady voice.

"Where does this tirade fall in regards to you serving me?"

The pooka froze, genuine alarm tempering the anger in its eyes as it remembered that Lyan now held a power over it equal to Nachyne. It opened its mouth, hesitated, and then said, "I presented an answer to an implied question regarding how to find the other elf. Master."

Lyan gazed at the pooka. *Are my thoughts still open, or is my mind private now?*

The pooka shifted uneasily under Lyan's gaze, and didn't respond to the silent question.

"Can I heal the pooka's arm?"

The first means that Equinox presented was to summon Nachyne to heal the pooka. Lyan rejected that immediately. *"Don't you think the god of monsters is angry enough at me already? Not Nachyne. Another way. Less dramatic. I just want the pooka's arm healed and whole."*

Another possibility came to mind. With an effort, Lyan resisted the urge to use the power before he understood all the effects. *"No. Tell me what ways I could use to mend it and how they work, so I can decide. Stop rushing."*

Equinox relented, though it left Lyan with the impression that the Spear was sulking. Lyan gripped the Spear to steady himself as knowledge filled his mind—countless methods he could use to heal the pooka, from simple to unbelievably overdramatic.

Consequences. Everything leads to something else. As an astrologer, I should know that better than anyone. What has the best consequences? There—that one. That will work.

The pooka still watched Lyan with fear. Lyan realized his conversation with Equinox had only taken a few heartbeats. Lyan stood straight. "You did make a good point. I haven't been using the Spear as I should." Equinox glowed in his hand. "And I'll learn by using it."

The pooka cried in pain, sinking to its knees and clutching its broken arm.

I could make it feel every moment as the bones knit. The pooka has tormented me since I left Eilidh Wood. Now, finally, I can repay it.

The pooka, pale, choked back sounds of agony and squeezed its eyes shut, biting into its lip to stop its cries, as it had when Nachyne punished it.

Lyan caught himself. *What am I doing? Torturing a helpless, injured creature, just because I can? Even when the pooka chased me, I had some chance of escape, however slim it seemed then. The pooka has no choice.* Sickened at himself, Lyan willed Equinox to numb the pooka's pain.

The pooka started, head jerking up to look at Lyan. Then it turned its gaze to its splinted arm.

"Don't move it yet," Lyan said. "It hasn't finished healing."

"Then why did it stop hurting?" the pooka responded, more suspicious than appreciative.

"Equinox numbed it."

"Why?"

"You'd rather be in pain?" Lyan asked.

The pooka's jaw tightened. After a moment, it answered, "No. Master." It wiped blood from its mouth.

Lyan looked around the forest again. In a low voice, he said, "Shadowstar, I'm safe. Please find Kithr and help him find me." He started walking, and the pooka followed. Lyan glanced over his shoulder to it. "I was right; you were bound by someone when you followed Cailean."

"Yes, master," the pooka answered sullenly.

"Ewart?" Lyan asked.

The pooka snorted with scorn. "Ewart couldn't bind his own shoes, much less one of my kind. He is nothing more than a tool to Porephyn."

"Porephyn, then."

"Yes."

"Why did you challenge me to bind you?" Lyan asked.

"Because I believed you could, master."

Lyan stopped. "What?"

"I was forbidden from telling even my god why I begged to be released from the mage's hold. But I knew full well I was bound by a devotee of the Mad God." Anger colored the pooka's voice. "Do you think I *wanted* to be a part of a plan to strengthen and release my god's enemy?"

So you taunted me and challenged me, because if I bound you, it would break the previous hold. "No," Lyan answered. "I'm sure you had no wish to do so."

He started walking again. After a moment, Lyan asked, "Do you have a name?"

"Only such as you choose to give me, master," the pooka said, voice cold.

"Doesn't your kind have names?" Lyan asked, frowning.

"Names belong to free creatures, *master*," the pooka said in an angry growl. "One who is not a free creature has only the name given by his master."

"Is there a name you want to be called?" Lyan asked. *To be so completely stripped of freedom that you can't even call your identity your own.*

"That. Is. Not. My. Choice. Master." The pooka made each word a statement of its hate.

"And I can't ask your opinion on a subject?" Lyan countered.

"What answer do you want?" the pooka asked, sullen.

"An honest one," Lyan answered.

"You're an idiot." The words escaped the pooka's mouth before it thought them through. The pooka froze, expression suddenly fearful again.

Lyan smiled wryly. "Well, that was certainly your honest opinion, even if not an answer to the question I asked."

"Master, I…"

"You answered honestly," Lyan said. "I don't fault you for doing what I told you. But I'd like an answer to the original question. *Do* you have an opinion or preference to a name?"

The pooka eyed him warily, still expecting a trick or punishment for the insult. "My only preference, master, is that the name you give me not be the one I claimed as a free creature."

Lyan frowned. "Why?"

The pooka stood stiff. "The name of any monster who is no longer a free creature becomes a word of scorn and insult. I do not wish that shame on my name."

That's why he wants me to choose. Lyan searched for a word or name that wouldn't be forever tainted in his own thoughts by this knowledge. A word came, one unfamiliar to him, in a language he didn't know. "Praett."

The pooka frowned. "Does it mean something, master?"

"Equinox suggested it," Lyan said. "I think it implies 'trickster'."

The pooka inclined his head. "As you wish, master."

They walked without conversation for a time. Praett broke the quiet. "Master."

"What is it?" Lyan asked.

"I told you I was ordered to capture you."

"Yes."

"When I succeeded, I was to meet a band of soldiers at the forest edge, and they would be an escort to the keep. We are near their camp."

Lyan paused and looked at Praett suspiciously. "What, exactly, are you thinking?"

He listened to the pooka, and only one thought ran through his head. *Kithr is going to kill me for this.*

14

Trickster and Shadows
For hunter and prey
Trickster and Shadows
A new game they play

Lyan glared balefully at the Tathren before him. The man stood slightly shorter than Lyan, but far broader in the shoulders. He wore a uniform that must have meant something to those knowledgeable in Tathren livery. His face was grizzled and his eyes hard, brown hair cropped close to the scalp. He studied Lyan, then Praett.

"This the one you were after?" He sounded dubious.

Praett's eyes narrowed. "You *doubt* me?" The honeyed voice dripped venom.

The man took an involuntary step back. Grizzled veteran of countless battles or not, the pooka clearly left him ill at ease. "Uh, no. But I do have my orders."

"So do I," Praett hissed. "And none mention for me to leave your head attached to your shoulders."

Lyan twisted at the cords binding his hands behind his

back, but not too fiercely, and glowered at Praett. In Elven, he muttered, "I still can't believe I let you talk me into this."

To Tathren ears, the words probably sounded like curses or insults. The man in front of Lyan eyed Praett again. "What about elf magic? And does he understand us?"

"What does it matter to you if he does or doesn't understand?" Praett responded. The smooth, taunting tone was calculated to send shivers down the spine of anyone hearing it. "And elf magic isn't your concern, either. I don't recall *asking* for your presence."

"No more than we asked to be your escort," the man countered darkly. "But since we both have our orders from our lord, we'll both follow those orders, so we can be done with this pretense of cooperation. Then you can go back to terrorizing small children, or whatever it is you do for fun, and we can go back to protecting our lord's keep."

Praett's narrowed eyes remained focused on the man, and the creature didn't say anything at all. The Tathren broke from the pooka's gaze and gestured to the other nine men. They broke camp with swift efficiency, avoiding Praett and Lyan.

Praett spoke in Lyan's mind. *"If you will it, master, I will gladly slaughter these sheep before they know they are in danger. But doing so will reveal the truth and my new allegiance, and will close the easiest path by which you can reach the prisoners."*

"I know." Praett couldn't read all Lyan's thoughts, but if Lyan directed one, the monster could hear him. Lyan kept the next thought private. *This sounded like a good idea—a workable plan. I just didn't realize how much being bound, being a prisoner even in appearance only, would remind me of Vynzent.*

To avoid the suspicion a shorn head would earn from anyone knowledgeable in bindings, Lyan had given Praett permission to make his hair long enough to tie back in a short tail. His arm had healed enough to make the sling unnecessary, though he still favored the limb. The remains of the pooka's shirt still hung in shreds, while blood, bruises, and burns marked his skin. Praett's glare challenged any to comment on his tattered appearance.

Lyan had scuffed and dirtied his clothes. Streaks of mud and grass stains on his clothes and face gave him a look almost as ragged as Praett's. Locks of red hair kept slipping down to hang in his face, irritating him. He shook his head in an effort to toss a particularly persistent one out of his eyes. The cords around his wrists were loose enough that he could wriggle free if needed, but their presence kept pulling Lyan's thoughts back to fire and scalding metal pressed against his bare skin. The worst aspect of the role he played, though, was that to present the image of being a captive, Lyan had been forced to leave Equinox hidden in the trees.

Lyan had consented to Praett's idea only after he had reassured himself several times that he could summon the Spear in an instant. Equinox didn't care for the separation any more than he did, but Lyan absolutely refused to let the pooka carry the Spear like some battle trophy.

Even thinking about the Spear made Lyan struggle against the urge to call Equinox. *"Remind me to keep to the plan!"* he ordered sharply.

"You are safe, master, and I will let no harm come to you. If I return to the keep without the company of these sheep, I will immediately be called into the presence of the priest, possibly with you still in my company. At a look, he will know the truth of my bonds, as these ignorant sheep do not. Reaching the prisoners will become far more difficult if he knows I am not his. So long as we enter with the sheep he ordered onto me, they will report to him, and he is unlikely to call for me, master. Then you will be able to free the prisoners." Praett made an effort to remind Lyan of all the arguments in favor of the plan. After a moment, he added softly, *"I cannot and will not betray you, master."*

Lyan drew a steadying breath. His hands trembled. He watched the Tathrens load their gear on the horses. They would be ready in moments. Lyan whispered to the wind in

Elven. "Shadowstar, when you and Kithr find me, don't attack, and don't let Kithr attack. I know it's going to look like I'm in trouble, but I'm not. I'm safe. Trust me."

"What's he whispering over there?" demanded one Tathren. "Some elf magic?"

Praett gave the man a bored, annoyed look. "If he is, it's only that your wits rot away. Since you have none, I doubt you'll notice any difference."

The Tathren was younger and rasher than his companions. He had a sword half out of the sheath before the leader stopped him, resting one hand over the blade's pommel.

"Let it go," the leader ordered.

"But sir!" protested the angry young man.

Praett simply watched, smirking. "Come now, let him draw. Give me an excuse to play."

"Let it go," the leader ordered again, voice hard. "Try to fight that thing, and you'll be lucky if it kills you quickly. If you're not lucky, you won't die until after it's broken every bone in your body."

The hot-headed young man hesitated. Praett sighed and yawned in exaggerated boredom. "Must have seen my last toy. A pity, that one. He still had at least ten bones I didn't get to before his heart stopped."

All the men shifted uneasily, and the younger warrior pushed the sword back into the sheath. Lyan cast the pooka a sidelong glance. *"Did you really do that?"*

Praett didn't even blink. *"I hated being forced to serve Porephyn, master, and I found every possible means to express it."*

As if the near-incident hadn't happened, the leader of the men addressed Praett. "Our orders are that the prisoner is to ride the horse we brought. You can travel however you like."

Praett's voice became honey again. "Oh, I'll ride with the elf, of course. So none of you will have to fear his dreaded magic."

Angry mutters answered him, ignored by both the pooka and the leader of the Tathrens, who silently pointed to a horse.

Praett smirked, took Lyan's arm, and in the Trade tongue said, "Come along, little elf."

Lyan jerked away. "Rot in the Mad God's Pits," he snapped in the same. He noticed the slight relaxing of tension from some of the Tathrens as they made the assumption their prisoner didn't speak or understand their language.

Praett just chuckled, and yanked Lyan to the horse. He freed Lyan's hands long enough to climb into the saddle, surrounded by wary, armed Tathrens. Lyan glared at them. The men stumbled back several steps.

They're as afraid of me as they are the pooka. Nylas and his like have certainly kept the fear of elves alive.

Praett bound Lyan's hands again, then swung onto the horse behind him. The horse shifted uneasily, disliking the pooka, but didn't try to throw off the riders. The leader of the Tathrens took the reins and tied them to his saddle, obviously not trusting Praett any more than he did Lyan. They rode north.

As the afternoon grew late, Praett shifted uneasily behind Lyan. *"Your friend is near, master. And his arrow is aimed at me."*

Lyan's eyes swept the land, but he couldn't see Kithr or Shadowstar. He could, however, feel the itch he associated with being followed. If Kithr hadn't attacked yet, Shadowstar must have had some success in holding Kithr back. *"Can you speak to his mind?"*

"I can."

"Then tell him a message exactly as I tell you."

"Yes, master."

"Lyan says to tell you to wait. He has a plan, and he's safe. He says

we're playing Trickster and Shadows. He's the bait and you're the snare, like we used to." Lyan thought of the game he and Kithr had played so often as youths. If Kithr were thinking clearly, he'd recognize the pooka couldn't know such things. "*Tell Kithr that.*"

Silence for a moment, then Praett responded. "*He says I'm a lying, treacherous, misbegotten bastard, and that he will see to it that I die a slow, painful death in agony. He demands to know why he should listen to any of my lies.*"

That sounded like Kithr, certainly. But he hadn't started loosing arrows yet, so he was listening, or at least being cautious now that he knew the pooka was aware of him. "*Tell Kithr this: Lyan says he can call Equinox with a thought and Nachyne with a word. The pooka is bound to serve Lyan by the will of his god, and if he disobeys that, he will welcome the slow, painful death you promise over what Nachyne will do to him.*"

A shudder of fear ran through Praett, and he whispered aloud. "I will never betray you, master."

"Tell Kithr what I said," Lyan ordered in an undertone.

"I have, master. He demands that he speak to you directly."

"Can you arrange that tonight?" Lyan asked.

"Easily," Praett answered.

"Let Kithr know."

"It is done." After a moment, Praett relaxed. "*His arrow remains on the string, but is no longer drawn or aimed at my head. I've felt the bite of his arrows before, and would prefer not to repeat the experience.*"

Kithr seemed willing to consider the possibility that Praett told the truth. Lyan at once wished for and dreaded the conversation to come.

He's probably going to punch me. And I am going to completely deserve it.

The Tathrens didn't press much further. Though the land offered little shelter, they stopped at a site that had been used recently, judging from the trampled ground and dark remains of a fire pit. The men dismounted and set up camp. Praett pulled Lyan off the horse, then left him for a moment and spoke to the leader of the Tathrens in a low voice.

The man looked irritated. "Not satisfied with having the ride to torment him?"

"It's no fun when he *knows* he can't get away," Praett purred in a tone Lyan knew all too well.

"Our lord ordered that he arrive whole and mostly unharmed," the Tathren said sharply.

"I just want to play a little game. I won't hurt him… much."

The man's mouth curled in a disgusted sneer.

Praett's voice grew colder, still keeping the playful tone. "You wouldn't want me to get *bored*."

The man stiffened. "Fine. But it's your head if something happens to him."

The pooka only smirked and pulled Lyan from camp, speaking in the Trade tongue. "Let's play, elf."

Lyan didn't need much acting to portray revulsion as he tried to jerk away. Praett's tone sent shivers down his spine every time he heard it. "What makes you think I have any wish to play your twisted 'games'?"

Praett grinned wickedly. "If you don't play, I win."

Once they were away from the camp, Praett's demeanor changed. He loosed Lyan's hands and bowed his head. "I beg your forgiveness for my behavior, master. I know it causes you distress."

What other reaction does he expect, having heard that voice taunting me at any unexpected moment? Lyan shook his head. "You're playing your part, and you play it well. You're doing what you should to avoid suspicion."

"Yes, master." Praett didn't sound convinced.

"If I didn't act like it bothered me, I wouldn't be doing my part in the ruse either," Lyan said. "They're watching me just as much as you."

Praett nodded again, a little more at ease with the idea that some of Lyan's reaction played into the deception. "Your companion awaits this way, master."

They walked four or five yards when Shadowstar nickered and trotted up to Lyan from a shallow dip in the land. The stallion roughly shoved his nose against Lyan's chest. Lyan laughed softly and rubbed the stallion. "I'm sorry I worried you, Shadowstar. Thank you for finding me and helping Kithr."

Shadowstar snorted, tossed his head, and stepped aside. Kithr emerged from the growing shadows, and cautiously slung his bow over his back. He eyed Praett with suspicion. The pooka remained several steps back and behind Lyan. Kithr looked from Lyan, to Praett, back to Lyan.

"You idiot mooncalf, what in rot and ash are you thinking?" Kithr demanded in a low voice.

"It seemed like a good idea at the time?" Lyan offered.

He saw the punch coming and braced himself. Kithr swung, but Praett darted between Lyan and Kithr. Kithr's fist hit Praett's arms, raised to block the blow.

"What in…?" Kithr began in disbelief, shaking a stinging hand.

Lyan stepped around Praett and rested a hand on the monster's shoulder to move him aside. "Kithr's allowed to hit me, all right? For that matter, so is Cailean. I'm pretty sure I deserve it if either of them feels a need to knock sense into me."

Praett scowled. "You could have said that earlier, master." The tone implied the pooka would have been more than happy to see the blow connect.

"I didn't think about it," Lyan said. He looked at Kithr. "So, hello."

Kithr looked at both Lyan and Praett, for a moment

saying nothing. When he did speak, he was to the point. "Explain. Now."

"I failed to consider the implications of calling on Nachyne when attacked by a creature of his domain," Lyan answered. The nagging wish to have Equinox in hand rose in him again, and Lyan gave in to the impulse. The Spear suddenly appeared in Lyan's grasp.

Kithr jerked back a step at the abrupt appearance of Equinox. His eyes narrowed then. "You bound the pooka?" He glared at Praett. "And I should trust a creature that lives to deceive?"

Praett answered before Lyan, voice flat. "My lord Nachyne took my life, bound it, and made it a gift to the Spearbearer as my final punishment for disobeying the laws of my god. I can never again make the claim of being a free creature." He raised one arm, showing the black metal band around the wrist. "So whether or not you trust me, whether or not the Spearbearer trusts me, he is my master, and whatever he wills, I must obey."

Kithr drew a sharp breath. "Is this creature telling the truth, Lyan?"

Lyan nodded.

"Then what in all the gods' names are you doing surrounded by would-be warriors and useless thugs?" Kithr demanded.

"Cailean and his men have been captured and taken to the keep by the orders of the priest who cursed Cailean, Porephyn. That same man bound the pooka. He sent the pooka out with orders to capture me and meet with those men to take me to the keep as well."

Kithr held up a hand to stop Lyan. "One question first." He glared at Praett. "The *last* time you were near, we were close to the Shrine of Equinox. I know how we crossed moons' worth of travel in an instant. How did you get here?"

Praett sniffed dismissively. "What you call a moon's ride is barely a day and a night of running for me, if I wish to travel swiftly. Porephyn called me back when you entered the Shrine and I couldn't follow." Praett folded arms across his chest. "Our time is limited, master."

"These men think I'm the pooka's prisoner," Lyan said before Kithr could ask anything else.

"And this is a 'plan'?" Kithr responded.

"As a prisoner, I can walk into Cailean's keep and down into the dungeon. Then, I can free Cailean and his men without Porephyn or his underlings realizing I'm not their captive, and without them knowing the pooka serves me and not him."

Kithr frowned. "You think you can free the Tathrens by yourself? Brazen. Still, given how narrow your last escape from this monster was, it's believable that you could be caught. As long as they believe that, you shouldn't be suspected." For several moments, he silently searched the idea for flaws. Finally, he scowled. "Where do I fit into this plan?"

The question surprised Lyan. He'd been braced for an extended argument with Kithr rather than reluctant acceptance. "We know Cailean's keep has hidden entrances. Porephyn's men couldn't have found them all, and even if they did, they aren't likely to have heavy guards on all of them," Lyan said.

Kithr continued to frown. "You're thinking one elf can sneak in more easily than a company."

Lyan smiled. "Can you get inside a mere Tathren's stronghold unnoticed and find the dungeons?"

"Bah, is that all you want? Rot it, Lyan. If all their men are as worthless as those guarding you, I could take half the keep by myself."

"I'm sure Cailean will want at least a little part in reclaiming his home," Lyan said.

Kithr waved a hand in dismissal. "Fine, fine, I'll wait for

you and your pet Tathrens. We'll meet at the dungeon entrance, and if you're not there, I *will* hunt you down."

Lyan nodded. "Understood."

"And I will be following you. If anything happens, I won't wait for a second explanation."

Lyan nodded seriously. "Thank you, Kithr. Also, Cailean's been caught, and we still don't know who the traitor is. So be careful."

"You do the same." Kithr responded.

"We must return, master, before the sheep decide to come searching," Praett said.

Lyan walked to Shadowstar and slid Equinox into the straps on the saddle designed to hold the Spear. "I'm leaving Equinox in your care until I need it, all right, Shadowstar?"

The stallion tossed his head and snorted, then nuzzled Lyan. Lyan scratched Shadowstar's ears. He hated to leave Equinox again, but leaving it with Shadowstar eased some of his anxiety. He knew the Spear would be safe. "I'll see you again soon, and I know you'll be here when I need you." Lyan looked toward the orange glow of light where the Tathrens camped, and he drew a deep breath. "All right. Let's go back."

Kithr didn't say anything, but Lyan felt his friend's eyes follow him the entire walk toward the camp, and that gaze made Lyan question again his decision, his plan, and his ability to do what he said he would do.

No, I can do this. I'm not going to be on my own. I have Praett helping me, and I can call Equinox. I won't be alone.

Praett bound Lyan's hands again. "They may wonder at the quiet."

Lyan thought quickly. "The simplest explanation would be if I appeared unconscious or nearly so."

"I can arrange that," Praett said, a little too eager.

Lyan just gave him a withering look.

Praett huffed. "Or I can sling you over a shoulder and leave you to pretend unconsciousness."

"Better," Lyan said.

"But not *nearly* as satisfying," Praett muttered.

Fawning obedience or sullen resentment—Lyan wasn't sure which attitude he would rather endure. He didn't comment. Praett picked Lyan up with little effort and walked to the Tathren camp with Lyan slung over his shoulder. Lyan kept his eyes closed and listened.

"Have your 'fun'?" snapped the leader, irritated.

"A satisfying enough chase," Praett answered in the taunting, honeyed tone. Lyan wondered if he got some satisfaction provoking and deceiving these men.

Praett lowered him to the ground. Feeling the fire's warmth nearby and seeing the dancing light through closed eyes, Lyan shuddered.

Vynzent isn't here. These men fear me. They aren't going to torture me. He held the thought, repeating it to himself over and over. Noise in the camp grew softer as the men bedded down for the night. Lyan tried to find some rest. *Kithr's watching over me, and Praett can't go against my will. I'm not alone.*

Sleep finally came.

Morning brought a small meal of stale beer and tough jerky. The Tathrens even gave a couple strips of dried meat to Lyan, which was more than he'd expected. They broke camp with minimal talk. Praett left his thoughts unspoken.

The Tathrens set a harsh pace, pushing the horses hard. As he rolled stiff shoulders and tried to find a comfortable spot on the saddle, Lyan asked Praett, *"How far are we from the keep?"*

"The men would like to reach it tonight, but even at this pace, we won't arrive until tomorrow," Praett answered. *"Barring any unexpected trouble."*

"Unexpected trouble? As opposed to what? Expected trouble?" Lyan responded.

Praett chuckled aloud, drawing sharp and wary looks from the Tathrens. He smirked at the men, not explaining the fit of humor. To Lyan he replied, "*Any trouble would be unexpected. The men who hold the keep have a solid hold on the countryside. At the most, trouble would come only if Cailean [...] to attack. And they are unlikely to do so, given the size of this group.*"

More tidbits of information for Lyan to stash away. Cailean still had some loyal men holding out for his return.

Through the day, Lyan watched the land. They passed villages and farms, and people scrambled from the path of the horses with little more than glances at the riders. The farms looked, to Lyan's inexperienced eye, healthy. Ripening grain filled the fields. He wondered if Ewart's men had raided the farms and villages when they attacked, or if they had focused only on their goal.

As evening neared, the Tathrens began to grumble. The unhappiness grew when the leader finally ordered a halt for the night.

"But sir, it's not that much further," one protested.

The leader glared at them all. "And how many of you forget night is the time for elves? The time when they attack? We are stopping, and we are stopping *now*. I am not riding on until some elven trick sends us plummeting into a chasm. We have our orders, and our orders are to deliver the prisoner alive and whole, and that will not happen if we are dead. Is that understood?"

"Yes sir." The reluctant response lacked enthusiasm.

"Good. Make camp." The man turned to Praett. "And as for you, I don't care how boring it makes your night. You can and you will, survive one night without 'playing' with the prisoner. Is *that* understood?"

Praett yawned. "Fine, if you insist. But I expect to be compensated for a night of boredom."

The man tensed and answered stiffly. "You'll have to take

that matter up with the lord, tomorrow. If you deserve any compensation, that's for him to decide."

Praett smirked. "I'll ask for the hot-headed one. He'd be an entertaining toy while he lasts."

The Tathren's hands clenched in fists, but he only said, "That is for our lord to decide." Spinning sharply away, he marched across the camp and took his part in preparing for the night.

15

The die is cast,
The act is begun.
The curtain rises,
The end known to none.

Men and women in plain, rough-spun clothes scurried from the path of the horses. Lyan watched them, seeing how they cleared the village streets and ran into their houses, shutting door soundly behind them. The people barely glanced at the riders. Lyan doubted many even noticed him. The glowers on the faces of Cailean's people showed no fondness for men in Ewart's service. He wondered whether anyone in this village at the foot of the keep knew of Cailean's capture.

His eyes moved to the stone fortress. It didn't loom as Ewart's keep had when they freed Nylas and his men, but the closer they rode, the more an unseen, undefined air made Lyan's skin crawl. Something dark lurked within the walls, like a fat, venomous spider on its web.

From the keep itself, Lyan sensed age, and he could well believe it held entrances no one knew about. From the different colors and weathering of the stone, he judged where additions had been made and walls extended. The oldest parts were gray, worn and weathered. Ancient lichen filled the crevices, as integral to the walls as the rocks and mortar. If the inner keep had been built like the outer wall, over many years by many different hands, it could hide passages long forgotten and rooms without access.

The horses clattered up the cobbled road and through the first gate. Lyan tensed. Fear closed around him as they continued through the second gate. On all sides, Tathrens turned to look at the arrivals, and some murmured in surprise.

"Hey, is that…?"

"Heard they got sent out to meet that damned monster, but I didn't hear why. A prisoner? He doesn't look Tathren."

"Can't you see those ears? That's a damned *elf!*"

Lyan turned to the whispering knot of men. They instantly fell silent under his gaze. Several made signs of protection against evil.

Lyan's eyes narrowed and he spoke in Elven. "You want protection from evil? Guard yourselves against your own leaders, not me."

Praett smirked and spoke in the Trade tongue. "Come now, little elf, they'll think you're trying to curse them."

"Rot in the Mad God's Pits," Lyan muttered sullenly in the same.

"An elf, here." Someone said the words anxiously.

Praett rolled his eyes and spoke in Tathren with exaggerated boredom. "Yes, a dreadful, terrible elf. Just as your lord ordered. But don't worry, I have him contained, for now."

"Enough." the leader of the escort snapped. "We have a report to make."

"No," purred the pooka. "*You* have a report to make. *I* have a captive to see locked away." He cocked his head at the men. "Unless you really desire my company a little longer."

They stiffened, and their leader answered. "You have your orders, monster. Take care of them."

"So dull, so lacking a true spirit of adventure," Praett sighed. "I do pity mortals sometimes."

"We'll do just fine without your pity or your interest," the man snapped.

Praett laughed and jumped from the horse. The monster pulled Lyan down, looking rough and careless enough to spur a curse from Lyan. Despite the appearance, Lyan had no trouble keeping his feet. He glanced around, and Tathrens shifted back.

I almost think I should thank Nylas for keeping the fear of elves alive among Ewart's men.

Taking a firm hold on Lyan's arm, Praett pulled him across the courtyard. Lyan made a show of trying to jerk away, the image of a sullen, angry captive.

Scorch marks blackened stone walls, and some walls had been destroyed, leaving rooms exposed to the elements. Canvas draped the gaps, and men carried loads of bricks and stones under the watchful eyes of soldiers. Stray chickens scratched at the dirt, scattering when someone kicked a stone at them. Lyan fought the urge to gawk at all the activity.

Praett didn't hesitate to enter the main building, Lyan in tow. A few men scowled as the pooka chose to enter by one of the gaping holes in the wall rather than a door, taking them into a parlor, but no one objected. The few servants scrambled from Praett's path. The pair moved into a hall.

A set of stairs led down, watched by a pair of guards. Praett ignored them as he descended. The men cast uneasy looks at pooka and prisoner both. Lyan expected to see something like the dungeon where Nylas and his men had been held, but these stairs opened into a guardroom. A fire crackled in the hearth to combat the chill, and torches burned in sconces on the walls. A weapon rack stood against one wall beside a large, scowling man wearing a leather jerkin over his shirt.

The man looked them over, then spat on the floor through stained teeth. Lyan thought he could smell the man's breath from across the room. "You just got to be special, don't you? Can't catch this one along with the rest of the prisoners, have to bring him in late? Fine, you've delivered your prisoner. I'll take him from here." He stood.

Lyan tensed. If Praett left him now, it could jeopardize the whole plan.

Praett gazed at the man. "No, I think not."

The warden glowered. "I don't care what you think. You follow the rules as our lord's given them, and that means I take charge of prisoners."

"No." Praett's voice grew icy. "Not this one. This one is mine. A pathetic waste of fat like you is not worthy to be in the same room as this elf, much less lay a hand on him." Praett's gaze held the warden's. "Give me the keys."

The warden folded his arms over his barrel chest. "I've gotten no orders that allow you access to the dungeon."

"And *I* have been given no orders that your arms must remain attached to your body," Praett countered, not blinking. He held out a hand for the keys.

The warden held the pooka's gaze longer than anyone else associated with Ewart or Porephyn had. Finally, with ill grace, he jerked a ring of keys from his belt and slapped the jingling ring down on a crate. He shifted his glare to Lyan.

"Keep him away from the other prisoners. Especially the Dev'gilla whelp—our lord's ordered he stay in isolation."

Praett smirked. "I know my orders."

"Sure you do. And we all know you twist your orders any way you can." He spat again. "Get moving."

Praett scooped up the key ring. "Come along, elf." Taking Lyan by the arm, he walked to the door at the end of the room.

Lyan jerked away from the touch. "I can walk without your help."

Praett smirked. "Big words, little elf." He pulled Lyan through the doorway, swinging the heavy wooden door shut behind them.

Torches lit the long hall. Praett unbound Lyan's wrists and spoke silently. *"If you will allow, I will give your hands the appearance of being bound a little while longer, master. Guards patrol the dungeon and I would trust Porephyn to hide spies where they can listen to the prisoners."*

Lyan hesitated, rubbing his wrists, then he nodded reluctantly.

Praett wound the rope around Lyan's wrists, and tied them loose in front. Lyan tested them, and knew he could free his hands. He looked down the long hall lined with closed doors and shuddered. Being cut off from the sky in Nylas's camp had felt stifling, but this place stank of pain and despair, promising to swallow anyone given to it, never to see the light of day again.

Cailean and his men are trapped here. I have to endure a little while in this hole if they are going to be free.

Praett waited until Lyan gave a nod that he was ready. They walked between pools of torchlight. Cell doors stood flush against the walls. Unless an escapee hid in another cell, he would find no shelter to conceal himself from guards. The cell doors were thick wood, with a swinging panel at the base for food to be pushed in, and a small barred window at eye level. The smell of musty straw lingered in the hall, and bits of straw littered the floor around the cell doors. Lyan watched the windows for signs of his friends.

As they neared one cell, he heard movement within. Praett paused without Lyan asking. The cell's occupant moved to the window and exclaimed a dismayed, startled curse, then, "Lyan?"

Lyan saw Shiolto. The Tathren's face bore bruises and

streaks of dried blood. Shiolto gripped the bars of the window like he needed them to steady himself. Lyan spoke. "Shiolto? Are you all right?"

"We were ambushed. Yion… he's hurt pretty bad. I'm just banged up, mostly." Shiolto's eyes flickered from Lyan to Praett, and the glare he fixed on the pooka burned with anger. "What did that *thing* do?"

"I'm… I'm all right, Shiolto." Lyan wanted to say much more, to tell the truth and reassure his friend, but Praett's warning of spies hung with him.

"Is this the best 'rescue' you can manage, elf?" The question came from a raspy voice across the hall, one door further down. Ragged coughing followed the question.

Lyan started and turned. He saw slow, pained movements on the other side of the window, and drew a sharp breath. "Aikan?"

The older man leaned heavily against his cell door. Dark shadows ringed his eyes, bruises swelled his face, and dried blood crusted his thinning hairline. A long cut ran over his right eye. He'd been hit in the face several times, to judge from the bruises. His eyes moved from Lyan to the pooka, back to Lyan, and he repeated his question.

"Shiolto holds some grand delusions that you can free us. Is this the best you can do?"

"It seemed like a good idea at the time," Lyan responded.

Aikan's brow furrowed in a frown. Praett press something into Lyan's hands. Glancing down, Lyan found a stick of charcoal. As he maneuvered it, he asked, "Aikan, where is Cailean?"

"I saw Lord Cailean being taken deeper into the dungeon when he was brought in."

"You were caught first?" Lyan asked.

Aikan nodded. He watched Lyan, still frowning, suspecting something was more than it seemed, and decided to share a little more information. "I heard the guards receive orders that no one be allowed to Lord Cailean's cell except to bring water. He was unconscious when I saw him, and I don't know if he was injured."

Lyan cast a questioning look back to Shiolto, who shook his head, voice tight with anger. "I don't know either. I was. I wasn't in a position to know if Lord Cailean was hurt or not." He gripped the bars and glared at the pooka. "You might not have had any hand in our capture, but if you've hurt Lyan, I swear I will tear you apart!" Shiolto lunged out and grabbed at Praett.

Praett only smirked, standing well out of reach. "Now why would I do that? It would spoil my fun if I broke my toy."

Shiolto shouted in inarticulate rage. Lyan turned away from him and met Aikan's gaze, then raised his hands to show his palm and the rough Tathren letters he'd written on his skin.

"Trust me."

Aikan's expression didn't change but for a slight narrowing of his eyes, and his head moved in a small nod. He held Lyan's gaze for a long moment before speaking.

"Enough, Shiolto. You're only amusing the creature."

Praett smirked, pulling Lyan into motion again. "There, you see, little elf? Just as I told you—your Tathren friends aren't hurt… much."

The pooka's tone never failed to send a shiver down Lyan's spine, and it drew far more reaction from Shiolto, who slammed against his cell door with an angry shout.

"My brother would have bled to death, and now you bastards aren't even giving us food! What do you mean, 'not hurt much'? Get back here! I'll rip your throat out!"

Lyan had never heard Shiolto angry before. The horse-tender had always seemed at ease, not holding grudges even against Kithr, who had nearly hit him with an arrow. Lyan drew breath to reveal the truth, explain the plan, but choked the words back. He looked away, eyes to the floor. *I'm sorry, Shiolto. Please forgive me for hiding this from you.*

He spoke to Praett instead. "Since your claim about the Tathrens seems doubtful, what about Yion?"

Praett hesitated only a moment. "The mercenary will live."

Shiolto's shouts faded as they walked on. Praett finally stopped. "It is safe to speak here, master."

Lyan rubbed his hands together, erasing the words from his palm. "How badly is Yion hurt?"

Praett shook his head. "He is in better health than the Tathrens, master. My senses say the blessing of his god healed the injuries he took. He is awake, alert, and calm in his cell, choosing to portray the illusion his captors expect."

"What about Dalrian?"

"Despite what his brother says, he is hurt but in no immediate danger of death. His wounds were bound and tended, from what I sensed. He is weak, though."

"And Cailean?"

The pooka slid the ropes from Lyan's wrists. "His cell is ahead, master, where the torches burn dim. He's weak, but I cannot tell more than that." Opening the key ring, Praett considered, then selected five keys. "These should open what you need."

Lyan accepted the keys and fought down the fear that formed a lump in the pit of his stomach. His hand trembled as he clutched the keys. "So I guess this is where I'm on my own."

"You can call Equinox to you at any moment, master. And if you issue me an order, I will hear. It is even possible, if you wish it, for you to see through my eyes, though doing so will leave you unaware of your own surroundings." Praett gazed at him. "Do not become a coward now."

Lyan forced a strained, soft laugh at the last words. "You're a font of encouragement, aren't you?"

Praett scowled. "I hate this place. My well-being depends on your success, master. Right now, I have every reason to do all I can to support your efforts. However, to continue the ruse, I must not linger here."

"I know," Lyan said. "Help Kithr if he needs it, and make sure he finds his way to the dungeon. Otherwise, you don't need me to tell you how to keep suspicion off you."

"Do I have permission to kill if needed, master?" Praett asked.

Lyan hesitated, then nodded. "If it's necessary."

The pooka's eyes glittered with satisfaction and anticipation. "Of course."

Feeling as if he had just released a wolf on a flock of sheep, Lyan turned his back on Praett and walked to a cell door half in shadows. Nothing moved inside, but someone's breath broke the quiet. Sweat dampened Lyan's hands as he fumbled with the keys until he found the correct one for the lock. The door squealed open, making Lyan wince. The smell hit him next, like a filthy latrine. Grimacing, he stepped into the dark, narrow cell. Not even dirty straw softened the hard stone floor as it had in other cells.

Praett swung the door nearly shut behind Lyan, dimming the thin light further. Lyan tensed, for a moment fearing that he had somehow been deceived, and he'd walking into a trap.

He let the idea go. *No, Praett can't betray me.*

The cell was barely large enough for a man to lie down. Even elven eyes struggled to see in the faint light, but Lyan glimpsed movement at the back of the cell. A shape that slumped against the wall shifted weakly. Chains rattled. Cailean's voice whispered—a thin, strained croak.

"Back so soon? Do what you will. You won't find Solstice."

Lyan stepped closer, shoving the keys into his belt pouch. "Cailean, it's Lyan."

"Good try, mage. Sounds just like him. Not going to fall for your tricks."

"Taking lessons in doubt from Nylas?" Lyan responded. "At least you aren't calling me a mooncalf yet."

"If you are Lyan, prove it."

Lyan knew one undeniable way to prove his identity. He stepped back and raised his arm. *Equinox!*

The Spear appeared in his hand with the thought, glowing like a beam of moonlight. Cailean winced from the sudden light, but his cracked lips curved in a relieved smile. The Tathren lord looked as if he'd been dragged behind a horse—his clothes were filthy and ripped, blood staining the cloth, his face bruised and dirty, his hair a tangled mass. His eyes were sunken and exhausted. His arms hung in chains from the wall.

"Lyan? You really are here? How in the gods…?"

"The short version is that the pooka is bound to me, and feigned to capture me so I could get in here without suspicion. Kithr is sneaking in—I'm sure he can find a way. I'll go into details some other time." Lyan pulled a water skin from his belt. The Tathrens hadn't been willing to get close enough to him to search him. Lyan held the skin to Cailean's mouth, and the Tathren lord drank deep gulps. The guards might have been given orders to bring Cailean water, but they clearly had not been giving him enough.

When the skin was empty, Lyan asked, "What happened, Cailean?"

"Solstice. I had to use the Spear." Cailean let his head rest back against the cold wall while he caught his breath, as if even speaking exhausted him. "Lyan. My men. Safe?"

"They're bruised, imprisoned, angry, and worried. I saw Shiolto and Aikan, and the pooka said Dalrian will be all right. Yion isn't hurt as seriously as their captors think."

Cailean lifted his head. "Aikan too? How is he?"

"He looks like he fought when he was captured." Lyan didn't want to say more about Aikan; captivity obviously wasn't treating the older man well.

An absence finally struck Lyan, overlooked earlier in the

fear and worry about his friends. Lyan looked at Cailean and continued. "I didn't see, and no one spoke of Torqual."

Cailean's expression twisted in anger, confirming the suspicion creeping through Lyan's mind. "You were right. Aikan didn't betray me."

"Torqual did," Lyan whispered. He saw Cailean try to speak again, and held up a hand to forestall him. "Wait, Cailean." *Equinox, I need food and more water for Cailean.*

A leather satchel appeared on the floor at Lyan's feet, a water skin beside it. Using Equinox, Lyan cut the chains holding Cailean's arms to the wall. He crouched beside Cailean and opened the satchel, finding bread, cheese, and dried meat within. If the cell hadn't stunk so, Lyan's stomach would have complained about being empty, but he felt little appetite. When he handed the food to Cailean, the Tathren devoured everything ravenously.

After draining the second water skin, Cailean found his voice, and sounded a little stronger. "Gods, I'm so damned *helpless*. Haven't eaten since I woke here."

His captors have been making sure he doesn't regain his strength. "What happened, Cailean?"

"We rode into an ambush." Anger burned in Cailean's eyes. "I was furious. Maybe there was some other answer, but I doubt it. I *had* to use Solstice to protect my men. We beat them back. Then, Torqual showed his true allegiance. Went after Yion first, and fast. None of us expected..." Cailean shook his head sharply. "When he attacked, the rest of the ambush struck." He cursed. "Torqual knew. He knew there were enough that I could have killed most using Solstice, but not all, and it would drain the last of my strength."

"Why didn't you?" Lyan asked.

"The bastard knows me too well. He ordered me to surrender. If I did, he promised no further harm would come to my men, and their injuries would be tended. No one would die." Cailean closed his eyes. "Yion was down, bleeding badly. Dalrian was wounded and pinned, and Shiolto… I think Torqual hit him with a poisoned blade." His hands clenched in fists, and his voice shook with anger. "If I didn't surrender, Torqual swore he would make sure I was conscious and helpless while he tortured my men to death in front of me."

Anyone who knows Cailean knows he would do anything to protect them.

Cailean opened his eyes. "He thought he could take Solstice, but *that*, at least, I denied him. I sent the Spear to a safe place, and neither he nor his master will get their hands on it."

"A safe place?" Lyan repeated. Cailean just smiled slightly and nodded. Lyan blinked, eyes opening wide. "Cailean! Did you send Solstice…?" He didn't finish the thought aloud. *Did you send Solstice to the Shrine of Equinox?*

Cailean only nodded. "It took more strength that I thought. After that, I remember his men holding me up and him hitting me, demanding the Spear. I think he tried to make me walk behind his horse. Don't think that lasted long. Woke up here. Haven't seen Torqual since, just a guard and sometimes, Ewart's master."

"Porephyn," Lyan said.

Cailean nodded. "He's trying to force me to reveal where I hid Solstice." He shuddered with the memory. "Is there a plan?"

Lyan nodded, about to answer, when a thought struck. His eyes opened wide and he paled. Cailean's words: *The bastard knows me too well.* "Oh gods. Torqual will hear I've been captured. He knows Kithr won't sit idle."

"Lyan?" Cailean asked.

Lyan turned, his eyes locked on Cailean's. "How many times when they sparred did Torqual tell us he can predict Kithr? That Kithr still uses the same tactics the elves used before. Gods." Lyan saw understanding fill Cailean's eyes, and the Tathren paled. Lyan's thoughts flew to Praett. *Find Kithr! Warn him! Torqual is the traitor.*

Cailean tried to stand. "We have to get to him."

"We don't have time, Cailean." Lyan's stomach twisted in a knot. His closest friend was in danger and death threatened, and Lyan couldn't reach him. His only chance, his only hope: place his trust in the creature that had tormented him since he left Eilidh Wood. Lyan sat on the filthy floor.

"Lyan, we have to do *something*." Cailean urged.

"I *am*," Lyan snapped, more sharply than he'd intended. "But I can't talk at the same time."

"Sorry." Cailean looked abashed. "Do what you need to; I'll stop distracting you."

Lyan closed his eyes, gripping Equinox to his chest. *"Where is Kithr?"* he demanded of Praett.

"I am near, master," Praett answered.

Lyan suddenly saw through eyes not his own. The world swam with colors and shapes that glowed in shades of red, blue, green, yellow, or even dull, flat gray. Nothing had a form he could comprehend, and the foreign sight made his stomach lurch as he fought nausea.

"Your pardon, master. I am able to see the auras and energies of my surroundings. I will keep to a sight more familiar to you." The swimming colors shifted, becoming walls and people.

Lyan didn't respond, only watched as Praett swept down halls. He didn't seem to hurry, but Lyan would have been running to match his pace. The pooka stopped in the shadows of a doorway into a small courtyard nestled between the outer wall and the castle's keep. The branches of scattered trees bore ripening apples, and a small fountain spat intermittent bursts of water. Stone benches invited visitors to sit and enjoy the view of trampled flowers that must have been tended at one time. Archers lined the walls, arrows to the string, looking down into the courtyard at the prone figure on the ground. Torqual stood among them, smirking with an expression not unlike the one often found on Praett's face.

Torqual spoke, voice clear in the stillness. "Don't think I've forgotten the lesson you so graciously refreshed for me, Kithr. Not one arrow hit you—I was watching. Get up and surrender. Keep playing dead, and I have more than a dozen archers who will ensure you aren't pretending. They might not be as good as you, but they can hit a prone target."

Kithr didn't move.

"Archers."

The archers drew bow strings tight. Kithr launched to his feet and sprinted to the nearest stone bench before the first shaft hit nearby. The archers murmured in surprise and fear. Torqual smirked.

Help him! Lyan told Praett. *How you do so is up to you.*

"Yes master," Praett murmured, watching the scene.

"You're fast, Kithr, but you have no way out," Torqual said. "I told you before, using the same tactics only works until your enemy learns your tricks. I've known what you would do every step of the way. Why do you think that entrance wasn't as guarded as the others? You've done everything just the way you would have done seventy years ago."

"Not quite *everything*," Kithr snarled. "Seventy years ago, I wouldn't have trusted a *Tathren*."

Torqual laughed. His humor was cut short as he dove for cover. Kithr's arrow nicked him. A volley of arrows rained onto Kithr's position, and he darted behind another bench. Only one archer scored a hit.

"No need to drag this out, Kithr. I know why you're here —you came because we have Lyan." Torqual wisely stayed behind shelter as he spoke.

Kithr snarled at the bloody gash on his leg. His burning eyes raked the wall in search of Torqual. "Where is he?"

"Unharmed, for now." The gloating sneer in Torqual's voice implied the threat. "Do you want him to stay that way?

You know what Tathrens do to elves. But do you know what disciples of Murdo will do to one?"

A shiver ran up Lyan's spine. The words hung in the still air, finally in the open. The archers didn't even react to the Mad God's name.

Pure hate blazed in Kithr's eyes. "You dare. If you lay one finger on Lyan, I'll rip out your heart and feed it to the dogs."

"Brave words, when you're the one surrounded and trapped, and I'm the one who knows where your friend is. You want to see him, Kithr? You will. What state he's in, though, depends on you. My lord is far more imaginative than Vynzent."

An involuntary tremor of fear ran though Lyan at Vynzent's name. Kithr shook with rage.

"Surrender, Kithr," Torqual ordered.

"Where is Lyan?"

"In a cell, in the dungeon. The same place you'll be going."

Kithr's narrowed eyes judged the walls, the defenders, and his own chances. "Don't think I'll forget your treachery, Tathren." He laid his bow and quiver on the ground, then his knife, and he stepped from his meager shelter.

The archers tensed, but none loosed arrows. Torqual spoke, still not visible. "I don't believe those are all your weapons, Kithr."

"Then come get the rest yourself," Kithr countered.

"Search him," Torqual ordered one of the men.

Praett flowed from the shadows in view of all of them, letting his form shift from human to horse and back as he approached Kithr. "Allow me," he purred.

Kithr stiffened, eyes narrow. "You."

On the wall, archers and soldiers shuffled uneasily. Murdo's name hadn't discomfited them, but the pooka did. Torqual spoke sharply, as surprised as the rest, worried by the reactions of his men. "Who and what are you?"

Praett's movements were so swift and effortless, he seemed to appear behind Torqual, from the ground to the wall, by magic. "You don't remember me? A pity. I spend so much time stalking your group along your journey."

Torqual spun, blade in hand. Praett's glowing red eyes held his gaze, and Torqual restrained himself. "You… the pooka."

"What did you expect, a dragon? *I* will take care of this elf." Praett smirked. "I hope he'll be as entertaining as his friend."

"Playing *games*?" Torqual sneered.

Praett continued to smirk. "My games caught the elven Spearbearer. The only thing yours have caught is one fighter, and you wouldn't have been able to do so without my success."

"You have no claim to my prisoner," Torqual snapped.

Around him, archers and soldiers edged away from Torqual, casting anxious looks at one another. Praett took a step closer to the Tathren and spoke softly, menace in his voice. "Do not threaten me with boredom unless you wish to become the target for my entertainment, mortal."

Torqual seemed to realize, finally, the danger that loomed over him and the pleasure Praett would take in toying with him. He stepped back, stumbling against the wall. "If you let Kithr escape…" he warned.

"Then you will have the opportunity to catch him again," Praett responded. "And I won't interfere if that happens. You know if he gets loose, he'll come for you first."

Torqual locked gazes with the pooka's glowing red eyes, but the Tathren looked away first. "Let him see Lyan, but don't put them too close together."

"I know my orders." Praett swept back down to Kithr, who glowered under the wary watch of the archers.

"Treacherous scum," Kithr snapped as the pooka searched him, confiscating three more blades.

"Do you mean me, or the Tathren traitor?" Praett asked, leaning close to whisper in Kithr's ear. "My master watches through my eyes and ordered me to help you."

"Did you know this filthy bloodlord was the traitor?" Kithr snarled.

"Not until my master learned it from the Tathren Spearbearer."

"Then I don't mean you." Kithr jerked back, but the monster seized his arms and pinned them behind his back.

"I thought you *wanted* to see your little friend," Praett purred loud enough to be heard by Torqual and the others. "I didn't hurt him, much."

Kithr twisted angrily, but he didn't break free of the pooka's hold. "I will return any harm done to him ten times over."

"Promises, promises." Praett bound Kithr's wrists with a quick twist of cord, collected the weapons from the ground, and pulled the elf along. Kithr stumbled, his injured leg objecting to the abuse. Praett steadied and supported him while appearing to all but drag Kithr through the doorway. Three guards had gathered to block any escape attempt, but they scattered before Praett.

Everyone's afraid of you, Lyan observed.

"I dislike being here, master, and they learned quickly that my methods of entertaining myself came at their detriment," Praett responded, voice barely audible.

"What?" Kithr asked, suspicious.

Praett cast a quick look around to ensure they were alone. "My master addressed me, and I answered. You wish me to take you to him?"

"Why don't you ask the mooncalf where he wants me?"

Tell Kithr the mooncalf can hear him just fine, and I thought he had a plan once he got inside.

Praett paused, then repeated in a puzzled tone, "My master says the mooncalf can hear you just fine? And he thought you had a plan once you made your way into the keep."

Kithr gave a soft, amused snort. Praett pulled him into a secluded hall and released Kithr's hands. Kithr retrieved a rag from his belt and bandaged his leg. "My plan encountered difficulties when it became obvious a certain Tathren bastard anticipated it. My way isn't going to work." Kithr scowled. "I'm predictable. So now it's your turn. Where do you want me?"

Lyan thought quickly. *"Meet us at the dungeon entrance, if the way is clear."*

"It will be, master," Praett promised.

16

Mist in shadows
Fear no bonds

Lyan blinked and gulped in a deep breath, awareness returning to his own body and Cailean's cell. Cailean crouched beside him, face lined with worry. "Lyan? Are you all right?"

Lyan nodded. The movement made his head throb. "I'm all right, I think. Kithr's safer now."

"What happened?"

"Torqual anticipated Kithr, even the route Kithr would take inside, and set a trap."

Cailean cursed. "What happened? What did Torqual do? You stopped him?"

"The pooka intervened. The people here still believe he's bound to Porephyn and following his orders, and everyone is afraid of the pooka, so they don't try to argue with him."

Cailean stiffened. "The pooka? Lyan, that creature has been chasing and tormenting you since we first met. How can you trust it? Even if you bound it, as… as Ewart's master did, that doesn't change its nature."

Lyan gazed at Equinox, and spoke quietly. "I didn't bind him, Cailean. I made a mistake that has lasting consequences for both me and the pooka. I learned that Nachyne, the god of monsters, must answer when the Spearbearer of Equinox calls on him. Then, when the pooka had separated me from Kithr and attacked me, without thinking my response through I called on the god of monsters to protect me from a creature of his domain."

"Ahebban's Hammer," Cailean whispered, sitting up straighter. "The god of monsters? The one who's temple we stumbled on? How? What does he have to do with Equinox?"

Lyan shook his head. "That's best explained some other time, Cailean. The result, though, is that the pooka serves me, whether or not he wants to, and unlike the binding a mere mortal can perform, this is permanent." Lyan paused a moment, then continued. "I got the impression Nachyne has laws forbidding his monsters from attacking or interfering with the Spearbearers. He was furious, and didn't care that the pooka had acted under the orders of the one who bound him."

Cailean only listened, watching Lyan's face.

"Nachyne punished the pooka. The conclusion of that punishment was to bind him to serve me. He isn't a free creature anymore, Cailean. By the will of his god, the pooka belongs to me."

"Punishing the pooka, or punishing you?" Cailean asked with a thin smile.

"A little of both," Lyan answered. "But more the pooka than me. Probably." He slowly climbed to his feet and held his hand to Cailean. "So, I trust he will obey me. Kithr and the pooka are on their way, and will meet us near the dungeon entrance."

Cailean slumped wearily against the wall. "What about my men, Lyan?"

"I have the keys to their cells. I know Porephyn probably

has spies near them, but we'll have to deal with that sooner or later."

Cailean gazed at Lyan, not yet taking the offered hand. "Lyan, free my men and meet Kithr. I know I'll be more hindrance than help right now."

Lyan's face darkened. "Mad God's Pits, Cailean, I didn't come here to leave you in this stinking cell. To say nothing of the fact that your men would never agree to a rescue that didn't include you. I am not leaving here without you. Now get up! Wait too long, and Kithr will come looking for me, and I can assure you, his mood is bad enough already."

"Lyan, I'm too weak to be any use to you. You'd be better to go without me."

"Horse turds," Lyan responded flatly. "This is *your* keep, *your* home, and you are infinitely more familiar with it than I *ever* will be. Haven't you told me often enough knowledge is as valuable as fighting skills? I *need* your help, Cailean. We need to know the things only the lord of this keep can know." He caught Cailean's arm and tried to pull the Tathren to his feet. "And I am *not* explaining to Aikan why I left you behind, dammit. He dislikes me enough already."

Cailean struggled up, getting his feet under him with Lyan's help. The Tathren panted for breath and winced. "All right. Whatever your plan is, I'll do what I can. I can't promise it'll be much, though."

My plan? My plan didn't extend past getting us all free and reunited. I expected Kithr to take charge after that. Everyone's depending on me?

Lyan offered Cailean his shoulder to lean on. Cailean accepted gratefully, sagging against him. Lyan pushed the cell door open and helped Cailean limp out. The Tathren's face was drawn with pain.

Equinox, can you heal Cailean, like you did Praett?

Braced for another flood of potential answers, Lyan didn't expecting a "no." He stared at the Spear in disbelief, feeling almost betrayed. *What do you mean, no?*

The Spear struggled to explain through impressions and incomprehensible images before finally resorting to speech. *"I can heal you—you are my bearer and I am bound to you. Solstice could heal Cailean, but I cannot."*

Lyan shook his head. *"You healed Praett!"*

"That is different. The pooka is not a mortal, but a creature of magic."

"What difference does that make?" Lyan demanded.

"All the difference," Equinox answered. *"My brother and I are not from this world, and our magic is not part of it. Creatures like the pooka can tolerate foreign magic and survive, albeit uncomfortably. But if I try to heal a mortal other than my bearer, that magic will kill them— even another Spearbearer."* A long pause, then, *"Believe me, Lyan. We have tried before. Even magic has rules. Different rules than those you know."*

"Can you at least numb his pain? Give him strength?" Lyan asked.

He sensed agreement from Equinox, and a tingle of energy ran down Lyan's arm. Cailean started and stood a little straighter.

"Save your strength, Lyan. You'll need it."

"Don't worry about me, Cailean. You're the one who's hurt," Lyan told him.

Cailean smiled. "Stubborn elf."

"As stubborn as a Tathren," Lyan agreed. "Come on."

Cailean still needed Lyan's support, but he didn't limp, and his face regained some color. Lyan listened for guards but heard none, even as they neared the cells that held Cailean's men. Cautious, Lyan helped Cailean to one wall and motioned for him to stay there. Cailean nodded understanding, watching Lyan continue toward the cells. Both tensed in anticipation of a trap. Lyan moved with all the stealth he could muster.

He spun around, heart pounding in alarm, when a familiar voice spoke without warning. "Do not fear for guards or spies, Lyan Stargazer. They will not trouble us any longer."

Lyan wasn't the only person the unexpected announcement startled. From Shiolto's cell, someone scrambled to their feet. "Yion? You're all right? What are you talking about? Lyan was taken further into the dungeon. And weren't you in a different cell?"

Yion answered, his voice ever calm and steady. "Your concern is appreciated, Shiolto. I am well, and yes, I was given a different cell than this present one. I found it necessary to leave the first in order to remove some hazards from Lyan's path."

Aikan moved to the window of his cell and looked out. The older man fixed his best scowl on Lyan. "You took your time, elf!"

Lyan shook himself and took a deep breath, wishing his heart didn't slam against his ribs. "Sorry, Aikan. I'd have been back sooner, but I had to convince Cailean he isn't going to be a burden."

"Lyan!" Shiolto exclaimed from his cell. "How? What in the gods names…?"

Lyan found the keys Praett gave him and unlocked Aikan's cell door. "My capture wasn't what it looked like, Shiolto. The pooka serves me now."

"You couldn't have told us a little sooner?" Shiolto protested.

Lyan flinched and opened his mouth, but couldn't make himself justify the deception to his friends.

"Of course he couldn't," Aikan said sharply, opening the cell door slowly and stepping into the hall. "He needed the ruse to last until he found Lord Cailean." The older man eyed Lyan and hesitated. "It seems I owe you my thanks, Lyan."

"You probably shouldn't thank me until we know whether or not I've gotten us all into worse trouble," Lyan said wryly.

"No." Aikan's voice was firm. "I owe you my thanks, not simply for your actions today. I owe you my thanks and… an apology, if you will have it."

Lyan hesitated, then nodded. "I will. You are welcome, Aikan."

He opened Shiolto's cell next. The door groaned open. Shiolto stumbled and barely caught himself. Lyan steadied him and looked at him with concern. "Cailean said you were stabbed. Are you all right, Shiolto?"

One of Shiolto's hands strayed to the bandages wrapping his shoulder. "I'll be all right, Lyan. Gods know why, but they patched us up before locking us in here."

"They did because those were the terms under which Cailean would surrender," Lyan said.

Shiolto's head jerked up. "What? Lord Cailean surrendered? Because of us? But…" He closed his eyes for a moment, then nodded.

Lyan moved to the next cell, and found Dalrian inside. Shiolto's brother had scraped straw into a pile and lay asleep on it. Lyan shook his shoulder.

Dalrian groaned, voice weak and strained.

"Dalrian," Lyan urged. "Wake up."

Dalrian's eyelids fluttered open. "Leave me alone."

"Dalrian, it's Lyan."

Another groan, and Dalrian blinked blearily in the dim light. At Lyan's silent command, Equinox glowed, illuminating the cell. "Lyan? Gods, good to see you. You get the bastard who betrayed Lord Cailean?"

"Not yet," Lyan told him. "I had to find all of you first. Can you walk?"

"If I have to." Dalrian sat slowly, wincing with each movement. Lyan helped him stand and stumble from the cell.

Shiolto ran to his brother's side, draping Dalrian's left arm over his shoulder and lifted him from Lyan. Lyan looked back down the hall and saw Yion had joined them, a cell door open near him. The mercenary cleaned a sword with a rag, his expression placid. Lyan almost asked where he'd gotten the sword, then decided against doing so. The answer was obvious enough: its previous owner no longer needed it, as he no longer needed the knives now gracing Yion's belt. Dried blood stained Yion's clothes a rusty red color. Looking up and seeing Lyan, the mercenary smiled.

"Well met, Lyan Stargazer. I am glad to see you safe and whole."

"It's good to see you too, Yion. You're looking better than rumor claimed," Lyan replied. Yion's clothes attested to wounds and spilled blood, but Yion himself looked as healthy as Lyan had ever seen him. *How did he escape his cell without anyone noticing? What skills does Yion have?*

Yion nodded. "My god was gracious to his unworthy servant, healing me and telling me to await your arrival. When you passed us, I saw the pooka and recognized the nature of its bindings." He considered Lyan speculatively. "When you have opportunity, I should like to know the full tale of how it lost its freedom."

"I already owe the story to Cailean," Lyan said.

"Where *is* Lord Cailean?" Aikan asked pointedly.

Cailean moved from the thin shadows where he lurked, watching his men. "I'm here."

"Lord Cailean!" Shiolto exclaimed in relief.

Cailean smiled, but his gaze moved to Aikan. He stepped toward the older man, then hesitated, looking at the bruises that darkened Aikan's face. "Aikan, I…"

Aikan collected himself, and fixed a stern gaze on Cailean. "My lord, I hope you are not struggling under some mistaken idea you must publicly apologize to one of your men under your own roof. It's unfit for a lord."

"A lord can publicly apologize to one of his most loyal men under his own roof when he's been an idiot and isn't afraid to admit it," Cailean countered. "Gods, Aikan, what happened?"

"I could be far worse, my lord. Fortunately, Ewart has been occupied with other matters so he kept his visit brief."

Cailean tensed. "Ewart?"

"The 'reward' he promised me, my lord, is not what those words led you to think," Aikan answered. "You didn't believe Ewart simply accepted my rejection of his offer, but you didn't allow me to elaborate. You were right, he did not take kindly to my refusal. I offered it not with words, but steel. We fought in my chambers. He mocked me and called me a fool. Told me I was too late to save you from your doom. I stabbed him in the chest. I hoped the wound would prove fatal, but I didn't dare continue to cross blades with Ewart when you were in danger. I left him bleeding and ran in search of you, my lord. The first soldiers I met, I ordered to your chambers. They were fresh, and I am not young anymore. I prayed they would find you in time."

Cailean drew a startled breath, eyes opening wide. "The men, their timely arrival… You sent them. Gods, Aikan, I'm a fool. You saved my life by sending them to me, and I repaid you with this."

"You had every right to judge me, Lord Cailean," Aikan said. "When I found Ewart's final, mocking message after we escaped the keep, it chilled me to the bone. Seeing it, I knew I had failed, and he lived. I feared to tell you. To explain how I found myself in single combat with Ewart would require telling everything leading to our battle. After I left your camp, I resolved to return here and finish what I had failed to do— end Ewart's life. His men captured me before I reached the keep." Aikan shook his head. "Ewart paid me only a brief visit —long enough to inflict bruises. He put off more damage until he had time to enjoy his work. And, I suspect, until he had other prisoners for an audience." Aikan's eyes met Cailean's.

Lyan heard quiet steps approaching on the stones. Kithr spoke sharply. "Lovely reunion. Are you done yet? We have minions of the Mad God to kill."

The Tathrens started and turned. Kithr stood, bow slung

over his shoulder, injured leg bandaged tight. Behind him, Praett waited. Lyan smiled in relief to see them safe, surprised he'd been worried, at least a little, about the pooka.

Aikan scowled at Kithr, but without much venom. "I'm surprised you allowed Lyan to enter without you."

"Just as well I did. Now the treacherous bastard thinks we're all cleverly contained," Kithr said, his voice cold. "Apparently, my plans are as predictable as my fighting style."

"Torqual," Cailean's voice grew icy, his eyes angry. "He knows me too well, and he knows elves too well."

"No," Kithr said. "He knows the ways of those like me or Nylas, those who invaded your country. He knows the ways of the Lost. He does *not* know the ways of elves." Kithr looked at Lyan.

Certain this moment would come, Lyan dreaded it. His hands closed tight around Equinox.

Dalrian leaned heavily against his brother. "Lord Cailean, are we going to withdraw and find the rest of your men, to take back the keep?"

The idea tempted Lyan. He could let Cailean take charge, and find his men, so they could... what? Besiege this keep? Try to attack against an enemy who held the favor of Murdo? "No," he heard himself say. "No, we're not going to retreat. We're not going to leave this evil to fester and rot until it spreads so far there's no stopping it. I came here to fight the forces of the Mad God that are trying to take root in your very home. Didn't you? Isn't this why you set in search of Equinox, to have a weapon strong enough?"

Eyes gazed at him, but no one spoke until Kithr stepped to Lyan's side. "Well, this sounds like it will turn into the sort of plan I'll enjoy."

Praett sighed. "I'll do as you will, master." He too joined Lyan.

Yion spoke next. "I have no need to ask my lord what he

would have me do. I will fight with the Spearbearer of Equinox."

"Mad God's Pits, Lyan, I *said* I would do what I can to help you, whatever the plan is," Cailean protested. "No need be melodramatic. But is there any chance you can explain the plan somewhere a little warmer than my dungeons?"

"The guard room at the dungeon entrance is clear," Praett said. "And you will find weapons there."

"Good. Lead the way." Lyan glanced at the Spear. *I hope you or the gods can give me some kind of help in making a plan that won't get us all killed.*

17

Strike the heart,
That the body sprawls
Strike the head,
That the spirit falls

Kithr walked beside Lyan. They followed Praett back up the hall. Kithr watched Lyan, then spoke quietly in Elven, the slightest hint of humor lurking in his voice.

"You don't have a plan, do you?"

"I had a plan," Lyan protested. "It got us this far, didn't it?"

"It did," Kithr agreed. "And did your plan go any further than this?"

Lyan didn't answer.

"That's what I thought."

"You're not really helping, Kithr," Lyan said.

"I can't be as much help as you want me to be, Lyan. I can't craft a scheme that will fool our enemies. Not when that bastard knows how I think."

"And he *doesn't* know *me*?"

"He *thinks* he knows you, but he underestimates you,

Lyan." Kithr forced a thin smile. "As far too many of us have done before him. He could never imagine you would find a way to enter the dungeons in the guise of a prisoner. He couldn't imagine I would have been willing to let you do so."

"I didn't think you'd agree to go along with my plan, so I'm not surprised no one else would expect it," Lyan told him.

They climbed the steps into the guard room. The jailer's chair sat empty, but the room showed no evidence of a fight.

Praett answered Lyan's question before he asked it. "The jailer's body rests in a cell, master. We took him by surprise."

Cailean studied the room, then walked to the far wall and opened the chest on the floor. "Good. His men didn't steal all the gear."

"Weapons?" Kithr asked. He assessed a rack of blades, and another of spears.

"Armor," Cailean responded. "They took the mail, but left the leather." He lifted a thick jerkin from the chest and smiled grimly. "Probably because my family crest is prominently dyed into the leather."

That thought stirred an idea in Lyan, and he abruptly turned to Praett. "How many servants and other people here are loyal to Ewart?"

"Loyal? Very few, master. They serve under fear, and keep their heads low so as to avoid attention. Whether any have courage enough to help their true lord, I doubt. Those who had that courage either fled to find Cailean's forces, or they learned firsthand the consequences of open defiance." Praett considered. "At the most, I expect many would turn a blind eye to the presence of men in their lord's colors."

"If they let us use the servants' passages to get around the keep, that'd help by itself." Shiolto eased Dalrian, pale and weary as his brother, down to the floor near the crackling fire. Shiolto eyed the pooka warily, then looked to Lyan. "Can we really trust what it says, Lyan?"

"Yes, Shiolto. I'll explain why later."

"Well, if you say we can believe it, I guess that's good enough," Shiolto said, still cautious.

"Such doubt," Praett purred. "I'm hurt."

"Sure you are." Shiolto scowled.

Aikan stiffly walked to the rack of sheathed swords and drew one. "So, two elves, Lord Cailean, and his four men are going to retake the keep?" He gave Lyan a dubious look.

"I don't know about retaking the keep," Lyan admitted. "But I know we need to kill Ewart and Porephyn."

"Who?" Shiolto asked.

Aikan, however, stiffened. "What part does that black-hearted mage have in this?"

Lyan glanced toward Cailean. The Tathren lord had pulled on the leather jerkin and straightened it so the vivid emerald crest, a large cat carrying a spear, showed clearly on his chest. He met Lyan's gaze.

"Cailean, I don't care if you like it or not, I'm telling your men the truth. You *not* telling them didn't help—your loyal men weren't prepared, and Torqual obviously knew already."

Cailean's jaw tightened, but he didn't say anything.

"Do we have time for this, Lyan?" Kithr asked.

"They need to know." Lyan looked to Aikan, Shiolto, Dalrian, and Yion. "Porephyn is a priest of the Mad God. When Ewart's men attacked and took the walls, Porephyn attacked and cursed Cailean. Whenever Cailean uses the powers of Solstice, it drains his strength. Torqual knew of the curse when they ambushed you. He knew Cailean would be too drained to stop him after using the Spear."

The Tathrens exclaimed in surprise. Yion nodded grimly, as if he had known at least some, if not all, of what Lyan revealed. Cailean closed his eyes.

"So, we kill Porephyn to break the curse, we kill Ewart to break the leadership of his pitiful excuse for an army, and we kill Torqual to hang his filthy corpse from the battlements,"

Kithr said, breaking the silence. He shifted his bow. "So, where do we start?"

Cailean found a faint smile. "Ever to the point, Kithr."

"If I'm not, you'll stand around talking until someone dies of old age." Kithr drummed his fingers with an impatient glower.

"I can use Equinox to shield us from notice, like I did when we rescued Nylas and his men," Lyan said. "It's not a perfect protection, but it's something. Torqual knows that trick of Equinox, but that won't help him find us." Lyan considered, then looked to Praett. "Where are Ewart and Porephyn likely to be found?"

"During the day, any number of places. At nightfall, both retire to their shrine," Praett answered.

"What shrine?" Cailean demanded.

Praett's expression darkened. "The shrine to the Mad God that Porephyn built in the back courtyard. He often required me to report to him there. I suggest purifying the site with fire."

"I agree. I can feel the foul taint from here. How many guard this shrine?" Yion asked.

"At night, two men at the courtyard gate, five patrolling the grounds, four outside the shrine itself, and four more who follow Ewart like dogs, with about as much wit. The courtyard remains lit all night, but the servants avoid it as much as possible. Investigative ones disappear." Praett's voice was flat.

"Is it guarded during the day?" Lyan asked.

"The courtyard is closed and warded during the day, master. Porephyn will know the moment someone attempts to enter."

"They spend the entire night there?" Aikan scoffed.

"Neither man appears to require sleep," Praett said. "It seems nights spent in worship and rituals to the Mad God revitalize them. However, Ewart struggles more by the end of the day than Porephyn. If he's careless, a wound on his chest begins bleeding. For some reason, it does not heal. He is at his weakest when he first enters the shrine, shortly after nightfall."

"We don't have to wait *here* until night, do we?" Shiolto protested.

Lyan shivered. "No, I'd [illegible] place where I can tell when it *is* night. Equinox can hide us." He turned to Kithr and spoke in Elven. "Am I overlooking anything?"

Kithr considered, then replying in Tathren. "Actually, yes. Cailean, you have men waiting for word from you outside the keep?"

Cailean nodded.

"They ought to have scouts close enough to know if something important changes. Maybe spies among the servants, if they have any wits." Kithr turned to the pooka. "Are there any?"

Praett considered. "Many were discovered and dealt with, but a few remain."

Cailean sat down with a weary sigh. "I'm not sure where this is leading, Kithr."

"Find one of these servants. Send him to tell your men you're here and that once Ewart and Porephyn are dead, you might need a little help cleaning up his men," Kithr said blandly.

Cailean stared at Kithr in surprise, then a laugh escaped. "Are you sure you can't handle them all yourself, Kithr?"

Kithr snorted. "No doubt I *could*, but I haven't yet found an enchanted quiver that never runs empty."

"If I ever encounter one, it'll be my gift to you." Cailean pushed to his feet. The banter surprised Lyan, as if they discussed an upcoming festival. But he had to admit, it made him feel more at ease, as if they faced some minor difficulty.

Cailean continued. "Aikan, Shiolto, Dalrian, find armor and weapons, assuming Yion hasn't somehow secreted an entire sword rack on his person."

Yion smiled. "No, Lord Cailean. Most of the blades are

too long—I could at most hide four without inhibiting my movement."

Aikan already had a sword belted around his waist, and moved to the chest for armor. Shiolto helped Dalrian to the rack. Dalrian took the nearest blade, belting it on with an effort. Shiolto searched a dusty weapons pile close by and emerged with a mace much like the one he'd carried during their travels. Cailean lifted a spear from the rack. It wasn't as long as Solstice, but none of the available spears were. Cailean took several experimental jabs at the air before nodding. By his expression, he wasn't wholly satisfied with the weapon, but it would suffice.

"Should I wear one of those leather jerkins?" Lyan asked Kithr.

Kithr considered. "It wouldn't hurt. Shouldn't weigh you down much. Try to find one that *doesn't* have a bright green target on the chest."

Lyan looked, but he didn't find any without Cailean's crest. Taking one that seemed close to the right fit, he struggled into the heavy sleeveless jerkin. Kithr helped him pull it on and grunted approval.

"Better than nothing, even with the target."

"Better to be wearing Cailean's colors than to be attacked by his men when they arrive," Lyan replied.

"I'll take my chances with them," Kithr said.

Lyan's hand tightened around Equinox. *Hide us, please.*

He felt the Spear's power. Trusting Equinox but anxious all the same, Lyan led the way up the stairs, eager to escape the underground. His friends trailed him, moving with less haste.

Lyan almost froze when he stepped from the stairs and into clear view of the guards standing on either side of the doorway. Their eyes drifted lazily over him, glazing slightly. Kithr pushed Lyan in the back when he stopped, making Lyan stumble forward. He barely caught himself before he tripped into a woman carrying a full basket of clothes. One of the guards chuckled softly, making Lyan turn sharply. The man's eyes were still glazed, and he didn't seem aware what he'd found humorous.

Lyan swallowed hard, then motioned for the others to follow. He directed his thoughts to Praett. *"Find a servant who can carry a message to Cailean's men."*

Praett nodded and turned to the right, the same direction the woman with the basket had gone. "Follow me." He walked swiftly. The Tathrens struggled with the pace, and Kithr tried not to limp. Lyan sensed Praett's annoyance as he slowed for them. As they passed a window, Lyan looked out and guessed the time at halfway through the afternoon.

We don't have much time.

Praett turned down halls with confidence. Lyan quickly lost any sense of where he was in the stone building, and he wondered how anyone found their way through a place like this.

The pooka opened a door into a room that stank with piles of clothes waiting to be washed. Lyan boggled at the endless stacks, wondering how a place could even produce so much washing, much less how someone could be expected to keep up with it. The pooka turned to face them.

"Master, you and Cailean will find the washer woman in the next room. The others ought to wait here—too many people, and she will lose her nerve."

Lyan nodded, willing to trust Praett's judgment. Cailean frowned. "A washer woman? She's trustworthy?"

Praett shrugged. "I have the sense that someone, a brother, or father, or son, is one of the scouts watching your keep."

"Cailean, if we stop to double-check everything the pooka says, we aren't going to have *time*," Lyan snapped. He walked toward the far door.

Cailean pushed the door open. A wave of steam hit them. Large cauldrons sat over grates on the floor, filled to the brim with water and laundry. A haggard-looking woman moved between the cauldrons, stirring them with a massive paddle. She glanced over when the door opened, but her eyes passed over them.

Let her see us, Lyan told Equinox.

The paddle dropped from the woman's hands to clatter on the floor and her eyes widened as large as dinner plates. "My… my lord? Lord Cailean?"

Cailean nodded, raising a finger to his lips. The woman bowed low, her eyes still wide in disbelief. She spoke in a whisper. "My lord, what… what can I do for you? How did you… We heard you'd been imprisoned by Ewart, my lord."

"I'm not a prisoner anymore," Cailean told her. "And I know you can contact my men who watch the keep."

She gulped, then nodded. "My brother, sir. Do they know you're free, sir? Did they find a way to reach you?"

Cailean shook his head. "No. Another of my allies helped me escape." He nodded to Lyan.

She looked past Cailean to Lyan, and her eyes, amazingly enough, grew even wider. She stumbled back several steps, one hand raised to ward against evil. "An elf?"

Lyan made a gesture of peace, and bowed to her. "Lyan Stargazer at your service, milady."

"I'm no lady, sir," she managed, tensed as if she would bolt at any moment.

"And I am no enemy to your lord," Lyan said. "Nor to you."

She swallowed hard and moved her head in a jerky nod.

"I need you to take a message to my men with all possible haste," Cailean said, drawing her attention back. "If I succeed tonight, Ewart and the one he serves will be dead. I need my men to be ready to strike once the leaders have fallen. Tell them the signal will be my standard flying above the keep. Can you do this?"

She nodded. "Yes, my lord. Of course! I'll go immediately.

Please be careful, Lord Cailean. We've been waiting, praying for your return."

Cailean nodded. "Thank you. Ahebban watch over you."

She curtseyed, and then quickly bundled clothing into a basket. Her eyes slid back to Lyan. He [illegible] gently at her, trying not to alarm her more. Cailean motioned to Lyan to follow him, and left by the door they'd entered. He pulled it closed behind them, and wiped his face free of the sweat born from the hot, damp washroom air.

"I hope she's safe," Lyan said quietly.

"She knows what she's doing," Cailean said. "Guards try not to annoy the washer women—they end up with holes in their clothes when they do. She'll be fine. As long as she gets the message passed on, everything should be fine."

Lyan wasn't so easily convinced, but he couldn't do anything to help a woman who nearly fainted at the sight of him. "Where should we wait for night? Not in here, if we can help it. Anyone would be able to smell us coming."

"No, not here." Cailean nodded to his men, and they roused from their brief rests. "But I know the ideal place. Almost no one goes there, and I doubt Ewart would change that, or even think about it."

Aikan frowned thoughtfully. "My lord, do you mean your late mother's suite?"

Cailean nodded. "Other than servants cleaning it once a week, the rooms are unused. It's the best place I can think to rest until nightfall."

"Less talking, more moving," Kithr said. "Lead the way, Tathren."

Cailean nodded. "Follow me."

18

Blessed are they who stand
Fearing not the coming night
Blessed are they who stand
Bending not to Murdo's blight

Lyan leaned against the stone wall, gazing out the window and running his fingers over the cool glass. Glass was rare in Eilidh Wood, and these small panes, fitted together in their frame, fascinated him. The crafter had colored some panes and used them to form patterns. Sunlight caught the colors as it flowed into the room, painting the floor and creeping up the wall as the day grew later.

The room smelled disused—dust in the air that regular cleaning couldn't dispel. Lyan also caught lingering hints of a floral scent, the ghost of perfume worn by the woman who had once called these rooms her own.

Behind Lyan, Kithr dozed on one of the thick rugs. Any sudden movement would wake him—bow and arrows rested close at hand.

Lyan turned from the window and looked toward the door into the bedchamber. He didn't hear any movement from there now, and resisted the urge to check on his Tathren friends like a mother hen on her chicks.

"You should rest, Lyan Stargazer," Yion said quietly. Aside from Lyan, he was the only one uninjured and keeping watch. Praett scouted the rest of the keep and listened for any alarm at their escape.

Lyan shook his head, though he did sit in one of the high-backed chairs. "I don't think I'd get much rest if I tried."

"You worry," Yion observed.

Lyan nodded and spoke quietly, as if the Tathrens might hear him from the other room. "I don't think Dalrian will be fit for a battle tonight. He's not bleeding to death, but he could barely walk here even with Shiolto's help. The stairs nearly undid him. Shiolto's in better condition than his brother, but even so, I don't know if he would be better staying with Dalrian. Aikan… he's hurting and he's been beaten, but I know better than to think he would stay behind. He deserves to be there, and he'll fight Ewart and Porephyn for as long as he's able. Then, Cailean." Lyan thought of the weariness he saw in Cailean, and the stiffness in his movements even with Equinox blocking his pain.

"You worry about entering this battle with only two of our warriors at full strength," Yion finished. "And wisely so. But do not forget advantages we still hold. You carry your Spear without the restrictions that bind Lord Cailean, and Torqual is foolish to dismiss the threat of Equinox or your wit. And in addition to the Spear, you control the pooka. Torqual believes in the power and strength of a warrior—in spite of what he has seen, he would not think to warn his master that you are a danger."

"Am I?" Lyan asked, feeling Torqual's doubts held more truth than Yion credited them with.

"We are here thanks to your plan, Lyan," Yion replied.

"You could have gotten out without any help from me,

Yion. You demonstrated that earlier. How did you get into the other cell without being seen?"

"My former life demanded the ability to move unseen, to open that which is closed, and to kill without a sound," Yion said. For the first time, his gaze moved to the window, avoiding Lyan's eyes. One hand rose to rub at the faint indentation in his forehead.

"And you still have those skills," Lyan finished.

"Not so honed as they were. Should I face others with the same training, they would be the faster, and I would not lay wagers on my victory. Especially if I faced more than one."

That thought both startled and chilled Lyan. Someone faster, more skilled, more deadly than Yion? "Do you think that would happen?"

Yion turned his gaze back to Lyan. His voice remained even, but this time, Lyan doubted the calm front. "Any encounter would more likely be only chance, and if they were not seeking me, I would have the advantage."

"Why did you leave, if you knew doing so would bring your own people hunting you?"

"Because a life of death is not a life, Lyan. I chose to spare a life that did not deserve to be taken, knowing that to do so forfeited my own in return. I fled from my land and saw the life I had spared to a place of safety. Then I prepared to face the hunters I knew would follow me." Yion paused, gaze distant. Then he smiled. "Before they found me, one far greater did so. He asked me to follow in his path—a path different from the one I had walked before. He called me to serve him and learn a new life, and he removed me from that place and those who sought my death. In turn, I pledged myself to him."

"And you became a mercenary?" Lyan asked.

"It is a simpler occupation to explain, and less presumptuous than describing oneself as a champion of a god," Yion said mildly. "And before you ask, he still wishes not to be named."

A champion. Not just a follower or a worshiper. A champion of… "He's a Tathren god, isn't he?" Lyan said suddenly.

Yion raised an eyebrow. "Why do you say that?"

"Because you're here, helping Cailean. And because Kithr and other elves who *do* know Tathrens at a glance say something about you feels Tathren, even though you aren't one. Not only that, it makes sense for a Tathren god to send someone to help protect the Tathren Spearbearer."

Yion smiled. "My lord says you are more clever than you give yourself credit for, Lyan, and that I may tell you that you are correct. Perhaps this will also answer some of Kithr's questions."

From the rug where Kithr lay, Lyan heard a muttered insult. Lyan wasn't surprised Kithr was awake and listening, any more than he was surprised Yion knew Kithr was doing so.

Lyan's own anger surprised him. "So why doesn't your god have you lead us, Yion? Why not grant you power to stop all that's been going on here? Murdo isn't even a real god, and *he* gives power to *his* followers! Why should we even have found Equinox? Everything that's happened, *why*?"

Yion's expression grew serious. "Because the Spears are the weapons that can battle Murdo, and they are not limited by the same confines as mortals. Murdo uses his followers as tools, giving little regard to the ravages his power wreaks on those he grants it to. Though I tried, I was unable to reach Lord Cailean before the curse fell upon him. Had my god granted me power while I stood amid Ewart's men, the followers of Murdo among them would have recognized the truth and cut me down. My skills are not those of one who leads. Others are far better suited to the task than I."

Lyan remained unsatisfied. "Since Cailean's keep fell, he's been chased by Ewart's men, had the pooka hunting him, and had a traitor in his midst. Your god couldn't have given you the means to intervene?"

"I did not know for certain that a traitor remained in Lord Cailean's company," Yion said. "My god granted me minor talents: the ability to ward our camp against those who would enter with intent to harm, the ability to turn the pooka's eyes away from us—as I was doing when we met you in Eilidh Wood—and the skill to identify the pooka's influence on another. As for Ewart's men, my own skills have been sufficient to deal with them." Yion looked at Lyan. "My answer still fails to satisfy you. Perhaps it will suffice instead to say that yes, my god could have given me power enough to strike down Ewart's men and the pooka and ease our path to the Shrine of Equinox, but doing so would have killed me as well. Murdo cares little what becomes of his followers, but my god would prefer his champions live long enough to see the battles for which he called them. Had he given me that power, Lyan, you would still face this battle with Ewart and Porephyn. Only you would face it without me."

Lyan said nothing for a long minute. Finally, he turned his gaze back to the window. "What about Porephyn? He uses Murdo's power to cloud the sky, and to curse Cailean. It hasn't killed him."

"He built a shrine to Murdo, and spends sleepless nights within it, Lyan. I expect he spends the time in rituals and sacrifices to counter the cost of the magic. Do you not know that magic works by rules? Every power comes at a cost."

Lyan remembered the first time he'd seen Nylas successfully make a plant bloom, and the evident strain his cousin had shown. He nodded slowly, but his gaze turned to Equinox.

If powers come at a cost, what price do the bearers of the Spears pay?

Equinox's voice whispered softly in his mind, startling Lyan. *"The price of our powers has already been paid. It was paid long ago by my brother and me."*

"Lyan?" Yion asked.

Lyan shook his head. "Equinox answered a question when I wasn't anticipating an answer." An answer that only raised more questions.

Yion nodded in understanding and leaned back in his chair, closing his eyes. Lyan returned to the window.

~

As evening neared, activity in the keep trailed away. Guards changed posts, a few servants finished final errands, but even watching from the window, Lyan sensed that everyone preferred to be safely in their quarters when darkness fell, if they could.

Lyan turned from the window. "It's time, Kithr."

Kithr nodded and sat up slowly.

Leaving him and Yion to prepare, Lyan walked into the bedchamber to wake his Tathren companions.

Two people could easily have slept on the bed, but only Cailean lay on it. Aikan dozed in a chair, while Dalrian lay on the divan and Shiolto sprawled in another chair. They all looked worn, exhausted. Lyan almost turned and walked back out. He made himself go over and shake Cailean's shoulder.

"Cailean, it's time."

Cailean stirred with a tired sigh. "Already?"

"I'm sorry," Lyan apologized. "But it's almost night."

He roused Aikan next. The older man opened his eyes, glanced to Cailean, then glowered at Lyan.

"I thought I told you to wake me first, elf."

"And Cailean told me to wake *him* first," Lyan replied. "I had to pick one of you."

Aikan scowled, but finally nodded. Lyan offered him a hand, which Aikan ignored.

Shiolto stirred before Lyan said anything to him, and peeled open his eyes. "Hey Lyan, how's Dalrian?"

"Still asleep," Lyan answered.

"Don't wake him, please," Shiolto said.

"We agreed Dalrian should stay here." Cailean climbed to his feet. "If anything goes wrong tonight, he can make his way out to my men when he's able."

"Does Dalrian know this?" Lyan asked.

Shiolto nodded. "It wasn't easy for him, but he agreed."

Lyan looked again at Dalrian. The Tathren's face was pale, and he slept despite the stirring around him.

Back in the sitting room, Praett had returned. "Are you prepared, master?"

Lyan snorted and gave the creature a dubious look. "Am I ever going to be?"

"Porephyn is preparing for something this evening, master. I overheard the guards discussing it. I would guess he intends to make use of the prisoners he thinks he has, probably intending to offer one or more to the Mad God."

Lyan stiffened. "When?"

"Late in the night. He hasn't sent anyone to the dungeon yet to check on the prisoners, and he didn't call on me to attend him."

Lyan nodded. "You said Ewart seems at his weakest at the end of the day. We can't wait until they discover we're not locked in cells."

"Ewart is at his weakest, and the guards and their dogs are at their most alert," Praett answered. "We will encounter patrols in the halls."

The thought of dogs reminded Lyan of the hounds that accompanied the reapers, and he shivered. He looked to his companions. "Are you ready?"

"If we're very lucky, we can get to the courtyard without raising an alarm," Cailean said. "Dogs could be a bigger problem."

"Kill Tathrens, kill dogs, kill the minions of Murdo, don't

get killed," Kithr said. "Do we need more of a plan than that?"

"If and when we do, we'll make it up as we go," Lyan responded. He felt Aikan glowered at the reply. He also read the tension in Kithr and the others; no one wished to fail.

Shiolto cast a look back over his shoulder toward his sleeping brother, then nodded to Lyan.

We're as ready as we can be.

Lyan opened the door cautiously and looked up and down the empty hall. He was tense, expecting a trap to spring closed around them at any moment. Lyan stepped to the side. Cailean took the lead, pale face grim and eyes hard, ready to fight whatever stood in their path. Aikan's expression matched Cailean's, and he gave a silent nod of acknowledgment to Lyan. Yion looked as he normally did, as if he dwelt in a private certainty of their success based on something known only to him. Shiolto fidgeted with the tassel on his mace handle. Kithr's face, unsurprisingly, said he was ready to kill something.

Cailean walked with confidence. Lyan trusted the Tathren lord to know his way through the keep; Lyan himself had no idea where they were or where their destination lay. At the top of the stairs, Cailean slowed and listened.

"Two guards around the corner at the bottom," he said softly.

"Allow me, Lord Cailean," Yion offered.

Cailean nodded. Yion moved down the stairs with the silent grace of a serpent. Lyan listened; he didn't hear any sounds to hint at violence or death. Yion returned as quietly as he'd left, and inclined his head.

"The path is clear."

"I'd ask you how you do that, but I'm not sure I want the answer," Cailean said.

"If you wish to ask, I respectfully suggest you do so later, Lord Cailean," Yion said. "We first have a task to complete."

"And yet he'll tell *you* the short version of his life's story," Kithr muttered in Elven in Lyan's ear.

"We weren't trying to sneak through this stone monstrosity at the time," Lyan whispered back.

"Bah. Details," Kithr scoffed.

A smile twitched the corners of Lyan's mouth as he shook his head. They moved down the stairs and rounded the corner. No guards remained. Casting a look around, Lyan noticed a closed door near them, and wondered if two bodies now lay on the other side. Torches lit the hall, reflecting off the pale stone walls.

Cailean looked forward. "I don't know of any servants' passages that will bring us close to the back courtyard. The best path is the direct route."

"Are these halls kept lit all night?" Lyan asked.

"Doubtful," Aikan told him. "The torches will either be allowed to burn out or be extinguished unless there's good reason for keeping them lit."

Shiolto looked at the torches uneasily. "These were recently replaced. They won't burn out anytime soon."

Cailean said nothing, but turned sharply to the right down another hall. He almost ran headlong into a patrolling guard. The men stared at each other for a frozen moment. The guard opened his mouth and grabbed for a weapon. Cailean slammed the hilt of his dagger into the guard's face. The man reeled back. Blood gushed from his nose. Cailean's other hand jabbed the throat and cut short the guard's cry. As the guard staggered, Cailean stabbed him. The guard sank to the floor in a clatter of armor, skullcap spilling off to roll across the floor. Cailean panted for breath.

"Lord Cailean!" Aikan moved to his side. "Are you hurt?"

Cailean shook his head. "No. No, I'm all right. I was careless, didn't even look first."

Aikan scowled. "If he had been more alert, my lord…"

Cailean just shook his head, grabbed the dying guard's

arms, and dragged him toward a door. Aikan opened it, checked inside, and nodded. Yion drew a rag and wiped blood streaks from the floor. Lyan tried to convince his racing heart to slow.

Cailean pulled the door shut. "I'm [sure]. [...] Kithr, would you scout ahead to the next intersection?"

Kithr answered with a single, sharp nod and moved ahead. Lyan almost followed, but stopped. He longed to be outside and out of these enclosing walls. That wish clawed at him until he struggled to think about anything else.

Kithr motioned them to follow. Lyan forced himself to focus. Tapestries hung on the walls, depicting scenes of men on horses chasing a deer, or fighting one another. In another, a man and a woman sat together, hands clasped, the woman looking up into the man's face. The torches burned lower in this hall than in the last one. Lyan didn't know if that meant it less-traveled at night than other passages.

At the intersection, Kithr stopped and peered around the corner cautiously. He waved them to join him. "Which way, Tathren?"

"Left here," Cailean said. "There should be two pairs of wooden doors about halfway up—we'll take the ones on the right."

Kithr nodded. "It's clear so far. I'll check ahead. Lyan, come with me."

Lyan started, but decided not to argue. He tried to imitate Kithr's silent steps with marginal success. Fewer tapestries hung in this hall, and doors leading into places unknown dotted the left wall. Lyan drew a deep breath, and wondered if he only imagined he smelled fresh air. The hall curved until he couldn't see Cailean and his men behind them. Kithr walked with bow in hand, an arrow on the string. Unease lay heavy in the pit of Lyan's stomach.

He saw the doors Cailean mentioned, unguarded. Lyan looked to Kithr, about to speak. He sensed movement in the air, then the sound of feet. The door he'd just passed swung open. Before he could spin around, a blade pressed against the side of his neck.

"Lyan and Kithr, how unexpectedly convenient. I was just on my way to fetch you from the dungeon."

Lyan tensed sharply. "Torqual."

19

By touch of darkness,
Let your eyes see.
Swear upon your life,
That death may never be.

S harp steel rested against Lyan's neck. His eyes moved to Kithr, who stood tense, ready to attack Torqual.

"Wait," Lyan mouthed.

"I'd suggest you drop your bow, Kithr," Torqual said mildly. "How did you get out? Ah, of course. Why didn't I think to find out what became of your Spear after your capture, Lyan? Probably because you have yet to demonstrate any skill with it."

"No, because you're ignorant of the Spears and everything about them, Torqual," Lyan answered coolly. "You should have realized already that a Spearbearer can both send the Spear away to safety and call it back in an instant."

"Give it to me." Anger colored Torqual's voice.

"Are you even *listening?*" Lyan wondered at his own bravado. He felt no fear, only anger at Torqual's arrogance.

"You *can't* take a Spear from its bearer. Didn't you figure that out already with Cailean and Solstice?"

"It's only a matter of time before Cailean reveals where he hid his Spear." Torqual started to reach forward.

Kithr raised the bow. "Touch the Spear and lose your hand, traitor."

"I warned you, Kithr—put down your bow." Torqual pressed the blade against Lyan's neck, breaking skin and drawing a thin trickle of blood.

"It isn't *my* weapon you should worry about," Kithr growled.

"I'm not—not when Lyan stands between you and me," Torqual sneered. "Give Equinox to me, Lyan."

Lyan seethed. *My village dismisses my skills, Nylas and his men do, and even my enemies do!* Lips curled back in a snarl. "The Spear is not yours!"

Equinox responded. A burst of power threw Torqual backward against the wall. Lyan spun to face the man, neck stinging from the shallow cut.

An arrow flew past and sank into the wooden door where Torqual's head would have been if he hadn't ducked.

Belatedly, Lyan sent a thought to Praett, knowing he should have done so the moment Torqual's blade touched his skin. *"Torqual's here."*

Torqual scrambled through the door. Kithr ran to Lyan's side. "Are you okay, Lyan?"

Lyan nodded. He heard Torqual's retreating footsteps, and gave chase with Kithr at his heels.

Lyan smelled fresh air, and glimpsed Torqual entering a courtyard. "Trap?" he asked in Elven.

"Obviously," Kithr said. "Guard against arrows?"

Lyan nodded, feeling a touch of power from Equinox. "Done."

Kithr nodded. "Leave the fighting to me."

Torqual stood at the far end of the courtyard and faced them. He'd picked up a buckler, and stood next to a pair of archery targets for cover. His eyes narrowed on the two elves.

"Done running, Torqual?" Kithr sneered. He ignored the archers on the walls and the [illegible] at the [illegible] entrances to the courtyard.

"You might as well put down the Spear, Lyan." Torqual indicated the image etched on the buckler—a hand gripping two spears. "This bears the blessing of my god. Equinox's magic cannot touch me now."

Lyan stiffened. *Murdo can stop the power of the Spears?*

Kithr snorted. "You'll believe anything the Mad God tells you, won't you? Not that it matters. Lyan won't be the one killing you. Any last words, traitor?"

Lyan glanced at Kithr, surprised his friend would offer anyone the opportunity.

"Last words? The last that you'll hear, perhaps. It didn't have to come to this." Torqual's voice grew deceptively pleasant, but eyes glittering with anger. "It shouldn't have become so messy. Everything was going well. Everyone fit their parts and played them perfectly. Except for one little snag. One minor piece in the game with delusions of grandeur that didn't move the way it was supposed to. One damned *elf* who won't act like an *elf!*" He fixed a murderous glare on Lyan. "Why in Murdo's name did *you* defend *Aikan?* The old fool spent the entire journey attacking you. You should have been like Kithr, ready to seize the first opportunity to be rid of him. If Cailean would have killed the old man, you two wouldn't have split away from the rest on some fool's errand to track him down."

Lyan's eyes narrowed. "There may be no love lost between Aikan and me, but if I'm going to see the last of him, it'll be because of something he does, not for a wrong he didn't commit."

Torqual shook with fury. "Act like an elf. Cut down your enemy while he's weak. What does it matter why?"

"Lyan *is* acting like an elf," Kithr cut in sharply. "Those you think of as elves—those like me, like Nylas and his minions—we're the ones who are Lost. We are the ones who have forgotten how to act like elves, traitor, not Lyan." His smile cut like ice in a winter gale. "You know what to expect from us. You know nothing of what to expect from an elf."

Torqual stiffened. His gazing moved to Kithr, then back to Lyan. His lips curled into a feral snarl. "This is *your* fault, Lyan! Archers! Go!"

Lyan awaited the arrows, trusting Equinox to shield them. The shafts never came. When Lyan raised his eyes to the wall, he saw the smug Praett leaning casually against a battlement, satisfied.

Torqual also looked up. From where he stood, he couldn't see the pooka, but he could see slumped bodies hanging over the edges of the walls. "What in Murdo's name?"

"One thing never changes about Tathrens," Kithr said, stepping between Lyan and Torqual. "They love to talk and boast when they should shut up and fight. And then they wonder how we outmaneuver them."

"Torqual." Cailean stepped over the slumping body of a guard and into the courtyard from the entrance to Lyan's left. "Surrender."

Torqual didn't even look his way. His expression betrayed only longsuffering annoyance. "Lord Cailean. Of course. You are simply determined to throw all plans into chaos, aren't you Lyan? I thought astrologers *wanted* order."

"There is no order when the Mad God is involved," Lyan countered.

"Of course there is. *His* order. The only kind that matters." Torqual abandoned the archery targets and lunged forward, glare fixed on Lyan.

Kithr dropped the bow and jerked his own blade free with barely enough time to block Torqual's attack. Swords clashed. Lyan stepped out of Kithr's way.

Torqual's expression said his true target was Lyan. He lunged again, and Kithr twisted away. Lyan had seen the move many times before, and felt a sinking dread in his stomach. He knew Kithr would follow with a cut at Torqual's back. Torqual knew it as well. Lyan opened his mouth to call out a warning.

Kithr stopped the swing before it started. His foot lashed out instead and slammed into Torqual's unprotected shin. The Tathren staggered. Kithr stepped in and grabbed the pommel of Torqual's sword. He twisted it up, trapping Torqual's arm and further unbalancing the Tathren. Torqual grunted and bared his teeth. Kithr jerked the sword from his grip and dropped it to the dirt.

Torqual glared at Kithr. "Seems even an elf can learn new tricks. So what are you waiting for?"

"You expect me to cut you down right now, don't you? It's what you'd expect of a bloodthirsty elven warrior lost to his people." Kithr spat in the dirt. "Cailean, Torqual's been your man longer than I've known him. That gives you first rights in dealing with him."

Cailean looked at Kithr in surprise. Torqual laughed, stepped away from Kithr and snatched his sword from the ground in the distraction. "You should have taken the chance when you had it, Kithr."

Cailean stepped toward Torqual, spear held ready. Torqual sneered and waited for Cailean to close the distance, then lashed at him. Cailean sidestepped the attack. Kithr moved back to stand by Lyan, picking up his bow. His gaze remaining on the two Tathrens.

Lyan's gaze was arrested by the duel before him. Torqual had stopped laughing, his expression as set and cold as

Cailean's. In the flickering light of the torches, Cailean jabbed at the man who had betrayed him. Torqual deflected with his buckler and slashed at Cailean. The blade tore through the edge of Cailean's shirt, but didn't draw blood. Cailean jabbed at Torqual's stomach. Torqual twisted aside and counterattacked. Cailean had the advantage of reach, but he was hurt and worn, while Torqual moved as if he'd spent all day resting for this duel. Flickering torchlight cast shadows around the courtyard, distorting shapes.

From the side, Lyan saw Aikan, Yion, and Shiolto watch from across the courtyard. Shiolto coiled to rush at Torqual. Yion whispered something to Aikan and vanished into the shadows.

"Your men are far too honorable, M'lord," Torqual scoffed. His blade darted out, catching Cailean in a shallow cut on the arm. "Leaving you to fight me alone."

"Better than being traitors and followers of the Mad God!" Cailean snapped, winded.

Torqual evaded Cailean's attack with lazy ease, opening a gash on Cailean's other arm. "Better than service to Murdo?" He laughed. "Well, Lord Cailean, while you are enjoying your honor in your grave, I'll be enjoying the rewards my god gives those who serve him." He slashed at Cailean.

Cailean's spear intercepted the blow. The shaft cracked. Cailean staggered back. Torqual slashed again. The blade scarred Cailean's leather coat, but didn't cut through.

Aikan shouted in anger and lunged into the fray. Torqual turned, forced to answer the new attack before he could finish Cailean. Lyan sucked in a sharp breath and called on Equinox to shield Cailean. Murdo might protect Torqual, but if that effect didn't extend to others near him…

Torqual sneered, then gasped in surprise as Cailean stabbed the head of the spear under Torqual's mail shirt and into his stomach.

Cailean panted for breath. "Don't get too cocky, you traitorous bastard."

Torqual snarled, lifting his sword. His arm shook. Cailean tore the spearhead free and stumbled back from Torqual, holding it like a dagger. "Damn you, Cailean Dras'dellal!" Torqual hissed. "Die!"

He swept the sword down. Aikan shoved Cailean aside, and Torqual's attack missed both men. Aikan lashed out. His blade sliced deep into Torqual's sword arm, drawing fresh blood. Torqual shrieked and lost his blade again.

He staggered back from Aikan, clutching his arm. Blood ran between fingers. More stained his stomach. His eyes darted around, finding enemies on all sides.

Aikan pulled Cailean to his feet, watching Torqual with narrowed eyes.

Torqual's lips moved as if in plea or prayer. "Lord Murdo, help me."

Kithr's bow creaked. A raven-feathered arrow flew straight and true. Lyan drew a sharp breath as it passed through Torqual to stick in the archery target beyond. Torqual turned a pained, wicked grin to Kithr. "Should have taken the chance when you had it."

Shiolto ran at Torqual with a cry of anger, swinging his mace. As if Torqual had less substance than a ghost, the weapon passed through the air and met no resistance. The torchlight shone through him, and where he stood, no shadow fell. Even the blood flowing between his fingers didn't stain the ground.

Torqual's face was pale with pain, but he still found a smirk. "Thank you, my lord." Raising his eyes, he looked directly at Lyan. "A gift, until we meet again."

The soldier vanished without another sound. Equinox blazed a warning through Lyan's mind. He stiffened, clutching the Spear as something crawled up his spine, oozing malevolence. He doubled over, feeling it digging its claws into his back.

"Lyan!" Kithr said in alarm, catching his shoulder. "What's wrong?"

Get it off! Get it off me! The words ran through his mind, but couldn't find voice.

Feet thumped on the ground and rushed to them.

"What are you doing?" Kithr demanded.

Praett answered. "Killing what you cannot see, mortal." A strong hand ripped the thing from Lyan. Lyan heard a crunch, like a beetle underfoot, and he could breathe again.

Kithr pulled him onto his feet. "Lyan, what happened?"

"Something attacked me." Lyan turned to Praett. What was *that*?"

Dark liquid dripped from the pooka's hand. His fingers curled around something invisible. "A banespawn fiend, master. A creature of Murdo." Praett glared at Lyan. "Next time you use the Spear's powers to protect the other Spearbearer, think about extending the same protection to *yourself*."

"Are you all right, Lyan?" Cailean leaned against Aikan for support. "Where's Torqual?"

"My master is mostly unharmed. Torqual is wherever Murdo chose to take him," Praett answered. "But I don't sense him anywhere in the keep."

Cailean grimaced as he bent to pick up Torqual's sword. He drew a deep breath, and trembled with fury. He clenched his free hand into a fist, then relaxed. "Then we'll worry about Torqual later. Time's slipping away. Where's Yion?"

"Here, Lord Cailean." Yion's voice drifted from across the courtyard. "The remaining guards ran to raise an alarm, but I prevented them from doing so."

"All the noise we've made, and no alarms raised yet?" Kithr said. "Ewart's defenses are deplorable."

"The servants probably know," Shiolto said. "They just aren't going to say anything or stop us."

Cailean nodded sharply. "Let's move. Torqual already proved Kithr's point about talking rather than acting."

"Lead the way," Ivan said.

Naked blade in hand, Cailean gave another sharp nod and took the lead.

20

*Two to bear the weight
Of all the fates of men*

Lyan fought the urge to scratch his back. The sensation of claws still crept up his spine. He glanced at his companions and wondered what else might attack them. If it did, could he protect them before someone else was hurt—or killed?

Kithr saw his anxiety and rested a hand on Lyan's shoulder. "You all right?"

"I didn't think something invisible would attack me," Lyan answered.

"Lyan." Kithr said his name firmly. "You aren't going to expect everything, and you don't have to. You've got the rest of us to watch your back for a reason. Blight, resent it though that monster might, the pooka *has* to protect you. He might complain, but he'll find something to complain about even if you do everything perfectly."

Praett snorted. "As if *that* could happen."

Lyan found himself smiling. "Thanks."

"Just remember that you're not alone, Lyan," Kithr said.

Only Kithr would know the importance of those words to Lyan. He nodded and said again, softly, "Thank you."

Cailean paused, hand raised for silence. Lyan listened, but nothing sounded strange. Cailean looked to Praett. "No night watch to patrol the halls?"

"In nights past, there has been," Praett answered, frowning. "Except on nights when they performed certain rites to their god. Even Ewart's hired thugs dislike the constant screams as victims are offered up."

A shiver ran up Lyan's back. "Torqual intended to retrieve Kithr and me. He didn't say why, but a Spearbearer… Wouldn't that be a powerful sacrifice for the Mad God?"

The others stopped and looked at him so suddenly Lyan wondered what he'd said wrong. "Oh blight," Cailean breathed. "Ewart's master told me the time was nearly right, and he would show me the truth 'when he held the Spear in his hand'. I assumed he meant Solstice, but if he meant Equinox instead…"

"Some later time, my lord, we can all thank Torqual for underestimating Lyan," Aikan said. Lyan looked at the older man in surprise. Aikan scowled back, and, realizing he had almost issued a compliment, added, "Or, we can thank Lyan for making it so easy for Torqual to underestimate him."

"He couldn't have taken Equinox from me, in any case," Lyan said. "Just like I told Torqual. Even killing me wouldn't put Equinox into his hands."

"I'd believe Torqual doesn't have any power that could take the Spears from their bearers," Cailean said, "but as for his master, I'm not so confident he couldn't do something if one of the Spears lay in his reach." He started walking again.

Kithr suddenly cursed, and eyes turned to him. "Don't stop," he said sharply. "I heard a shout."

Cailean hurried his steps. "They won't know where we are, though they might guess where we're going."

"They do not have to know where we are, Lord Cailean. They have only to let loose the dogs," Yion said.

Lyan shivered. The last dogs he'd seen had been the black hounds of the reapers. The thought chilled him to the bone. His steps quickened of their own accord. "Are we close, Cailean?"

"We're almost..." Cailean trailed off. "Oh, blackened blood."

Nails clattered on stone, and a wave of large, black shapes rushed from around the corner. Seeing intruders, they stopped and bared gleaming white fangs. Their eyes were yellow, their teeth smooth, but Lyan's blood froze all the same. He caught himself listening for the whispers of the reapers. Behind the first group, another pack gathered. For a long moment, neither men, elves, nor dogs moved. One sleek black dog barked and lunged at them, the rest of the pack on its heels.

Lyan froze. These mortal dogs were not the same as Murdo's spawn, but his thoughts still mired in fear. Yion hurled a throwing star into one dog. It tumbled with a yelp.

The lead dog leapt. Lyan raised an arm to protect against the fangs.

The dog slammed hard into something invisible, as if the air itself became solid. It staggered, dazed. Those behind scrambled to stop without success. They slid into the barrier in a pile of legs amid yips, snarls, and growls. The second pack met the same fate. Lyan stared, knowing he hadn't had wits enough to call on Equinox for help.

A solid, strong hand smacked Lyan on the head. "Oww!" he protested. He spun around, intent on returning the hit. His mouth opened, but no words came.

"Damn fool, stubborn, bull-headed *mortal!*" Nachyne said, exasperated. Muscled arms folded across bare chest. "When did you plan to invite me to this little party?"

"Uh, I didn't," Lyan managed. "So how...?"

The god of monsters snorted. "Just because I *must* come

when you call doesn't prohibit me from being where I wish any other time."

On either side of them, slavering dogs clawed and bayed at the force that blocked them. Nachyne cast them a look of mild annoyance and waved his hand in a dismissive gesture. "Silence."

The dogs stopped. Heads drooped and tails tucked between legs. Several dogs whined softly. They milled uncertainly, then lay down, heads resting on paws. Nachyne nodded approval.

No one else moved, just stared at the tall, bronze-skinned, winged god. Nachyne still wore the green silk loincloth, to Lyan's great relief. Torchlight seemed drawn to Nachyne. He gleamed as if cast from metal. Leathery wings folded back, and his feline tail twitched idly as he gazed back.

Lyan cleared his throat and licked dry lips. "Um, Nachyne, my companions: Cailean Dev'gilla, Spearbearer of Solstice, and his men, Aikan Unne, Shiolto Rona, whose brother Dalrian is elsewhere in the keep, and Yion. You already met Kithr."

"And your pet has been behaving himself?" Nachyne asked, eyes shifting to Praett, who did his best to act invisible.

"I have no complaints," Lyan said.

"Good. So, this is the Spearbearer of Solstice." Nachyne considered Cailean.

Cailean found his voice. "I am Cailean Dev'gilla, Earl of Ihvako. And what interest does the god of monsters have, to bring him into my home?"

Nachyne raised an eyebrow. "Ah—so Lyan hasn't gone telling the tale. Well, in that case, let's simply say I have a personal interest in Equinox."

"Time's been a bit short," Lyan said. "And still is."

Nachyne ignored the implied request. He looked over Aikan and Shiolto without comment, and then studied Yion. The god blinked and stood straighter. "Well. This is a curious sight. In one place, the elven Spearbearer, the Tathren Spearbearer, and Saiboti's most recent champion. How curious that the Tathren god of warriors should choose a champion so obviously *not* Tathren."

Yion sighed. "My lord did not wish his identity to be revealed, Lord Nachyne."

Nachyne snorted. "Then he should have told me so."

"I doubt he expected that I should encounter you, Lord Nachyne," Yion answered.

Nachyne folded arms across his chest and scowled. "He sent you to guard the Spearbearers, didn't he? He damned well *should* have expected you to encounter me!"

Yion's god is Saiboti, Lyan thought back to the tales Kithr had told him about the Tathren gods. *The god of warriors, and brother of Ahebban. Ahebban hates elves because of some dispute he had with Soldarr, but Saiboti doesn't sound like he holds the same grudge. Why would a Tathren god of warriors and honor take a foreign assassin as a champion?*

Lyan pushed aside his inner doubts. "Nachyne, not to be rude, but we don't really have time to talk about this right now."

Nachyne's expression grew serious. "Murdo's meddling here. I can feel it. So, you weren't planning on calling on me, Lyan."

"Well, given how angry you were the last time, no, I wasn't," Lyan answered.

Nachyne waved a hand. "Even gods have bad days. That happened to be one. As you said, talk will wait until Murdo's minions are dealt with."

Cailean hesitated. "You intend to accompany us, Lord Nachyne?"

"Why? Is it a *problem*?" Nachyne returned.

"No," Cailean allowed quickly. "Only unexpected."

"The gods have no love of Murdo and no wish to see his plans reach fruition, Cailean Dev'gilla. At times, a direct approach is more efficient. And why should I leave all the fun to mortals?" As Nachyne walked, the dogs whined and fell in around him, tails low. The animals kept glancing at him as if hoping for some word of approval. The god of monsters snorted. "Don't look at me for praise. The Aethon's champion. Dogs are his creatures, not mine."

The dogs paid no attention to Yion as they trailed on Nachyne's heels. Lyan looked at his companions with an expression half apologetic as he followed Nachyne. Cailean leaned over and said in a low voice, "I do hope there will be *some* explanation when this is over?"

"I can explain Nachyne's presence," Lyan answered. "Yion, on the other hand… that's his tale to tell, because I don't know."

Cailean smiled faintly. "And here I thought you knew everything."

Lyan only smiled in return.

Nachyne strode around a corner, unconcerned with subtlety. Two men guarded a metal latticework gate into another courtyard. The evening breeze teased through the hall. They stared at Nachyne. One found his voice, raising his sword in a shaking hand.

"Who in Murdo's name?"

Lyan couldn't see the god's face, but he read anger in the tensed muscles and twitching tail. Nachyne didn't break stride. Fingers curled. Shimmering, impossibly long claws extended. The guards shouted in alarm and attacked.

Lyan winced. Claws tore through armor and flesh as easily as through parchment, cutting short the shouts. The two men fell to the floor, lifeless and bloody. Nachyne stepped over them and paused at the gate. Around him, the dogs whined and cowered. They slunk back around the corner and away from the courtyard. Lyan looked through the gate, gripping Equinox.

Torches lit the area, illuminating a stone building in the

center. Paths of paving stones curled across bare ground. The building itself appeared unremarkable—unworthy of the dread Lyan felt as he gazed at it. Minimal adornments, nothing to indicate a place of worship. The presence of guards at the entrance and patrolling the ground, however, implied an importance greater than the exterior appearance.

The guards watched the gate warily. Either they didn't see the intruders on the other side, or their orders to hold their posts were stronger than the need to investigate shouts outside the courtyard.

Or they knew something Lyan didn't.

Nachyne reached to open the gate, then drew up short. Pure fury flash over the god's face. Nachyne's eyes narrowed and his tail lashed back and forth. "You are not so clever or original as you fancy yourself, Murdo."

Cailean glared into the courtyard, and his hands twitched. Lyan knew he wished he held Solstice. "What have they done in my home?" The Tathren's voice quivered with anger.

"His minions have defiled this ground," Nachyne said. "And recently, as well. Any mortal not a follower of Murdo who sets foot on that ground will suffer debilitating agony." The god's mouth curled in a sneer. "The gate itself is enspelled to inflict it on anyone who attempts to open the gate without the proper token, blessed by Murdo. A trick he has used before, in different forms."

"Perhaps, Lord Nachyne, you can enlighten us on the best way to proceed?" Yion asked.

"I can counter the effects of the desecration," Nachyne said as if it were a minor concern. His next words, though, told Lyan that what Nachyne said was not accomplished as easily as he wanted them to think. "Doing so will occupy my attention, so dealing with the minions is up to you."

"What about the gate?" Shiolto ventured, the first words he'd spoken since Nachyne appeared. His voice trembled, wide eyes staring at Nachyne.

The god of monsters laughed. "I said the *gate* is enspelled. I said nothing about the wall around it." With the precision of an artist, Nachyne raised one claw and carved through the stone around the frame of the gate.

Ailan opened his mouth [illegible] before he remembered who he was about to chide for damaging Cailean's keep. The elbow Cailean jabbed into his side helped remind him. The older man straightened and drew his sword. The metal gate fell forward, crashing to the ground inside the courtyard. Guards gaped as the winged, bronze-skinned, nearly naked god walked over it. The metal groaned and twisted under his feet.

"Intruder. Intruder!" The shout rose in the courtyard, and guards charged.

The first caught Kithr's arrow through his helmet's eye slit. The second received two of Yion's throwing stars in the neck.

Praett's voice whispered to Lyan. *"Master, permit me to take care of the rest of these sheep."*

"Go," Lyan said.

He glimpsed Praett's wicked smile as the pooka sprang past him to meet the guards. Lyan felt no sympathy for the men. *You chose this path.*

"Spearbearers, do your job," Nachyne said sharply. Beads of sweat formed on the god's skin, though he otherwise showed no sign of strain.

Lyan looked to his companions and nodded. Equinox held tightly, Lyan ran across the courtyard into the shrine dedicated to Murdo. Like a smothering blanket, he felt the weight of a presence surround him, angry, resentful, longing to wrench Equinox from him. Swallowing hard, fear sitting like a rock in his gut, Lyan sent silent prayers.

Soldarr, Tesseia, Feyra, protect us. Ahebban, pardon an elf invoking your name, but watch over Cailean and his men, please. Saiboti, thank you for sending Yion to us. Equinox, please, please help me to fight!

21

Between the heavens and the earth they stand,
Betwixt gods and men, they walk the line.
Bearing the Spear of Peace, one holds Solstice in hand.
Bearing the Spear of War, one by Equinox seeks the sign.

Lyan saw his reflection in the polished stone floor. Rough, unfinished blocks formed the walls, giving the short entry hall an incomplete appearance, as if the craftsman had been interrupted. A heavy curtain hung at the end of the hall, blocking out most light from beyond, though slivers crept around the edges.

Kithr straightened, pretending he hadn't been limping slightly. Shiolto gripped his mace in white-knuckled hands. Yion's eyes didn't hold their usual relaxed confidence as he bore a slim blade in either hand. Aikan's gaze smoldered. The flickering light of the torches emphasized the bruises that colored his face.

Cailean rested a trembling hand on Lyan's shoulder—not fear, but weakness. Sweat beaded Cailean's face as he whispered.

"I know you're using some of Equinox's power to help me,

Lyan. But if you need that power in the battle ahead, take it. I'll be all right. Don't hesitate. Stopping Ewart and the priest is more important."

"I know," Lyan whispered.

Cailean nodded, drew a deep breath, and stepped forward. With the flat of Torqual's sword, he pushed aside the curtain and stepped within. Lyan followed on his heels.

Elven glow-lamps lit the chamber, and mirrors reflected the light to create an illusion of a wider, larger space. Despite the light, Lyan couldn't shake the sense that gloom filled the chamber and shrouded it in darkness. At the far end of the room, an ornate altar of polished black stone rose from the floor. Images had been carved in it, inlaid with gold and silver. Though Lyan wasn't close enough to see the finer details, he did recognize that in the altar's center, a figure sat enthroned, holding a spear in either hand.

Rage flared from Equinox. The desire to tear the altar to pieces flooded Lyan. But between Lyan and Murdo's altar stood obstacles he couldn't ignore.

In the center of the room, a man dressed in maroon robes knelt on the cold stone at the edge of a circle of mystic symbols. Light shone off his bald head. His voice rose and fell in a low chant. In one hand, he held a jagged knife, the blade stained with dried blood. Caught up in his ritual, he didn't acknowledge the intruders.

Near the doorway stood another man, facing the altar and flanked by four guards, focused on the rites rather than the doorway. The man's hair was beginning to gray, but he was still fit. He stood slightly hunched, as if in pain. A sword hung from his belt, but he wore no visible armor. A thin metal circlet rested on his head. One hand constantly rose to finger the pendant hanging on a chain around his neck, and he murmured along with the chant.

The man spoke without turning. "You're late, Torqual."

Cailean's face twisted with anger. "Torqual's going to be a

good deal more than 'late', Ewart. But do give him my regards when you see him in the Pits."

At that, the man turned. Lyan stiffened. Ewart's face was like a mirror to Vynzent's, aged, but bearing too great a resemblance to ignore, even to the same cut of hair and beard. Ewart's eyes narrowed. "Well, if it isn't Cailean, fancying himself a lord because he inherited a toy he can't use. Another spoiled Dev'gilla brat, given everything he wanted."

Cailean seethed. "And refusing to grant your child anything unconditionally worked *so* well with *your* son. Where *is* Vynzent now?"

"He's become a reaper's plaything, as any treacherous bastard deserves," Ewart spat, eyeing them. "It seems Porephyn's vaunted wards are worth less than the breath it took him to boast about them, if you and your pathetic allies simply walked in."

"Enough talk, Ewart," Cailean snarled.

Aikan stepped in front of his lord. "Your pardon, Lord Cailean, but I believe I have unfinished business with this man."

For one heartbeat, Lyan questioned if Aikan was, inexplicably, about to betray Cailean. But the steward's voice turned hard as steel. "The last time he and I spoke, I was unable to make my point clear to him." Metal glittered as Aikan drew his sword.

Ewart's eyes narrowed. "You made the wrong decision, Aikan."

"I made the wrong decision when I first responded to your invitation to treason, Ewart," Aikan answered. "An error of judgment I will now rectify."

Ewart's four guards stepped forward. Shiolto moved to Aikan's side, and Yion joined him. "We'll take care of this, Lord Cailean," Shiolto promised.

Cailean hesitated only a moment. "I know you will."

Through the confrontation with Ewart, the second man's chanting had not wavered. Now it stopped, and he rose from the floor, turning to face them. His head was entirely hairless, lacking even eyebrows. His skin looked gray in the light. The color of his eyes seemed to constantly shift. Around his neck hung a medallion in the shape of a pair of crossed spears.

Weapons clashed as Shiolto, Yion, and Aikan engaged Ewart's guards, but the bald man's attention didn't waver from Cailean, Lyan, and Kithr. His smile could have frozen boiling water. "You think to challenge me in my own lair, Lord Dev'gilla?"

Cailean trembled with fury. "I will not allow you to continue this mockery. This is my home!"

"Will you attempt to reclaim it? Do come and try. Show me your might, Lord Dev'gilla. When you lie broken before our god, perhaps you will begin to understand the futility of your actions."

"I will never bow before you or Murdo!" Cailean shouted. He pointed the sword at the man. "I refuse."

"You don't even know how to free yourself of the curse laid on you," the other sneered. "Why don't you say my name, Lord Dev'gilla? I do enjoy watching you choke on it. You don't have the slightest understanding of the power that holds you."

"Your death will break the curse," Lyan said, cutting through the web of mockery around them. "And I *can* say your name, Porephyn."

The priest's gaze rested on Lyan. "Well. Who told you that, I wonder?" Porephyn mused. "Not Lord Dev'gilla, certainly."

"Someone else who hates you," Lyan said. "Though I'm sure *that* doesn't narrow the possibilities much."

"There will always be those who reject our god. What of you, elf? Murdo will welcome you into the ranks of his devotees."

Fury surged from Equinox again, and Lyan bared his teeth. "Your false god will never lay a hand on the Spears again!"

Porephyn's gaze narrowed as his mouth twisted in a dark smile. "A foolish decision, elf."

An arrow flew from behind Lyan toward Porephyn's chest. The shaft hit a barrier before it reached the priest, deflecting aside harmlessly. Kithr cursed.

"Do you think it would be so easy to kill a mage and priest of Murdo?" Porephyn sneered. "I'm well-versed in elves and their ways."

Lyan heard the same confident gloat as he'd heard from Torqual. *No, you're not. You don't know elves of Eilidh Wood. Equinox, I need your help, not your anger.* The wave of rage from the Spear made Lyan struggle to remain focused. If he had ever questioned the depth of Equinox's hate of Murdo, he never would again. Equinox ignored his thoughts, urging Lyan to rush in and drive the Spear into Porephyn's heart.

Which is exactly how he expects an elf to act. No! Lyan responded.

Kithr released another arrow, though he knew it would have no more effect than the first. Porephyn raised his ritual knife and pointed the tip at Kithr. A flash of light sparked from the blade. Lyan swung Equinox awkwardly into the spark's path. A jolt ran up his arm as the Spear connected, then cleaved through the attack. Wisps of magic drifted to the ground like mist.

Behind them, blades rang as Aikan battled Ewart. Lyan walked toward Porephyn. "I don't know what Torqual told you, and honestly, I don't care. If I'm really as incompetent as he claims, then I shouldn't be much challenge to a skilled mage. If I'm *not* so useless, who should you deal with first: the lord you cursed, the archer, or me?"

Porephyn smiled like a cat seeing easy prey. "Another novice Spearbearer. Truly my lord's favor shines on me."

"Lyan, be careful!" Cailean warned.

"I'll provide you with a little extra incentive, Spearbearer." Porephyn smirked. He waved a hand, and Lyan heard Cailean gasp in sharp pain.

He couldn't help but look back over his shoulder. Cailean doubled over on the floor, panting for breath. A trickle of blood ran from his nose.

Porephyn continued. "While I questioned him in the dungeon about Solstice, I gave Lord Dev'gilla certain gifts from my lord: spores from one of my lord's favorite plants. Balevines take root in living flesh and devour it for their nourishment. The immature plants are fragile, though, and can't survive outside of Murdo's prison without my enchantments. At my command, they have begun to grow. You could, of course, use the Spear's power to attempt to slow them, but doing so will draw from your strength. If you succeed in defeating me before they kill him, my enchantments will be broken, and the spores will die immediately. So, Spearbearer, what will you do?"

Lyan faced the priest, his face grim. "Kithr, help Cailean if you can and watch my back."

"Less talk, more dead priest," Kithr responded. "I'll keep an eye on the lordling."

Porephyn smirked and stepped into the center of the large ring of runes. With one crooked finger, he beckoned Lyan, taunting. Lyan stopped at the edge of the runes, not crossing them.

"Come, Spearbearer. Face me here. Or would you prefer we duel outside of these wards, where the splash of magic can strike everyone else as well?"

Lyan's eyes darted over the runes. He didn't know the meanings of all of them, but he recognized enough to know they were meant to contain, and magic used within the circle would not strike anyone outside it—a protection necessary for any manner of summoning, as this circle was probably used for. Though he suspected a trap, Lyan stepped within.

The runes flashed as he did so, a barrier springing into place around the ring. Lyan said nothing, his gaze fixed on Porephyn. The priest, in return, watched him. Lyan prayed his face didn't show the fear that settled like a rock in his stomach. He lunged forward, Equinox held to strike.

Porephyn avoided the clumsy attack and lashed out with his knife, opening a gash on Lyan's left arm. A rush of energy dulled the pain. Lyan tried one of the few attacks Kithr successfully taught him, and swept the Spear low at Porephyn's shins.

The shaft of the Spear hit hard. Porephyn fell back with a cry of surprise and pain. Lyan stabbed at him, but Porephyn rolled aside and up into a crouch. He flung his hand open, palm toward Lyan. A blast of wind and ice tore across the circle.

Lyan raised Equinox protectively, but while the barrier that could stop arrows blocked the ice lances, it didn't shield him from the frigid wind, nor did it prevent the stone underfoot from coating with frost and ice, becoming treacherously slick. Lyan fell back against the barrier, then cried in pain as heat scalded his back. He jerked away, trying to keep his footing on the icy floor. Porephyn loosed another burst of ice and wind at him.

Lyan dropped to his knees, bracing himself with Equinox. The cold bit and tore at him, even though the lances of ice shattered before they struck. Ice caked Lyan's red hair and fell from his clothes as he pushed back onto his feet. Porephyn smirked, mist gathering in his hands again.

Lyan acted by impulse, letting Equinox guide him. As the third blast roared toward him, he swept the Spear horizontally and felt a rush of air. The icy wind followed the sweep of the Spear, curving away from Lyan and rushing back around on the priest.

Porephyn made a sharp gesture, closing his hand and jerking his arm downward, and the wind died before the full brunt struck him. Ice shards still ripped the maroon robes, and the floor under Porephyn's feet shone with frost and water.

Lyan cast his [illegible] surviving battles against mages.

Porephyn wiped a trickle of blood from his mouth. In his eyes, Lyan read confidence. Lyan lunged forward, finding enough footing on the slick stones to keep his balance.

Porephyn sidestepped. Lyan jabbed Equinox's head into the stone floor and gripped the Spear's shaft as his feet hit the slick, wet patch where the priest had stood. Momentum swung him around into Porephyn. Elf and priest collided, both tumbling to the floor. Lyan lost his hold on Equinox as he fell. Pain met every muscle when he hit the ground. Porephyn cursed and shoved away from Lyan, struggling to untangle himself.

Lyan pushed up and saw the priest reaching for Equinox. The Spear vanished just as Porephyn's hands closed around the shaft and reappeared in Lyan's hold.

"Equinox is not yours!"

As if the air were a solid thing, a ripple snapped from Equinox into Porephyn, sending the priest flying back into the barrier.

If the barrier hurt Porephyn, his expression didn't show it. He did find a cruel smile, though, as a whip-like coil of fire appeared in his hand. "Torqual suggested you might have an aversion to fire, Spearbearer."

Lyan froze as fear raced through him. Porephyn flicked the blazing coil at Lyan's face. He reflexively blocked with Equinox.

"I'm not bound, and you're not Vynzent!" Lyan snapped.

The heat melted the ice and raised clouds of steam around them. From the corner of his eye, Lyan glimpsed shapes that might or might not have been his imagination.

Every move Porephyn made, they mimicked, and as the fire lashed out again, so did five tendrils of mist. Lyan twisted away from the flame, but one mist tendril tore his skin, then another. He staggered. More steam rose, forming a thicker mist.

Equinox drove into Lyan's thoughts, and he seized on the Spear's answer. Wind roared suddenly through the rune circle, catching the mist and lifting it overhead. *A storm. Give me a storm, and rain to quench the fire!*

Water poured down in a torrent, soaking Lyan to the skin. It added to the chill in his bones from the ice. Porephyn cursed and lashed at Lyan, but his whip sizzled, flickered, and died like a wet candle. The mist-figures had been swept up into the storm, torn apart. Energy crackled, like lightning hanging just over Lyan's head.

Porephyn raised a hand, grasping at the air as if to draw something down. The mist began to sink again. Lyan bared his teeth and pushed back. The mist roiled and twisted in turmoil as they struggled for control over it. Sweat ran down Lyan's face, and he shook. The mist ever so slowly sank closer.

"Lyan," Cailean gasped. Lyan's eyes shifted to the Tathren lord. Blood ran from Cailean's nose and trickled from the corner of his mouth, but he'd somehow pulled himself to the edge of the rune circle. "Remember what I told you." He panted for breath, pale and trembling.

"I carry my god's favor," Porephyn shouted, grasping the medallion around his neck. "I am the vessel for *his* will. You cannot stand against him. Not even the Spears of the Stars can stand against the might of Murdo!"

"You know nothing of the Spears or their might," Lyan said, voice chill. "And you know nothing of how an elf of Eilidh Wood does battle." *I'm sorry, Cailean. I need the strength I lent to you.*

A fresh surge of energy raced through Lyan as he withdrew the Spear's protection from Cailean. Suddenly reversing his tactic, Lyan stopped fighting Porephyn's efforts to draw the mist down. For a moment, mist choked Lyan, clawing at his face to steal his breath. Lyan squeezed his eyes shut and added Equinox's power to the downward force. Magic dragged the mist to the floor, then further forcing it between minuscule cracks where the stones had been set together. The surface was tainted and desecrated by the shrine, but deeper, Murdo's corruption hadn't yet reached, and there, Equinox found an acorn. Buried long ago, perhaps by some rodent, it still held life, hibernating and forgotten.

Wake. I need your help. Wake. Come.

Even Nylas and Patch working together not could have forced a seed to a mature tree in less than an hour. Equinox pulled the seed from its long slumber and it grew in an instant. Stones underfoot cracked, then shattered as the tree forced its way up, fueled by the water of the mist and by magic. Porephyn fell backwards, gaping in disbelief. Lyan looked at the tree spreading its branches upwards to tear through the shrine's roof, then he turned to the priest. He felt the tree's spirit, also woken from slumber, and felt it touch his thoughts.

The trees of Eilidh Wood kill those who would harm travelers who pass through in peace.

Lyan panted for breath, but spoke. "I am an elf of Eilidh Wood. I don't fight like the Lost."

Branches speared down: thick, straight branches with no leaves, only tips like spikes. Porephyn staggered back, hitting the barrier that now trapped him. The priest called a shield of fire around himself and grasped his medallion. "My lord, protect me!"

For an instant, the world froze around Lyan, and nothing moved. He heard a whisper echoing with mad laughter. "Porephyn, you have failed me."

Porephyn's fire shield sputtered and died. The medallion crumbled to dust. Branches drove into his chest, and he screamed, then began to choke, blood foaming from his mouth. The branches jerked free, and his body crumpled into a bloody heap.

The barrier fell, and Lyan stumbled to Cailean. Kithr caught Lyan's arm and helped him. The Tathren lay still on the stones, pale, his breathing ragged and strained. His eyes barely opened, and struggled to focus as Lyan stumbled down beside him.

"Cailean?" Lyan asked. "Cailean! Nachyne!"

Earth unmoving, boon of life,
Source of soil, source of stone.
Raise the walls, shield from strife.
Plow the fields, that seeds be sown.

At Lyan's shout, the god of monsters appeared beside him. Nachyne didn't ask why Lyan had called him—he looked at Cailean. His expression grew grim. "I'll do what I can."

Those words lacked the confidence Lyan wanted to hear. He bit his lip, unsure whether his response would come out as questions or demands of the god.

Aikan limped toward them. Blood spattered his clothes. When he saw Cailean, Aikan's face lost what color remained.

"Lord Cailean?" He dropped to his knees beside the man.

Cailean focused with an effort. "Ewart?" he asked in a raw whisper.

"Ewart Col'renn is dead, my lord."

"Good."

Aikan continued, though whether Cailean heard or listened was questionable. "The wound I dealt him at our last encounter never healed—he called it his price for the gifts given him by the Mad God. His greatest weakness, my greatest advantage. Are you listening to me, Lord Cailean?"

Cailean's eyelids fluttered. "I'm listening…"

Aikan scowled. "My lord, under no circumstances are you permitted to die before producing an heir."

"Been a little busy recently," Cailean managed. "Shiolto and Yion? Safe?"

"They're fine, Lord Cailean," Aikan assured him.

Lyan looked at Nachyne, and realized the god was as worn and exhausted as the rest of them. Sweat gleamed on his bronze skin, and his wings drooped even while folded back. Nachyne met Lyan's gaze and spoke quietly. "This might be beyond my abilities, Just Lyan Stargazer."

Lyan shook his head in denial. *Equinox? You must be able to do something!*

No spell of healing came to him. Lyan sensed the Spear's urgency, a mirror of his own as Equinox reached out to its place of power—its shrine. Venycia had told him the Spearbearer could compel the Guardians of the Spear to assist him. Any Guardian except the demigods, who had entered service to the Spear willingly.

Yet to the demigods Equinox called. Not an order, but a plea. Lyan wasn't sure if he actually heard words, or if his own mind interpreted the emotions he sensed in the Spear's cry. *Help the Spearbearers! Help my brother!*

The scent of pines and of lavender reached him. Lyan raised his eyes and saw her. Long black hair with white streaks, brown eyes, Venycia stepped through a doorway that, heartbeats before, had been merely a decorative arch carved into the stone wall. Of all the demigods, he'd most hoped she would answer. The sight of her chased the exhaustion from Lyan.

The doorway vanished behind her. The Guardian of the Spear shuddered as she set foot in the shrine, then hurried to the gathering around Cailean. Nachyne raised an eyebrow and stepped back, allowing her to crouch next to Lyan.

"Lord of Solstice, look at me," Venycia ordered.

Cailean turned toward her voice, but couldn't bring his eyes into focus.

"Call your Spear back to you," she said. "Lord of Solstice, call your Spear."

Cailean's brow furrowed in concentration, and his lips moved in silent words. One hand lifted, curling as if to grasp something, and Solstice, mirror to Equinox, appeared. Cailean gasped in surprise, then his eyes sank shut. Solstice began to glow. The light crept over Cailean until it covered him. Lyan found himself scooting back from the Tathren lord in response to a gentle but insistent push.

"Lord Cailean!" Aikan said urgently, the only one who refused to budge.

Venycia rested a hand on the older man's shoulder. "Rest easy, Aikan. Solstice is rejoined with its bearer, and will not permit him to come to harm. Lord Cailean will heal. Solstice will allow no less. The Spears are jealous in their protection of their bearers. The bond gives the Spears powers to heal and safeguard them, just as Equinox is doing for Lyan."

Lyan looked at his arm, where Porephyn's blade had gashed him, and realized it had already scabbed over.

"Even wounds that should be mortal, the Spears can heal so long as they are with their bearer," Venycia said quietly. "For now, Lord Cailean will rest. But be assured, he hears you, though it is difficult for him to respond."

Lyan nodded and smiled gratefully at Venycia. "Thank you."

She rested a hand on his shoulder. "Just because you cannot require us to help you, Lyan, doesn't mean you can't ask. Whatever the reason."

He swallowed hard. "I'll remember that." Lyan tore his

attention from her before he made a fool of himself and looked around the Mad God's shrine.

Overhead, the oak had driven through the ceiling to spread its branches in open air, hiding the night sky from sight. Pulverized rock dust drifted down on everyone. Lyan's gaze skirted away from Porephyn's mangled corpse as the roots began to crawl over the body. Near the doorway, blood trickled between the floor's cracks and pooled around the bodies of Ewart's guards. Ewart lay against the wall, blood staining his doublet, eyes open—blank, dead.

Shiolto sat against a wall opposite the corpses. Yion crouched beside him, winding a bandage around a gash on Shiolto's head. Shiolto looked dazed, eyes not quite focused. Praett stood in the doorway, silent. He inclined his head in a nod to Lyan when their eyes met. No one spoke.

Finally, Lyan climbed to his feet, steadied by Kithr. "Careful," Kithr cautioned.

"Sorry." Lyan caught himself. Exhaustion weighed down his limbs and he prayed no new threats assaulted them. Kithr, at least, was steady and fresher than the rest.

Lyan moved to the tree and rested a hand on the rough bark. Knobby roots broke and cracked the stones and crushed the runes of the mystical circle. At Lyan's touch, branches rustled, and leaves brushed his head. Lyan smiled faintly and leaned against the trunk. He hadn't sensed such a welcome from any tree since leaving Eilidh Wood.

"*What* have you created in my lord's keep, Lyan?" Aikan demanded. He eyed the tree with suspicion.

"It's... just a tree, Aikan. I didn't create it, only used Equinox to make it grow. The seed was already there, a Tathren acorn of a Tathren oak."

"*Tathren* trees don't move without wind," Aikan said.

Nachyne slumped wearily back on his elbows. "They could, if something woke their spirits. Any plant has some potential, really." The god of monsters addressed the air. "So, now that the damnable wards are finally gone, is anyone going to bother cleansing this place and thanking the elven Spearbearer for killing a high priest of Murdo?"

Lyan blinked, not sure who Nachyne addressed. He jumped when Murdo's altar [illegible] struck from above. In response, Equinox glowed in Lyan's hand. The ground trembled. Lyan expected tree roots. It wasn't the tree, but Equinox, determined to proclaim its hate for Murdo. A rock spike burst from the ground, slammed up through the altar's center, and split it in half. More cracks spidered through the black stone, and it crumbled into shards. The rock spike sank back into the earth.

Lyan closed his eyes a moment, drawing deep breaths. Fresh sweat dripped down his face as more weariness fell on his shoulders.

He sensed a change in the air, a new presence in the shrine, and his eyes snapped open. Beside Lyan, Kithr stiffened. The rubble of the altar crunched under the tread of a heavy foot, twisting to grind the rock into powder. Aikan's eyes opened wide in disbelief and he sank to his knees. Lyan's gaze, however, was arrested by the figure who eyed the shrine with obvious loathing.

He looked Tathren, but his presence filled the confined space and left Lyan feeling crowded and unwelcome. He stood two heads taller than Lyan, and wore a tunic and trousers of leather. A stylized bear reared across the front of the tunic, and his muscled body implied a life of labor. Short-cropped black hair did nothing to soften the hard face. Lyan felt as if he gazed at a stone wall—harsh, unyielding, unbending, and unsmiling. Cold gray eyes fixed on Lyan and the tree at his back.

"An *elven* tree, within one of *my* fortresses."

Kithr's hand rose toward his quiver in search of an arrow. "Ahebban," he whispered.

The tree rustled and shifted in response to the god's tone,

branches moving defensively around Lyan. Lyan leaned against Equinox and met the god's eyes. To his surprise, his voice held steady. "I thought it preferable to having a shrine to the Mad God in one of your fortresses, Lord Ahebban."

Nachyne laughed aloud. "He has a point, Ahebban."

The Tathren god's scowl didn't diminish. "An elven tree."

Lyan adopted a different tactic. He bowed as deeply as he dared without falling on his face. "I beg your pardon, Lord Ahebban. I'm not well enough versed in Tathren ways to know how your people would conduct such a battle. I only know the ways of my own people. I am an elf of Eilidh Wood."

"Yes, *that* is obvious enough," snapped the Tathren god.

"Not to mention he's the elf of Eilidh Wood who helped your Spearbearer, fought his way here, and killed the devotee of Murdo who raised wards powerful enough to keep you and the rest of the Tathren gods from entering this keep," Nachyne said in an offhand tone.

Lyan was starting to think Ahebban incapable of any expression but a fierce scowl. The Tathren god glowered at Nachyne. "I am aware of that."

The god of monsters pushed slowly to his feet, his expression growing dark. "Then try expressing a little *thanks* instead of acting like you're going to rip Lyan's head off."

Ahebban's jaw tightened. One hand clenched in a fist, then slowly uncurled. In a forcedly polite tone, he said, "Your assistance to the Tathren Spearbearer Cailean Dev'gilla, and your part in removing Murdo's blight, is appreciated, Lyan of Eilidh Wood. Now, if you would kindly consider removing this abominable *thing* from this keep, I would appreciate it."

Lyan started to speak, but caught himself. Protesting that the oak was only a tree was like saying Shadowstar was just a horse. He searched for some way, *any* way to politely refuse to do anything to the tree. Around them, not even Kithr spoke. Lyan wanted to look to his Tathren companions and guess their thoughts, but he couldn't do so without turning his back on Ahebban, and every instinct warned against giving offense to the god.

Soft steps crunched over stone shards. Venycia stepped up beside Lyan, and laid a hand on his [illegible] again. Seeing her, Ahebban drew a sharp breath as if to object, discomfited by the touch. Venycia looked at the tree, then her gaze met Ahebban's. "I think instead of trying to be rid of this tree, you should consider it as a symbol of reconciliation between Tather and Eilidh Wood. A sign of elves and Tathrens united against a greater enemy. Putting aside differences and old grudges. Don't you think it's about time to do so, Father?"

The god said nothing in response, but his eyes moved from Venycia to Lyan and back. Lyan's own mouth tried to drop open in astonishment.

When she told me her father was a god, I should have guessed. Kithr told me bears are sacred to Ahebban. But knowing Venycia's mother was an elf, I never thought her father could be a Tathren god. Certainly not THIS Tathren god.

"Isn't it time?" Venycia repeated. "We can all see Murdo has begun to act. This won't be the end—not when both Solstice and Equinox have Bearers once again. Isn't it time you stopped blaming Soldarr for a decision that was no one's to make but mine?"

Ahebban still said nothing.

"Um." Lyan cleared his throat. Venycia's presence, so close and warm beside him, chased thoughts from his mind. Ahebban and Venycia both looked at him. "In regards to the tree, I think Cailean ought to have some say in its fate. If he wishes it gone, then I'll see what Equinox and I can do."

As an attempt to move the topic away from divine family quarrels, it was pathetically obvious, but Ahebban showed the first hints of genuine appreciation. At least, he gave Lyan a nod, and his gaze wasn't so sharp and biting. "Very well—the matter of this… thing is between the Spearbearers to resolve."

"It was drawn up by the power of Equinox, and its health linked to the Spearbearer's. Cailean would be a fool to object to its presence," Nachyne said in an undertone.

Lyan leaned back against the tree again. "It's a tree," he murmured. "It's only a tree." He was sure he should say or do something more, but he was exhausted and his thoughts grew more and more muddled.

Praett snorted. *"Someone ought to start teaching you advantages of being a Spearbearer, master. For example, the right to tell even the gods that their problems can wait when you need to sleep."*

Lyan blinked, startled by the silky voice, then he shook his head with a faint smile. *"Mortals don't say things like that to gods."*

"Spearbearers do, master. The gods are indebted to the Spears and Spearbearers. You are the only two mortals in the world who stand any hope of defeating Murdo and his minions. Without the Spearbearers, Murdo would have broken free long ago. The gods need the Spearbearers, master, and for that reason, yes, you do have the right to refuse their demands, and to tell them your own needs are more important than theirs."

Before Lyan could gather his thoughts to respond, Kithr spoke, addressing Venycia rather than Ahebban. "If you're done discussing a *tree*, we're still standing in a fortress filled with enemies who don't know their lord is dead."

"And Dalrian doesn't know what happened, either," Shiolto hesitantly put in.

Lyan turned toward his companions—his friends. For a moment, Lyan thought he saw two Yions and two Shioltos as the room wavered, but when he blinked, his vision steadied again.

"Kithr?" he asked.

"What is it, Lyan?"

"Can I leave the rest of this to you? Try, um, not to insult the Tathren gods too much." Lyan blinked rapidly and tried to hold onto the trail of thought.

"Lyan, are you hurt? Are you all right?" Concern filled Kithr's voice.

"I think I'm going to pass out pretty soon," Lyan told him, unsure if he sounded as calm about the matter as he felt. His legs felt as weak as willow branches.

Gentle hands caught him. "If you don't object, Kithr, I'll see to it that Lyan Spearbearer gets the rest he needs," Venycia said, her voice a musical chime in Lyan's ears, and her scent lulling him closer to the sleep he wished for.

Kithr looked at Lyan, then nodded, albeit with reluctance. "All right. I'll see you when you wake, Lyan."

Lyan stopped fighting. The darkness crept around the edges of his vision, and he sank into Venycia's waiting arms.

23

Two nations torn asunder
By the choice of one born of both.
Two peoples brought together
By the rage of madness come to life.

A crash of thunder tore Lyan from solid sleep, and he jerked up, confused and disoriented. Blood pounded in his ears.

"It's all right, Lyan." He heard Venycia's voice, and his racing heart calmed. Lyan fell back into soft cushions.

A cool breeze carried the smell of rain through an open window. Lyan blinked away grit and sleep. He rubbed his face and his eyes focused. Above him, men in armor brandished weapons, urging their horses onward as they charged to attack a horde of creatures twice the size of a man armed with gleaming claws and savage fangs. Lyan gazed at the painting for several moments, then pushed himself up to sit on the bed, taking a deep breath of the rain-saturated air. He shivered as cool air played over bare skin. His left ankle ached, but the fresh air chased away the feeling of confining stone walls around him.

Venycia sat beside the bed. The Guardian wore a long green dress. The loose, gauzy sleeves floated down sculpted arms to silver clasps at her wrists. Black hair hung loose, covering bare shoulders. Lyan flushed. He was naked under the blanket.

Another crash of thunder rattled the window panes. Fighting embarrassment, Lyan smiled at Venycia. "I have no idea how long I've slept, but evidently Toirni thinks it's time for me to wake up."

Venycia laughed warmly. "You've slept through the morning and a little of the afternoon. Kithr has been checking on you constantly since midday. Lord Cailean came by shortly after he woke, before Aikan dragged him off to attend other matters."

"Cailean's awake? Is he all right?" Lyan asked, straightening.

"Worn, but healed. A few days to rest, and he will be completely restored," she assured him. "He sent a servant with fresh clothes for you as well." Venycia indicated a neat stack on the table beside the bed, and then rose, walking to the window to look out and let him dress.

Lyan blushed again, and grabbed the tunic at the top. "What about Dalrian? Shiolto, Yion, Aikan? And what happened to Ewart's men?" He spoke quickly, trying to cover his discomfiture. He admired Venycia's calm, collected air. If she felt self-conscious, she hid it well.

"I know all your friends are alive, Lyan, but I'm afraid you'll have to ask someone else for the details," Venycia apologized. "I remained here while you slept." She glanced over her shoulder, then turned to face him again.

Lyan hadn't yet pulled on the breeches, but the tunic hung long enough to be nearly decent. Not as decent as he *wanted* to be, but he tried to keep his composure.

Venycia continued. "As for Ewart's men, many of his hired

soldiers surrendered on the spot with Ahebban standing over them."

"Your father?" Lyan asked tentatively.

She nodded. "He loved my elven mother, and she him. There wasn't always animosity between Tather and your people." Venycia paused, then sighed, turning to look out the window again. "At the heart of the conflict between Ahebban and Soldarr, Lyan, you will find me."

Lyan blinked. "But why?"

"Ahebban had plans and expectations he assumed I would accept. Soldarr asked—asked, mind you—if I would become a Guardian of Equinox." She shook her head, making her hair ripple like dark water. "Ahebban… my father blamed Soldarr for my decision, convinced he somehow deceived me, or forced me to accept." Venycia's shoulders drooped. "Nothing I said changed his mind, and I gave up trying. Soldarr continued talking to Ahebban, as stubborn as my father. They argued until both wielded words as sharp as swords, digging up old grievances and inventing new ones. Through the priests and elders, Ahebban and Soldarr stirred their people against each other, until Tather and Eilidh Wood reflected the animosity of their gods."

Lyan just stared at her, not quite comprehending.

She faced him again. "Yes, Lyan. The anger and distrust between your two people is because of me." Her voice shook. "Because of one choice I made."

In those words, Lyan heard guilt, and saw pain in Venycia's eyes. He crossed the room to her in quick steps and rested his hands on her bare shoulders. "Venycia, it isn't your fault."

She shook her head. "I could have changed my mind. I hadn't become a Guardian of Equinox when the argument began. But I was just as stubborn and set on my path as they were."

"And Ahebban could have accepted your decision rather

than trying to force you to do what he wanted. Soldarr could have stopped pushing the matter and let it die away instead of forcing it too far," Lyan countered. "Venycia, it's not your fault. Despite generations of anger and everything that's happened, I'm here help... Cal... ...and Kuli's starting to think not every Tathren deserves an arrow in the eye. I have Tathrens I call friends, and who call me a friend."

"Lyan."

He looked into Venycia's serious brown eyes. The scent of rain and lavender surrounded him. Lyan leaned close, his lips finding hers in a kiss that caught both of them by surprise. Lyan was further surprised when Venycia wrapped her arms around him and returned the kiss, lingering and relaxing against him. All other thoughts fled Lyan's mind until they separated and stepped back, suddenly awkward.

"Venycia, I..." Lyan hesitated, unsure what he'd been about to say.

She rested a finger gently on his lips. "Thank you."

"But I..." *I think you're the most beautiful, amazing woman I've ever known.*

"I've longed to kiss you since you entered the Shrine of Equinox, Lyan," Venycia said softly. "When you began the Trials, I wasn't sure whether I hoped you would succeed and become Spearbearer, or fail and remain at the Shrine. I believed you worthy of Equinox; I couldn't wish against that. I also knew you wouldn't be happy being caged." She smiled, pink flush rising in her cheeks. "Lyan, I'm glad you succeeded and chose to bear Equinox."

Something in her voice made Lyan think perhaps she did know, or suspect, that one temptation Equinox had put before him had been to stay at the Shrine, with Venycia, as a Guardian. "Thank you."

Thunder crashed, and a gust of wind swept a cold burst of rain over them both, breaking the awkward silence. Lyan laughed in surprise, and Venycia grinned back at him.

"I'm sorry, Lyan. I should let you finish getting dressed," she apologized. "Pardon me."

Remembering that he still wore only the tunic, Lyan turned bright red as Venycia opened the door and slipped out. As she started to close the door, Lyan heard her exclaim in surprise. "Oh! Kithr, I didn't hear you come in."

"Just got here," Kithr responded. "Lyan's awake?"

"He is, and dressing," Venycia answered. Then she closed the door. Lyan couldn't hear any more of their conversation.

Lyan quickly pulled on stockings and breeches, tugging on his boots. His ankle throbbed, but he pushed aside the discomfort by thinking instead of Venycia's lips against his. He started from his reverie when the door opened.

Kithr entered. "Finally awake, I see." He closed the door and walked to Lyan. "And it's about damned time you two kissed."

Lyan's head jerked up. He jumped to his feet, cheeks burning. "What? You…"

"The pooka told me you were awake and warned me not to come barging in. I figured out the reason when I got here."

"You… You…" Lyan sputtered.

"I could have guessed from one look at you, even if I hadn't seen anything." Kithr's eyes twinkled with amusement. "Your face doesn't hide much, Lyan."

Lyan shook his head in surrender. He couldn't deny he felt like he was standing on air rather than ground, and if his feelings showed on his face, then so be it. He took a good look at his friend. Kithr wore a heavy leather jerkin emblazoned across the front with Cailean's house emblem. "You're wearing Cailean's colors?"

"It leaves fewer questions about which side I'm on," Kithr answered. "Cailean's men hold the keep now, but they don't know me."

"Is everyone alright?" Lyan asked.

Kithr smiled. "While we fought the followers of the Mad

God, Dalrian got it in his head to act on his own. Rather than wait and rest like any sensible man in his condition, he found his way to the walls. Killed a few guards, managed to get a few more minor injuries. He tore down Ewart's standard and raised Cailean's over the keep. You might call it the sign Cailean gave for his men outside the walls to make their move."

"Dalrian did?" Lyan remembered how pale and drawn Dalrian had been when they'd left him.

Kithr nodded. "I didn't think he had it in him, but that Tathren is tougher than I'd expected, and he used the rest to gather his strength. He'll need time to heal. Shiolto thinks he'll be all right." Kithr's voice held new respect for the Tathrens. "Makes me start to wonder what our real grudge was with them to begin with."

Lyan walked to the window and pulled the shutters closed. "Venycia became a Guardian of Equinox instead of joining the Tathren pantheon. That's what started everything."

"What does she have to do with that?" Kithr asked, puzzled.

"Her mother was an elf. Her father is Ahebban. Ahebban made some plans for her future that were disrupted when Soldarr asked her to become one of the first Guardians of the Spear. Ahebban and Soldarr fought about it."

"The daughter of a Tathren god followed Soldarr?" Kithr asked dubiously.

"This was before the gods began feuding," Lyan said.

"And they fought over *this*? Over who was guarding the Spear? When they should have known the need for Guardians?" Kithr continued.

"Kithr, this was also before Murdo. Before he became the Mad God. Before he was even *born*. There were Spearbearers before him, and there were people who challenged the Trials and failed. Enough to give Murdo an army."

Kithr frowned. "Why would any Guardian have helped him fight the gods?"

"Because they had no choice," Lyan said quietly, his eyes moving to the Spear leaning against the wall near his bed. "They are bound to obey the Spearbearer—all of them except for those few who became Guardians by choice, like Venycia or Waldros."

"Murdo's Pits! So you could…?"

Lyan nodded.

"And you *didn't?*" Kithr demanded.

"I didn't think about it," Lyan said. He hoped Kithr didn't see past the lie. *I didn't call on them because they have no choice but to obey. I already have Praett in that position, and Nachyne, to a degree, and I never asked for either. I never asked for slaves. The idea of being bound to another's whim terrifies me. I can't bear to think of doing that to someone else.*

Kithr sighed, shaking his head and accepting the given answer. "Come on. I'm sure you want to see your Tathrens."

Lyan held out his hand, and Equinox appeared in it from across the room. He nodded to Kithr, who led the way. The doorway opened into a sitting room. Praett lazed in a chair, standing when Lyan entered. Venycia was gone.

"The Guardian took her leave, master," Praett said. "I didn't ask her destination, but she said she'd return when she is able. She gave the impression that might not be as soon as she'd like."

My thoughts really are easy to read from my face, it seems. "What about the gods?" Lyan asked.

"Lord Ahebban departed. My lord wants to speak to you sometime. Lord Toirni simply sent the storm rather than making a physical appearance. The Tathrens seem glad for the rain." Praett waited for instructions.

"Thank you for your help," Lyan said.

Praett raised an eyebrow, dubious. "I did as my god and as you, my master, ordered."

"And I'm thanking you for it," Lyan said. "Because neither of us asked for this. Now, because I can't change what Nachyne did, I have new instructions for you."

"As you wish, master," Praett said, stiff.

Lyan drew a deep breath. "As much as you can within the restrictions placed on you by your god, act as a free creature."

The pooka jerked, then stiffened, eyes opening wide in disbelief. He stared at Lyan, clearly waiting for some qualifier, some trick. After a long moment of silence, Praett asked, "Am I free to leave, master?" His voice held neither defiance nor scorn.

"Is there any chance you'll call me 'Lyan'?" Lyan asked.

"No."

"You're free to go, Praett," Lyan said. "In whatever form you want to take."

The pooka turned and strode toward the door, stopped, looked back, and said, "Thank you, master." He opened the door and was gone.

Kithr eyed Lyan. "Was that a good idea?"

"I don't know," Lyan admitted. "But I think it was the right one. Let's find Cailean."

They walked into the hall. Movement on either side of the door made Lyan tense; he gripped Equinox tight. Two men wore Cailean's colors, but he didn't recognize them.

Kithr spoke in Elven. "The Tathren lord insisted these men guard your door. It's Tathren tradition, and meant as a complement to visiting nobles or dignitaries."

And not an insinuation of distrust, as it would be in Eilidh Wood.

The guards shifted uneasily when Kithr spoke in Elven. Lyan turned to them with a friendly smile. "Hello. Do you know where we could find Cailean?" He caught himself, thinking it might give a better impression if he at least *tried* to remember to use Tathren conventions. "Um, Lord Cailean, I mean."

"Don't worry, sir—Lord Cailean told us that you, um, your people don't use titles much and he doesn't mind you calling him by his given name," the one on the right said quickly.

"And Aikan scowled the whole time Cailean said it too, I imagine," Lyan said.

Both men laughed, relaxing. "Well, Aikan is very…" One man searched for a word.

"Proper?" Lyan suggested. "Yes, he is, but he's a good man."

"Aye, he is," agreed both Tathrens. "You can probably find Lord Cailean in the Great Hall going through reports. Need us to show you the way?"

"We can find it," Lyan said with another smile. "Unless that's one of your duties? I'm not familiar with most Tathren conventions."

"We can guide you if you want us to, sir, but it's up to you," answered the man on the left.

"Lyan," he said. "I'm just Lyan of Eilidh Wood." He shifted Equinox into his left hand and extended the right.

"Gerrit, sir," said the man on the right, shaking Lyan's hand.

Kithr snorted. "He means he'd rather be called by name than sir."

Gerrit flushed, mumbling an apology.

The man on the left also shook Lyan's hand. "I'm Toman, s… Lyan. Nice to meet you."

Lyan was pleased to see that neither guard hesitated to take his hand. "A pleasure," he agreed.

They left the two Tathrens, Kithr in the lead. Lyan asked, "Ewart's men are out of the keep?"

"The surprise attack by Cailean's men, the death of their lord, and the presence of a couple gods discouraged most resistance," Kithr said. "Many surrendered. Some fought.

They died. The rest are waiting in the dungeon until Cailean decides their fate."

Lyan shivered, remembering the cold, dank cells. He didn't envy those men.

~

The halls of the keep bustled with life that had been absent the previous day. Men and women rushed about, though they were quick to avoid Kithr and Lyan. The activity disoriented Lyan. They finally descended a broad staircase into an open room and he saw the main doors, getting his bearings. The doors stood open, admitting a constant flow of people in plain dress, drab browns and the occasional splash of blue or green, tracking mud over the floors.

"One of the first things Cailean did was announce that he'd host a feast tonight to honor the retaking of the keep, Ewart's fall, and our help," Kithr told Lyan. "His people jumped at the chance to celebrate Cailean's return, so things are pretty busy here."

Kithr made for a set of wide doors, and Lyan hurried after him, pulling from his gawking. To watch Kithr's firm stride, he might not have taken a single injury from the fighting of the previous days. Servants scrambled from his path and guards tensed. Kithr didn't acknowledge them, opening the doors into a long hallway.

As they approached the other end of the hall, a door opened to one side and Aikan stepped out, head bowed as he sorted through a stack of parchments, muttering irately under his breath. Aikan's head rose when he heard steps on the polished stone floor, and he fixed the expected glower on Lyan and Kithr.

"It's about time you woke up! Lord Cailean's been worrying."

"How is he, Aikan?" Lyan asked.

Aikan paused. "Better." Another pause. "Far better, since Porephyn's death."

"Good." Lyan nodded, acknowledging the words Aikan wasn't saying as well as those he was. *You're welcome.*

Aikan pushed open the door into the Great Hall. The ceiling rose high above their heads, giving Lyan enough room to breathe, and windows along one wall let in light, though it was muted by the storm outside. At the far end of the room, a raised dais held an ornamented chair, but Cailean sat at the long table, studying charts strewn over it. Cailean gripped Solstice with a possessive air Lyan understood well. Yion stood near Cailean, pointing at something on one of the charts.

Cailean didn't look up as they approached. "*More* records, Aikan?" he complained.

"Records and elves, my lord," Aikan answered.

Cailean's head jerked up, and his expression brightened. "Lyan! Gods, it's good to see you." He jumped to his feet, moving with an energy he'd lacked before.

Lyan grinned. "Not as good as it is to see you alive and well, Cailean. And with Solstice."

Cailean nodded, expression sobering. "Thank you, Lyan. Without help from you and Kithr, I couldn't have regained Solstice or the ability to use it."

Kithr snorted, folding his arms over his chest. "And don't forget it."

"I won't," Cailean responded. "Believe me, I won't forget what you've done for me, and if there is ever anything I can do to repay my debt—"

"Friendship isn't a debt, Cailean," Lyan said. "I did what I could. I probably didn't do it as well as I could have, or as well as someone with more skill could have." He gave both Cailean and Kithr a wry grin. "And thinking of that, have you decided who gets to be the first to smack me upside the head for attempting single combat with a high priest of the Mad God?"

Yion spoke, his voice smooth and calm. "You fought well, Lyan Stargazer. Not even I could have won against Porephyn without aid my lord could not give me, because of the wards over the keep."

"Can some[illegible] wards powerful enough to deny the gods entry?" Lyan asked.

"With the blessing of the Mad God, and enough blood shed in sacrifice, yes, I fear they can," Yion answered.

"But Nachyne entered," Lyan argued.

Yion nodded. "Such wards take a great many sacrifices to create. The blood needed to craft enough of them to deny access to all the gods would leave no one left alive in the land to need such protection. Porephyn and Ewart built their wards to prevent the intervention of any god of Tather. They expected no other to have any interest in the matter, and certainly did not anticipate Lord Nachyne's entrance."

"Which you have yet to explain," Cailean added.

"Because of events involving a previous Spearbearer, Nachyne has a vested interest in making sure the Mad God never gets hold of Equinox again," Lyan answered. "A very personal interest."

Cailean scowled, but only briefly. "In any case, Yion is right, Lyan. None of the rest of us could have fought that priest. Porephyn." Cailean struggled with the name. "None of us could have fought him and won."

A sobering thought, and one Lyan was immensely glad he hadn't had before the battle began.

Cailean clapped a hand on Lyan's shoulder. "Now, I keep hearing about a tree and some argument over it?"

"Have you seen it yet?" Lyan asked.

Cailean shook his head. "Not yet. Aikan said we should wait for you. I admit I haven't been eager to go back to that site, but now, it's time. Yion, Aikan, if you would accompany us?"

Aikan set his papers on the table and nodded in sharp

agreement. "No one has disturbed the courtyard since we left it, my lord, at my orders."

Cailean led the way to the courtyard. Lyan recognized the halls as they neared, remembering the dogs rushing at them. A pair of nervous guards, damp from the rain, stood watch at the doorway into the courtyard. They snapped to salute Cailean.

"Lord Cailean, no one's tried to enter, sir. Or leave." The last was added with a note of fear.

"Thank you," Cailean told them. "Well done."

He stepped into the courtyard and walked over the ruined gate that lay twisted on the soggy ground. Lyan followed, using Equinox to steady himself. Rain poured down, washing away signs of battle. The bodies of Ewart's guards killed by the pooka were only slumped, dark shapes. Lyan climbed the low steps into the plain building. The shelter offered a brief reprieve from the rain, but when they entered the main room, water dripped down again. The oak's canopy spread over the hole it had ripped in the roof, but rain ran off leaves to fall on them. As Lyan entered, the branches rustled, spraying water like a dog shaking off after a plunge in a river.

While Lyan had slept, roots had spread across the floor. A knotted clump of them covered the spot where Porephyn had died. The rain-washed corpses of Ewart and his guards lay untouched, their fate left in Cailean's hands.

Cailean's gaze was arrested by the tree itself. "This killed Porephyn?" he asked softly. "It's moving. The trees in Eilidh Wood did as well."

"I woke its spirit when Equinox pulled it into maturity. The trees in Eilidh Wood are awake as well," Lyan said.

"And those in Malgor Forest?" Aikan asked sharply.

"Yes," Lyan admitted. "But unlike Nylas, I'm not Lost, and this tree knows me, not Nylas and his winterborn blooddrinkers. It won't attack my friends." He held out his hand, and a branch drooped low to brush his fingers like a horse nuzzling its rider. "Go ahead," he told Cailean.

Cailean hesitated, then imitated Lyan, holding out a hand. The branch shifted from Lyan to Cailean, teasing over the outstretched hand. L[illegible] in his palms. Cailean laughed softly.

"Lyan, your tree is a welcome resident to this courtyard, and one I will gladly accept over the previous one," he said. "I'll have this wretched building torn down stone by stone, but the tree stays."

"My lord approves of your decision, Lord Cailean," Yion said. He turned to Lyan. "He hopes the elves of Eilidh Wood and the people of Tather can take steps toward reconciliation despite the difficulties of the past. They should look toward their common enemy."

Cailean smiled wryly. "Lord Saiboti doesn't need to convince me, Yion, and I doubt Lyan requires convincing either."

"Then the Spearbearers have the task of carrying that message among their peoples," Yion told him. "The Mad God has lost this battle, but the war is not yet won."

"I know." Lyan's hand closed tight around Equinox. "But at least we know we can stand against him."

"True enough," Cailean agreed. "And tonight, we celebrate this victory and the beginning of an alliance between Tather and Eilidh Wood!"

Kithr snorted. "If you can call two elves and one Tathren stronghold working together the beginning of an alliance."

"It's more than we've had before," Cailean responded.

"True enough," Kithr allowed. "True enough."

24

Stars above, their secrets keep
The ways of men below, they see
Stars above, in silence weep
For every man who would be free

Cailean's people worked wonders, rising with enthusiasm to the challenge of preparing a feast in less than a day. Servants cleaned the Great Hall and decorated it with basket-loads of fresh plants and flowers. Not only the keep's kitchen, but kitchens all through the village below the fortress hill leapt into frenzied activity. Cailean spared little expense.

As evening fell, the feast began, filling the Great Hall with people, food, and music. Lyan ate his fill, conversed with his friends, and endured the scrutiny of gawkers. He left Equinox with Solstice resting in a spear rack on the dais. The Spears didn't draw nearly as much interest as the elves did.

Once servants cleared the meal, the room grew stuffy, even the wide walls and high ceiling not enough to eliminate a sensation of being closed in. When Lyan left the table to mill, he drifted toward the door until he found his way outside.

Boisterous throngs filled the courtyard, where more tables

had been set up to accommodate the people who couldn't fit into the Great Hall. No doubt some protocol dictated who entered the hall and ate with Cailean, but Lyan didn't attempt to figure it out. The crowds were thick, and bright torches lit the night. Lyan almost [illegible], keeping his head low and avoiding drawing attention. The glare of light would spoil the view of the sky, and he kept his eyes down, determined that his first sight of the stars after so long be unsullied by torchlight.

Even the guards relaxed. Lyan approached the steps to the outer wall. A man stopped him briefly, letting him pass when he recognized Lyan as one of Cailean's elven guests. With a nod of thanks, Lyan climbed the steps onto the broad wall. He walked toward the back side of the keep, away from the lights and the noise. Below and behind, he could still hear the echo of celebration, and he smiled. The wine filled him with a pleasant warmth, and summer wind blew across his face, teasing strands of red hair that slipped free of his braid.

Finally, he raised his eyes to the night sky. He stumbled, bumping against a battlement. The pleasant tipsiness faded in cold fear. The heavens above remained shrouded by thick clouds.

But Porephyn is dead. I killed him. His enchantment should be broken.

"So, you're Lyan, the stargazer from Eilidh Wood."

The unfamiliar voice made Lyan turn sharply. He was sure he'd been alone, but now another man stood nearby, though he'd neither seen nor heard the other approach. The man leaned casually against a battlement, as if he'd been there the entire time. A wide-brimmed hat shadowed his features, but his eyes caught the glimmer of distant torchlight, and his mouth curved in a smile. His clothing looked like silk, deep red swirled with gold.

"Who are you?" Lyan asked, stepping back.

"Not only a stargazer, but also the Spearbearer of

Equinox. An impressive feat no elf managed for hundreds of years. Well done. Well done indeed."

"Who are you?" Lyan repeated. *God or mortal? Who... what are you?*

The stranger stepped closer and, with a wave of a hand, ignored the question. "You've fought with such determination, and you've succeeded beyond your dreams. Beyond even my dreams, to tell the truth. You deserve a reward. No, don't say anything. I know what brought you out here, and I know what you seek." The stranger raised his open hand toward the sky, fingers curling as if he seized something. He jerked down, like a man pulling away a covering. Lyan saw the gleam of white teeth when the stranger smiled again. "My gift to you, Spearbearer."

Lyan frowned, but the man gestured at the sky, and Lyan looked up once more.

His mouth fell open in shock. As if they had never been, the clouds were gone and the night clear. Stars glittered.

"You... Who?" He couldn't manage to say more.

"I must thank you," the stranger continued, taking yet another step closer, voice growing lower, dangerous. Lyan's mind screamed a warning, but as if his will were not his own, he couldn't tear his gaze from the stars, or even focus fully on anything else. The stranger's words whispered in his ears like the night breeze. "Surely you didn't think Porephyn alone could maintain an enchantment that covered half the continent? Fool that he was, Porephyn never had the skill to solve the riddle and find the Shrine of Equinox, even if he'd had an elf's lifetime. But you, Lyan of Heartshrine Village, you did."

Equinox. Lyan knew it wasn't wine that muddled his thoughts, but something else, a force that denied him even the concentration to call his Spear. It overwhelmed him, demanding he gaze at the stars and follow the patterns unfolding before his eyes. He heard the stranger's words, but his mind filled with the signs burning in the sky above, now revealed. Lyan's lips moved in silent denials.

"You see? You see the works you have set in motion? Not even Porephyn's greatest schemes could have opened such possibilities."

"You wanted him to fail," Lyan whispered.

"I *knew* Porephyn would fail, if you lived up to your potential. I could read it in the stars. So I sent this minion here as well, to control the magic of the sky, freeing Porephyn and Ewart to focus on their petty plots and to drive you to greater lengths—to see if you could rise to my expectations. And you did, Lyan. Oh, you did."

"No. No, this can't..." Lyan tore his mind free of the smothering force desperately, one hand reaching out to the air. "Equinox!"

Nothing happened. Lyan's eyes widened and he fell back, hitting a barrier he'd been unaware of before. At his touch, it flashed with a sickly orange glow. Lyan recoiled from it, gasping for breath. Foul magic crawled across his skin.

The stranger's mouth curled in amusement. "You forget, *I* am the true Spearbearer. I know the powers of the Spears as you never will, and I know the ways to keep pretenders such as you from calling out to them."

"No." Lyan stumbled, falling to his knees. "Equinox is not yours."

"Look at me, Lyan, Stargazer of Heartshrine Village."

The power of the voice slammed him like a tempest. He could no more stop himself from obeying than he could bid the wind be still. Against his will, he raised his head and turned to face the stranger. His mind screamed for help, but no sound escaped his mouth. The stranger tilted up his hat brim. His eyes met Lyan's. A gasp escaped Lyan, and even that sound cut short as he stared into the depths of madness.

Chaotic colors swirled in eyes that had no white, no iris, no pupil. Somehow in that maelstrom, Lyan read anger, cruelty, pleasure in causing pain and torment. Cunning. Patience, and a temper poised to fly free at the slightest provocation.

No. This isn't possible. You're sealed away.

The stranger grinned wickedly. "I'm still imprisoned in the pit where the gods think they can hold me? For now. Only for now. But you, Lyan, you and your actions have brought the time of my release so much closer. And even the gods can't prevent me from using the bodies of my willing followers."

Lyan couldn't speak, only gasp for breath. *How could you read the stars? There are none in your prison.*

The other's smile darkened, growing savage. "I took the stars from you, and look at what lengths you went to have them back. Do you really think I would not find a way to regain them, even in the depths of my prison?" He loomed over Lyan, then crouched down. "But soon, it won't matter—I will be free. You can be by my side, or you can stand in my path, and I will reclaim my Spear from your soulless husk."

No. Terror held Lyan. He couldn't turn away from the chaotic eyes, but he would not—dared not—bow. *Equinox is not yours, and I will never serve you, Murdo.*

Neither the stranger's smile nor tone changed. "You'll regret those words, stargazer. Look to the heavens, and know the truth of what's coming. Know what you, with your own hands, have begun. See, and know despair unlike anything you have felt before!" Within the mortal body, Murdo laughed. "Ah, and your friends. Yes, your friends." His eyes narrowed. "Try to speak of this to anyone, to say anything of what you have seen, and your despair will be complete." His voice dropped to a whisper. "I give you the gift of knowledge, Lyan of Heartshrine Village, and the curse of despair."

Power coiled around Lyan, suffocating him. Gasping, he tried to call out, but still no sound escaped.

Murdo's possessed puppet never broke eye contact with Lyan. "Look to the sky, Spearbearer. See what will happen to your friends if you tell them what is to come—see what they will do, and how they will make their fates so much worse by their actions. Ah, but perhaps the stars themselves won't tell you enough." He touched Lyan's face, spread fingers resting just below Lyan's eyes. "You will *see* their fates."

Pain stabbed [illegible] like lightning bolts. He shuddered, but couldn't pull away. His mouth opened in a silent scream as fire tore through his head and burned into his eyes.

Fat droplets of blood splattered onto Murdo's arm, and he hissed a profanity. He jerked back from Lyan and broke contact. Lyan slumped, struggling to understand Murdo's words through the haze and agony.

"I must cut our meeting short. This loyal minion has reached the limits of his endurance." Murdo rose, lifting a hand to the body's bleeding nose.

Lyan lifted his head with an effort, bracing himself on hands and knees. Blood streamed from Murdo's nose and trickled from the corners of his mouth. Flesh shriveled and darkened.

Finally, Lyan found a whisper of a voice. "I will find…"

"This loyal follower?" Murdo finished for him. "No, you won't. Or, if you do, it won't do you any good." The Mad God laughed as his borrowed body climbed onto a crenellation, and grinned wickedly. "Until we meet again, Spearbearer." With a mocking bow, he stepped backwards, over the edge.

Lyan dragged himself to the edge of the wall, but when he looked down, saw only darkness. A heartbeat later, the barrier surrounding him popped like a burst bubble. He tried to stand, but the effort was too much. He slid to the stone floor and awareness fled.

～

Someone shook Lyan's shoulder, waking him. "Should have known I'd find you out here."

Lyan groaned, his head pounding like someone beat on it with a hammer. He tried to remember why, and a chill ran down his spine, but he couldn't identify the cause of his terror. Like a dream, vague images slipped through memory, eluding attempts to gather them.

He opened his eyes, and found Kithr smiling good-naturedly down at him. His friend held out a hand. "Sleeping under the stars when there are perfectly good beds?"

The stars. Again, that chill sense of something terrible and wrong. Lyan looked at the sky, but dawn had chased away the stars. He accepted Kithr's help up and wavered unsteadily. Leaning against a crenellation, Lyan looked down for reasons he couldn't explain, only a fleeting memory of something or someone going over the edge. If anything lay among the far-distant rocks, the morning mist hid it from sight.

"Are you all right, Lyan?"

He opened his mouth, words on his lips. Then memory pushed into his awareness, and a lie slipped free, safer than the truth. "I think I drank too much last night."

Kithr nodded, sympathetic. "Well, there's breakfast, if you think you can eat something.

What happened last night? What did Murdo do to me?

Lyan followed Kithr down the steps. He found no answers to his questions, but one certainty pressed into his mind, undeniable as the sun's rise. This battle wasn't over—it had just begun. Murdo moved closer to breaking free.

And Lyan knew it was his fault.

Chapter One
Kithr

"For all you have done to further my release, Spearbearer, I give you the gift of knowledge… and the curse of despair."

Kithr cast a look at his companion, trying to read Lyan's face for any clue as to his silence. The closer they drew to home, the more withdrawn Lyan became. His silence had grown pronounced since they entered Eilidh Wood late the previous day. Kithr was accustomed to quiet, and usually welcomed it, but to ride for this long beside Lyan without so much as a comment on the sky or forest from his friend grew unsettling.

"What's wrong, Lyan?" Kithr finally asked, breaking the silence when Lyan did not.

Lyan gave no indication of surprise when he answered. "Nothing."

"Horse turds. You've said barely two sentences all morning. We rode past three of your favorite stargazing spots on this end of the forest, and you didn't say a word. You haven't looked at the sky since last night, and just a glance then. What's wrong?"

A thin smile touched Lyan's mouth, but didn't reach his eyes. "How many seasons have you been telling me to pull my head out of the clouds and watch my feet? And now you're worried because I've finally done so?"

Kithr fumbled for an answer, but couldn't put his unease into words. He'd always been one for action rather than talk, and Lyan made his worry sound foolish. "I just… It feels like you're hiding something. Something you saw, or something that happened."

"How could I hide something I saw, when the things I see are the signs written in the stars for anyone to read?" Lyan countered.

Because you're the one who knows how to read the stars. I'm no astrologer. All I see are glittering lights. I don't know what they mean. "All right…," Kithr said aloud. "Then what does my fortune say?"

Lyan did tilt his head back and look to the sky, brushing loose locks of red hair from his face. "You'll have to wait until night to know. I can't see the stars during the day."

Kithr couldn't shake the sense that the clear sky overhead relieved Lyan. As if, for the first time in his life, Lyan didn't *want* to see the stars. As if, with the clearing of the clouds that had obscured the night sky for so many moons, Lyan's love of stargazing had been stripped from him.

"Tonight, then. I'll hold you to that."

"Why the sudden interest, Kithr?" Lyan asked. "You've shown little concern for your fortune before."

Kithr gave the first excuse he could think of. "If I'm going to be taking any more unexpected trips trying to watch a friend's back, I'd like a little warning." Warning Lyan had *not* given him before. Although, if Kithr was being honest, Lyan hadn't exactly invited him along.

Lyan gave him another thin smile. "Any trips you take in the near future will be ones you plan first."

"So you *do* know something of my fortune without looking at the stars."

"I know you, Kithr—[illegible]"

Are you telling me that something is going to happen that will make me plan to leave Heartshrine Village again? What could possibly make me want to do that?

Lyan drew his black stallion, Shadowstar, to a stop and combed his fingers through the horse's dark brown mane. "Kithr, when you returned to Eilidh Wood after the war, did you ever feel like everything had changed?"

That, finally, gave him some idea about what troubled Lyan, even if the comparison stirred up unpleasant memories. "Yes. But Eilidh Wood hadn't changed. I had." Kithr looked at Lyan.

At a glance, his friend looked little different than he had when he left Eilidh Wood in the company of Cailean and the Tathren lord's followers. Lyan's red hair hung in a short tail. He might be a little more lean and toned than when he left. No obvious scars. And yet, anyone who knew Lyan would see something had changed. The way he held himself. The shadows in his gaze.

And, of course, the Spear.

Lyan shifted under Kithr's scrutiny, and his hand moved to rest on Equinox. The only visible memento Lyan carried of their travels was strapped onto Shadowstar's saddle, though Lyan sometimes wore it at his back: a spear taller than Lyan. At a glance, it appeared to be a beautiful, deadly weapon forged of a silvery metal and etched with runes inlaid with gold. Even the wicked barbs on the spearhead added to its beauty rather than detracting.

The sight of Equinox, one of the two Spears of the Stars, legendary weapons powerful enough to defeat gods with the right wielder, being borne by Lyan, astrologer of Heartshrine

Village, never failed to jolt Kithr. Not that Lyan hadn't earned the right to bear it—he had. But for so long, Kithr had unconsciously thought his friend weak for his love of stargazing and avoidance of battle, and he knew Lyan had been more aware, and more bothered, by the dismissal of his skills than he'd let anyone know.

But he faced the Spear's Trials and earned the right to carry Equinox. I know he can use its powers, but even I'm still uncomfortable seeing him with the Spear of the Stars. Is that what's bothering Lyan? Is he thinking about the reception he'll get in our village when others learn that he bears one of the most powerful weapons known to us? The Spear is a burden he chose, but he didn't leave planning to become Spearbearer. And he can't just give it up again now that we've stopped the Mad God's minions in Tather. Equinox is his for the rest of his life.

Lyan turned Shadowstar off the main road and onto the narrow trail to Heartshrine Village. Kithr followed. No one challenged them, but Kithr heard whispers of movement as someone slipped away ahead of them to tell the village of their return. The elves who served as sentries were skilled in stealth, much as Kithr himself was, and he heard the watcher only because he knew what to listen for.

When they reached the shrine, Kithr untensed. Home. Five stones, each taller than an elf, stood in a half-circle around a low, flat altar. Intricate images of Soldarr, Feyra, and Tesseia, the three gods worshiped by the elves of Eilidh Wood, were inscribed into the stones. This shrine was older than the village itself—Heartshrine Village had taken its name from the presence of this shrine.

Both Kithr and Lyan dismounted and knelt. Stiff muscles protested as Kithr bowed his head and prayed. *Thank you for guiding us on this journey, and for protecting us.* Kithr paused. *And… thank you for everything we encountered on this journey, and for opening my eyes and showing me that I was Lost, and for guiding me back onto the path an elf of Eilidh Wood should follow. Thank you even for the Tathrens.*

A few months ago, Kithr would have scoffed at anyone who said he would be grateful for Tathrens. Only sixty years ago, Kithr answered the call to war against the human nation of Tather, as had most young men of his generation. The elves of Eilidh Wood invaded Tather, seeking to claim Solstice, the second Spear of the Stars. Though they failed to capture Solstice, the war had left deep scars on both lands, and on those who fought. Most humans who'd fought were dead or old men, but for the elves, it remained a fresh memory. Kithr had held to his hate of them, nursing his grievances like old, familiar companions. If he allowed himself, he could readily summon the litany of sins he'd laid at Tathren feet, foremost among them his father's death. Kithr cut the thought short before he followed it further.

Though only a few years separated Lyan and Kithr, Lyan was not called to war, too important to Heartshrine Village as the astrologer's sole apprentice. He never fought and killed Tathrens, never saw the war directly. And when a chance encounter with a group of Tathrens introduced Lyan to Cailean Dev'gilla, Lyan had been fascinated.

No, Kithr amended. *That's not fair to Lyan. He was eluding a pooka, fell into a ravine, sprained his ankle, and was rescued by the Tathrens. Inviting them to our village was the hospitable thing to do. The fact that he then left the village again with them... that was motivated by responsibility, not curiosity, no matter what I thought at the time. But thank the gods I did not know back then that Cailean bore Solstice. Whether or not I would have succeeded, I know I would have tried to kill him.*

Kithr waited for Lyan. His friend remained still and silent, head bowed, for so long that Kithr wondered if he'd dozed off. Just as Kithr was considering shaking his shoulder to rouse him, Lyan stood.

"I'm ready."

Kithr rose and dusted off his pants—not that dirt showed on his brown clothing. "We're almost home."

"Yes. Almost there." Lyan climbed into Shadowstar's saddle.

Kithr heard strained notes in Lyan's voice and hesitated. The way Lyan spoke, it sounded like a man preparing to say his final farewells. "Lyan…"

"We shouldn't keep the Elder waiting." Lyan didn't look at him, gaze instead fixed ahead, though Heartshrine Village couldn't be seen through the trees yet.

"Ash and rot Lyan, what is it? Do you not want to go back? Is something happening at home that you don't want to deal with?" Kithr struggled for words. "We don't have to return if you're not ready. Is there something else, some other place we should be?"

Lyan sighed. "You're kind to ask, Kithr. But I know you want to be home, and I'm not going to take that from you. It wouldn't make a difference, here or somewhere else. So we might as well go where one of us wants to be."

"Where do *you* want to be, Lyan?"

"I don't know." Lyan still didn't turn to face him. "The Elder is waiting for us."

"Why in Soldarr's name won't you tell me what is *wrong*, Lyan?" Kithr burst in frustration.

Lyan's whispered answer was almost too soft to hear. "Because it won't help."

GODS OF EILIDH WOOD

Soldarr: The one male of the three gods of Eilidh Wood, Soldarr wields a battle axe in combat and is said to be a fierce warrior. In times of peace, he is lover to both Feyra and Tesseia. In the past, he has also engaged in trysts with mortal women; however, no such unions have been reported since Tesseia threatened to castrate him the next time he did so. Soldarr and the Tathren god Ahebban bear a grudge regarding Ahebban's half-elf daughter Venycia and her decision to becoming a Guardian of Equinox rather than following the wishes of her father.

Feyra and Tesseia: The goddesses are sisters, and both wield bows in combat. They are said to have a stronger connection to Eilidh Wood than Soldarr, understanding the forest and its whims more easily. Some Tathren priests claim that in addition to being lover to Feyra and Tesseia, Soldarr is also their brother, however, the gods vehemently deny this claim.

GODS OF TATHER

Ahebban, Watcher on the Walls: Ahebban is the protector of fortresses. When a Tathren keep or stronghold is completed, the [illegible] ask his blessing on it. One part of the ritual blessing calls for the god's protection on the fortress to prevent anyone outside the walls from using harmful magic against the keep or anyone inside it. He bears a fierce anger against Soldarr, and, by extension, the elves of Eilidh Wood. The bear is sacred to Ahebban.

Saiboti: Brother to Ahebban, Saiboti is the Tathren god of warriors. He doesn't share his brother's fanatical anger against the elves of Eilidh Wood. He is known to be a god of honor, and expects those who follow him to act accordingly. The hawk is sacred to Saiboti.

Erskine: Erskine is the Tathren god of the fields and harvest, venerated by farmers and all who work the land. His exact feelings toward the elves of Eilidh Wood are unknown, though it's doubtful that he looks very fondly on the invaders who burned, destroyed, and looted farms and fields. The cat is sacred to Erskine.

OTHER GODS

Veil: Veil is the god of divination. Said to live on the moon, Veil possesses the power to manipulate how the stars appear in the night sky. Astrologers interpret those signs to read fortunes and predict the future.

Toirni, the Thunderer: Toirini is the god of the weather, commonly called the Stormlord or the Thunderer. The nomads of the Apperet Plains revere him as a deity in their pantheon. He is the god they appeal to for rain. The power that Murdo has given to one of his minions, to cloud the sky, trespasses into Toirini's domain, but the Thunderer seems to be prevented from dispelling the clouds that hide the sky at night.

The Horselord: The Horselord is the god of horses on the Apperet Plains, and primarily worshipped by the nomads there. Most depictions of him show him as a centaur.

Nachyne, god of monsters: Even the monsters have a deity. Nachyne rules over the monsters, including but not limited to dragons, fairies, pooka, and sirens. He's not known to care much for mortals or to any great shows of benevolence, even to his own worshipers. He tends to take the form of a dragon or a man with draconic wings, claws, and a tail.

Cantorelle, god of roads: Cantorelle is the patron god of travelers, and takes special interest in the protection of refugees, women, and children. He is often invoked before a journey. Cantorelle does not have temples, though sometimes travelers will build a shrine in his honor after completing a particularly difficult stretch of their journey.

The god of roads has an order of priests/defenders of the roads, called Freewardens. As the god of roads practices neutrality in national disputes, so do the Freewardens, and they are allowed to travel across any border, through any land, without being attacked or detained by the denizens of that land. Any people who they place under their protection are equally exempt. No wise person would abuse this protection, nor interfere with a Freewarden—Cantorelle is fond of his Freewardens, and angering the god of roads promises to make any future travels fraught with peril.

ABOUT THE AUTHOR

Sanan Kolva is a technical editor by day, and writer of epic and steampunk fantasy the rest of the time. She is the author of The Chosen of the Spears series and The Silverline Chronicles series. Her short fiction can be found in multiple anthologies.

When not writing, she can be found baking and decorating cakes, battling the forces of evil in various video games, and appeasing her feline overlords. Please drop in, leave a comment, or sign up for her newsletter at http://sanankolva.com.

If you enjoyed this book, please tell someone else who might like it, or leave a review on your preferred platform.

9 781732 587250